PRAISE

"I enjoyed this bittersweet novel with its accurate depiction of the lives of cowgirls in 1920s Montana and its tender portrait of a marriage." —Mary Clearman Blew, award-winning author of *Jackalope Dreams*, *All but the Waltz: A Memoir of Five Generations in the Life of a Montana Family*, and *Balsamroot: A Memoir*

"In her poignant tale of Nettie Moser's diligent pursuit of a dream, Heidi Thomas gives a stunning example of what it means to "Cowgirl Up." *Follow the Dream* is a dynamic story of a woman's strength and determination that is sure to inspire as well as entertain." —Sandi Ault, award-winning author of *Wild Sorrow*, in the *WILD* Mystery Series

" . . . A wonderful story of courage and endurance." —Mary Trimble, award-winning author of *Tenderfoot*, *Rosemount*, and *McClellan's Bluff*

" . . . Perhaps because Nettie is in fact author Heidi Thomas's grandmother, she is a vividly drawn character. Or it may be Thomas's writing voice that makes all the characters so vivid, and creates such a compelling read. Although this book has been marketed as YA, and is certainly suitable for that group, I've been an adult for more years than I care to admit, and I loved this book. Get it and learn about a piece of the west that isn't the typical bandits or cowboys-and-Indians stories written by (and for) our fathers!" —Lori Orser, author of *Spooky, Creepy North Dakota*

" . . . I couldn't help but think about the times of today. Our financial futures and/or lack of them. *Follow the Dream* has made me realize just how strong our families of the past had to be. The hardships they went through just to get us where we are today. And with each generation, we seemed to weaken just a bit. We have become soft in our tolerance of problems and pain. I don't believe I know of a person who would go through the hardships that Nettie, Jake, and their son Neil went through and still keep a family together. *Follow the Dream* is a wonderful, heartwarming story of love, not just of a family, but a love for life." —Martha Cheves, author of *Stir, Laugh, Repeat*

"It is . . . scenes and realism like this that [make] Thomas a beloved author that gets to the heart of her characters and by extension her readers. *Follow the Dream* is a call to action not just for Nettie and Jake but all of us as we try to hold on to our own." —C. A. Webb, "Conversations Book Club"

"The struggle to keep body, soul, marriage, and horse herd together marks the saga that is *Follow the Dream*. Thomas's books are classified in the 'young adult' category . . . which in this case means there's no cussing or violence. Thoroughly vetted, it should interest readers of all ages." —T. J. Gilles for *The Outpost*, Billings, MT

"To my great surprise this one was a scorcher. . . . Heidi Thomas crafts several strong and engaging characters. I was transfixed and in awe of her ability to get me so emotionally attached to a group of cowpokes." —Giovanni Gelati, Gelati's Scoop

"This book deserves a place on the bookshelf next to Ivan Doig's coming of age in Montana novels." —Dan A. Johnson, reader

FOLLOW THE DREAM
A Novel

HEIDI M. THOMAS

TWODOT®

GUILFORD, CONNECTICUT
HELENA, MONTANA
AN IMPRINT OF GLOBE PEQUOT PRESS

Names of real cowgirls have been used in the story, but the relationship to the main character is fictional: Marie Gibson, Fannie Sperry Steele, Prairie Rose Henderson, Margie and Alice Greenough. All other characters and events in this book are fictional, and any resemblance to persons, whether living or dead, is strictly coincidental.

To buy books in quantity for corporate use or incentives, call **(800) 962-0973** or e-mail **premiums@GlobePequot.com**.

A · TWODOT® · BOOK

Project Editor: Lauren Brancato
Layout: Joanna Beyer

Library of Congress Cataloging-in-Publication Data

Thomas, Heidi M.
  Follow the dream : a novel / Heidi M. Thomas.
    pages cm
  ISBN 978-0-7627-9701-1 (pbk.)
 1. Cowgirls—Fiction. 2. Women rodeo performers—Fiction. 3. Ranch life—Fiction. 4. Frontier and pioneer life—Fiction. 5. Montana—Fiction. 6. Domestic fiction. I. Title.
  PS3620.H62793F65 2014
  813'.6—dc23
                                                2014001415

Printed in the United States of America

10 9 8 7 6 5 4 3 2 1

I dedicate this book to my father, Don N. Gasser, who instilled in me a love for books and who told me the stories that built the framework for Follow the Dream.

Acknowledgments

I thank God for giving me the writing gene, my husband and family for their never-ending support and encouragement, the teachers who believed in me, all my critique group members who give me such valuable feedback, and my fellow Women Writing the West and Skagit Valley Writers League members.

CHAPTER ONE

Sunday, March 2, 1924
Mrs. Jake Moser

Nettie drew a heart around "Jake" and doodled flowers in the margin of the first entry in her new journal.

I'm married to my cowboy and we're going to rodeo together. Rodeo.
My dream is coming true.

Nettie brushed the dust from her shiny black boots, stretched her shoulders in the unusually warm spring sunshine, and breathed in the familiar animal sweat aroma. *I'll ride this steer, show my folks how good I am.* She could already hear the crowd's cheers in her head and saw herself accepting a Top Cowgirl trophy. *I will be a star, maybe even the next Marie Gibson.*

She turned to Jake. "Well, Mr. Moser, how about giving your bride a hand?"

Jake grinned. "Well, Mrs. Moser, I'd be delighted." He helped Nettie steady herself as she climbed down from the top of the chute onto the bare back of the big red steer. She snugged her hand under the surcingle rope, feeling the animal's muscles tense beneath her as it kicked against the fence.

Jake squeezed her shoulder. "Ready?"

Nettie took a deep breath. She tightened her knees and nodded. *Here you go, Mrs. Moser.* She almost giggled. Funny how she still couldn't get used to her new name even after three months.

Before she had time to think, the steer crashed through the gate, bellowing a protest at its burden. Nettie leaned back as the big animal kicked its hind legs toward the sky. *Gotta find the rhythm.* The steer twisted and leapt. Nettie's body snapped forward and back and flopped side to side. Every jump jolted her from her tailbone to her teeth. She fought to gain her seat on the back of this nearly half-ton of muscle and bone, hearing yells from the Model Ts parked around the corral. *Where is my rhythm?* The arena whirled around her. Choking dust rose from the ground.

Nettie opened her eyes and saw nothing but blue sky.

Jake leaned over her. "Honey, talk to me. You all right?"

She blinked, wiggled her toes, clenched and unclenched her fingers. "Uh, yeah. How'd I get here?"

Jake smoothed hair back from her face. "Well, little gal, I'm sorry to say, you got bucked off."

"Oh, fiddlesticks." Nettie let out an exasperated sigh. She accepted a hand up, dusted herself off, and retrieved her hat. Why did she have to fail today, of all days, when her mother was here watching? Nettie gave herself a mental slap. *I was daydreaming. I wasn't focused on the ride.* She tried not to limp as she exited the corral, rubbing her bruised hip and bemoaning her bruised ego.

Mama and Papa met them outside the corral. "Oh, honey, are you hurt?" Her mother reached out to gather Nettie in a hug. "That scared me."

Nettie looked over Mama's shoulder to see concern etched in Papa's weathered face. "No, no. I'm not hurt. This sort of thing happens." She shook her head and made a wry smile. "I wanted to show you how well I could ride. But I just couldn't find my rhythm. Sorry I scared everybody."

Mama sighed. "I know you're a good rider, honey, but I still think rodeo is far too dangerous for women."

Biting her lip, Nettie glanced at Jake. *Oh, great. This is exactly what she's been against ever since I was fourteen years old.*

"But you're a married woman now." Nettie's mother gave her a wan smile. "And I know you're following your dream." She squeezed Nettie's shoulder. "Just be careful, okay?"

"All right, Mama, I will." Nettie laughed. "See you later." She and Jake walked back toward the chutes.

"Hey there, Mr. and MISSUS Moser," came a familiar voice.

Nettie turned to see Marie Gibson and her husband, Tom. "Marie! Where'd you come from? I wasn't expecting to see you today." With a chortle of delight, she ran forward and embraced her friend. "I'm so glad to see you. Did you just get here?"

Tom chuckled. "Just in time to see your spectacular spill." He clapped Jake on the back. "How're you doin', old chap? Heard about you two eloping."

Jake grinned.

Nettie hung her head. "Oh, dear. I'm sorry you had to see that. It wasn't one of my better days."

Marie laughed and shook her brown curls under her tall-crowned hat. "Oh, pshaw! If that's the worst spill you ever take, you've got it made, girl. I could tell you stories all night long about my falls. Remember when I dislocated my knee at Madison Square Garden?" She tucked her hand under Nettie's arm. "C'mon, let's you and I go over to the cook tent and get us some coffee. I have something to tell you. See you guys later." They left the men talking about the early warm spell and making plans for the rodeo season.

Nettie glanced at the champion cowgirl from the corner of one eye. What kind of news could Marie possibly have that they would drive 150 miles from Havre to tell her? A baby? No, Marie's kids were nearly grown and she still looked slim. Besides, they wouldn't make the drive to a little informal neighborhood rodeo for that.

At the tent, they poured themselves cups of steaming coffee. Nettie turned to her friend. "Well?"

"I've been invited to go to London with Tex Austin's International Rodeo this spring," Marie blurted. Her face shone.

For just a moment Nettie was filled with a great rush of longing. *Oh, why couldn't it be me?* It was every rider's dream to go to the Invitational in Europe. Then delight for her friend replaced the envy. She turned to give her a hug. "Marie, that's so wonderful."

Marie took Nettie by the shoulders. "And, there's more." She paused. "Tex heard something about this young woman rider from Montana and told me I could invite her to go."

Nettie tried to process the words, but they bounced, all jumbled, inside her head. Who would that be? She couldn't think of anyone. Gosh, how lucky for whoever—

"And . . ." Marie looked directly into her eyes. "I'm inviting you."

"Me?" A wave of disbelief rolled over Nettie, leaving a roaring in her ears. She sat down on a log bench.

"London?" She stared at Marie, the realization finally penetrating. "You're inviting me to go to London?" A giddy bubble rose in her chest like the champagne she'd had after her wedding. She jumped up and did a little dance step. "Oh, my goodness. I can't believe it."

"Believe it." Marie's big grin reassured Nettie. "So, do you think you can go? It'll be so much fun. You and me together."

"Yeah, you and me. Oh." Just as quickly, the bubble burst. "I forgot. Jake. He won't want me to leave him."

"Honey." Marie threw an arm around Nettie's shoulders. "You've got that man wrapped around your finger. He'll let you go."

Excitement bubbled again. "When are you leaving and for how long?"

Her friend fingered the trademark red scarf around her neck. "Tex plans to leave in mid-May. We'd be gone a couple months."

Nettie's shoulders slumped. "I don't know if I could leave Jake after only being married a few months."

"Well, maybe he'd like to come along then. He could be our chaperone, keep us out of trouble." Marie chuckled.

"Yeah. That would be grand." She bounced up and down on the log. "And we could still plan our rodeo for August or September, after we get back. Perfect."

She gazed over the rodeo arena, excitement building inside like a snowdrift in a blizzard. Then Nettie remembered. Money. They didn't have any. "How much would it cost?"

"Well, you will have the train trip to New York, and you do have to come up with a couple hundred for the trip over on the boat from there."

"Whew." Nettie shook her head. "It would be twice as much if Jakes goes."

Marie leaned forward. "But you'll get paid."

"How much?"

"It's based on the proceeds of the rodeo for the thirty days we perform. I hear Tex brings in good money. We could end up making double our costs. It's the opportunity of a lifetime."

"I know." Nettie could already picture herself parading in front of the judges' stand, accepting her award.

"Tom's so excited to be going back to England. He can show us where he used to live, go to Westminster Abbey, maybe we'll see the Queen." Marie jiggled her booted foot.

Euphoria overpowered Nettie's thoughts of practicality. "I want to go. I have to go. Maybe I just won't tell Jake. Don't say anything. Until I figure it out?"

Marie nodded. "We'll sleep on it. You'll figure out a way to get Jake to agree." She winked.

"Yeah. Oh, you'll come stay with us tonight, won't you?"

"Of course. We'd love it." Marie smiled.

Nettie chewed on a fingernail. *How can I make this work? Maybe I could sell my new boots.*

CHAPTER TWO

Monday, March 3, 1924

Life. Such a tease. London. With Marie. Tex Austin. Can't believe the opportunity. How can I come up with the money?

Nettie put down her journal as the first gray light of dawn outlined the window. Maybe her parents would give her the money. After all, she'd saved them a lot by eloping. No. She couldn't ask. And if Jake didn't want to go . . . *I'll go without him. I have to.*

She eased out of the warm bed, shivering in the frosty cold. Careful not to disturb Jake's light snores or their guests in the spare bedroom, Nettie put a wool wrap around her flannel nightgown and crept downstairs in her already stocking-clad feet to stoke the stove and make coffee. Her eyes felt gritty, head heavy. She didn't think she'd slept a wink all night.

When the coffee boiled, she poured a cup, hunched over it, and breathed in the steamy aroma. Life was so complicated. The kitchen clock ticked in the silence. Nettie sighed. First, she'd had to overcome Mama's objections to rodeo. Now, when she thought she was on her way to achieving her dream with Jake, money stood in the way.

How could she ask to go to London? She wasn't being fair to her husband. They were partners. *We don't have the extra money for this.* Even if she could borrow enough for herself, when it came right down to it, she couldn't just leave without him. Nettie set her coffee down with a thump that sloshed hot liquid over her hand. *Oh, jiggers!*

The stairs creaked and Marie entered the kitchen. "Coffee smells good. Did you tell Jake yet?"

Nettie shook her head.

"Any ideas come in your dreams?"

"Nothing but doubts."

"Maybe we could lend you—"

"No. I could never take a loan from you." Nettie jumped up to put the skillet on the stove. Then she turned. "Wait a minute. Would you be willing to buy Toby and Blacky for the amount I need to get to London?"

Marie slapped her thigh. "Great idea. Of course. I knew you'd come up with something." She stuck a hand out and shook Nettie's. "Deal."

"Yippee." Nettie's feet seemed to take on a life of their own as she danced in front of the stove.

When the bacon sizzled its tantalizing aroma, Jake and Tom clumped downstairs to join them.

Marie poured the men coffee and Nettie served pancakes and bacon. She poured molasses over hers and passed it to Tom. "So, you've been to London, right? What's it like?"

The Englishman slathered butter over his hotcakes. "Well, it's been many years since I lived in England."

Jake peered at Nettie from beneath quizzical eyebrows.

Tom poured molasses liberally. "Anyway, the city is dirty. It's foggy. Nothin' like Montana. Pure air. Beautiful skies."

"But they like rodeos."

Jake looked at Tom, then at Nettie. "Rodeos? In London?"

Tom took a big bite and closed his eyes. "Mmm. Good." He chewed and swallowed. "Yeah, they admire cowboys. Think the bloody Wild West is romantic." He chuckled.

Jake still had a puzzled look. "What's this talk about London?"

"Nothing." Nettie shrugged. "Just curious, that's all." She caught Marie's amused grin and turned away before Jake could see her own.

That evening after Tom and Marie had gone to bed, Nettie lingered over a cup of coffee with Jake. She circled her thumb around the rim of her cup. *I have to tell him. Can't put it off forever.* Clearing her throat, she blurted, "Marie is going to London with the Tex Austin Rodeo Troupe."

Jake raised one eyebrow. "Ah, so that's what the talk was all about this mornin'."

Nettie put on a bright smile. "Yeah, and guess what? She's asked me to go with her."

Jake sputtered in mid-sip. "You?"

Nettie nodded. "That was my reaction too. Little ol' me?"

"Whoa." He shook his head as if to clear it. "Well, that's quite an honor."

"And I want to go." Her knee jiggled in excited anticipation.

Jake took a breath and blew it out pursed lips. He glanced toward the papers he'd been scribbling on the day before. "I'm sure you do, little gal, and I wish you could—"

"I know we don't have the money," Nettie interrupted. "But I have it all figured out." She leaned back with a big smile. "Marie and Tom are going to buy Toby and Blacky, and that'll be enough to pay for the train and boat over."

Her husband's jaw dropped. "You'd go without me?"

"Oh, honey." His hurt look loomed before her, heavy and dark. "I didn't mean—" She jumped up, came around to his chair, and encircled his shoulders with her arms. She nuzzled his ear. "I don't want to leave you. Maybe my folks would lend us enough and you could come too." Her voice rose in a hopeful plea. "This is what I've been looking forward to, since I was fourteen. It's a chance of a lifetime."

Jake stood and scrubbed a hand through his sandy blond hair. "I can't go. Gotta stay here and take care of the horses, the ranch." He grabbed his hat and headed for the door, letting it slam behind him.

Nettie felt the air go out of her as if she'd been kicked by a steer. A hot tear escaped and trickled down her cheek. This was no better than dealing with Mama's objections to rodeo. *Gosh, am I just being selfish?*

Nettie tossed and turned all night. Pictures of horses and cowboys on a huge ship flashed through her mind, interrupted by Jake's hound-dog look. London. A big city. A big chance. But she and Jake were partners now. Married. She sat upright in bed. Jake's side was still empty. *Is this going to hurt our marriage? It can't. I love him so much.*

After Marie and Tom left the next day, Jake lingered at the breakfast table over his coffee. "Listen. I know what an opportunity this is for you." He blew on the hot brew and took a sip.

"You're right. I may never get it again." Nettie attempted to swallow the lump that rose in her throat. *Here it comes, the NO.* "I'd only be gone a couple of months. You could go if you wanted to." She turned her face away, gazed out the frosted window.

"Been doin' a lot of thinkin'. Tom came downstairs and we talked a long time last night."

She shivered. *He's going to try to let me down easy.*

"You can't sell ol' Toby and Blacky. We've got a couple pairs of draft horses we can prob'ly sell." Jake took a folded sheet of paper from his shirt pocket.

This was it then. Might as well get used to the idea. She'd probably never get any farther than Miles City in rodeo.

She barely heard Jake's voice. "I think they're bringing about thirty to thirty-five dollars a head nowadays. Should bring enough to cover the train and boat tickets, anyway."

"What?" Nettie snapped her head back to face Jake. "Sell draft pairs?" She stared at him, at a loss for words for a moment. "Say that again. Did you say boat ticket?"

He nodded.

Her mouth dropped open. "I can go?" Nettie jumped up. Dear sweet man. He was willing to help her.

Then guilt shattered her excitement. Nettie paced the length of the kitchen. Her mind buzzed, filled first with elation, then with despair. This was her dream, so close, and yet . . .

"I don't know. You weren't planning to sell them, and anyway, we could use that money to fund our own rodeo instead." How could she even ask Jake to consider it? "I can't take that." She sat heavily beside him.

"Sure you can." Jake put his arm around her shoulders. "What are plans for, but to be changed?"

Doubts prickled through her. "Oh, Jake. I can't ask you to do that. Besides, how could I get ready in time? If we'd had a year to plan—"

Jake laughed. "For someone who was just about to tell me where to go, you sure turned skittish all of a sudden. Besides, I know you. You'd probably sell your boots to go, maybe even me."

Face flaming, Nettie looked down at the table. She'd been acting like a spoiled child, not thinking like an adult.

"As far as you gettin' ready, we could scrape the mud out of the corrals, have your brother bring some steers over and you can start practicing tomorrow, if you want. Bein' muddy, well, so much the better. Just gives you more reason to stay on." He winked at her.

The icy swirls on the window suddenly glinted with the rising sun.

Jake was willing to sell the teams. He had a plan to help her go. She wanted this so bad. Nettie jumped up and smothered his face with kisses. "Thank you, honey, thank you. I love you so much." Then her shoulders slumped. "But you. Couldn't you go too?"

Jake shook his head. "No, I can't leave the ranch and the horses. But I think you oughta go."

Nettie felt dizzy. Including travel, she'd have to leave Jake for two months. She surely couldn't stand being away from him that long. But it was a dream come true. How could she turn it down? She closed her eyes, and her heart beat faster. "No. I can't. I won't go without you."

"Okay, then. It's settled. We'll both stay home." Jake stood up and carried his coffee cup to the dishpan.

"No! Wait." Nettie rushed to his side. "I take it back. I'm going."

She looked up at Jake, and a wide grin lit up his face. "Well, make up your mind, little gal." He laughed and reached out to tickle her.

She giggled. It was all right with him. Her boot toes beat a happy tattoo on the linoleum. "Yes. I do. I want to go." Nettie ducked her head. "I'll miss you."

"How much?"

"This much." She stretched her arms out wide. Jake wrapped his arms around her.

Her husband, her best friend.

CHAPTER THREE

Thursday, March 6, 1924

Today I ride again. Can't wait. London, here I come.

Nettie clambered atop the log fence as Jake hitched up the team to scrape the mud and an overnight skiff of snow out of the corral. Her breath steamed against the cold gray sky. Any minute now, she'd wake up and find this all a dream.

She yelled out to him, "I can't believe I'm really going to London with the Tex Austin Wild West Show." He grinned and tipped his hat toward her.

Butterflies swarmed in her stomach. She'd been no farther from home than Miles City when she went to the Roundup with Marie two years ago. What a huge adventure that had been, to travel across the state by train with all the horses and cowboys, to watch the best riders in Montana compete.

She absentmindedly massaged the wrist she'd broken when the steer had thrown her at that rodeo. There was always the chance she'd be injured again. But even though that broken bone had sidelined her for months, it had been worth it. *I'm not going to let anything stop me from riding.*

Jake plowed the first swath, piling the muck in one corner of the corral. Nettie fidgeted on her perch, itching to be on the back of some ornery beast, one that would challenge her winter-softened muscles. She had a lot of riding to do in the next couple of months to get ready.

The next morning Nettie awoke early and launched herself out of bed. She hurried through breakfast and left the dishes for later. As she and Jake walked out to the corral, her brother Ben arrived with ten head of steers. "Looks like you're gonna have a rodeo. Need some help?"

Nettie hugged him. "Yeah. Thanks for bringing the stock."

He and Jake penned the animals, cut one out, and held its head down by the ears to prevent it from thrashing around.

"Whoa, now." Jake spoke softly to the animal.

Nettie eased herself down from the corral fence onto the back of the red steer. Squirming to get a solid seat, she slid her gloved hand under the rope rigging to anchor her fist. The gut-roiling memory of her very first ride washed over her. With her other hand, she pulled her hat down tight. *I can do this.*

She looked at Jake, who grinned and raised his eyebrows. "Ready?"

Nettie mentally tamped down the fluttering in her stomach and nodded. *Ready or not, here it comes.* Jake and Ben let go of the animal's ears. The big steer leaped forward, bawled its disgust, and kicked its heels to one side while its head twisted to the other. Nettie bounced hard a couple of times, her teeth rattling, before she settled into a rhythm. After a very long eight seconds, Jake blew a whistle; Nettie slipped from the steer's back and ran to the fence to get away from the still-bucking animal.

"Yahoo." Ben waved his hat in congratulations. "Great ride."

Jake grinned and gave her a hug. "Good job, little gal. I can hardly tell you've had the past few months off."

"Of course." A glow of satisfaction warmed Nettie. She hadn't forgotten how. "I can still ride." She let a giggle escape.

Day after day, hour after hour, Nettie mounted one steer after another. She gave the go-ahead signal again and again, and tried to adjust herself to each animal's unique moves. Sometimes she rode until Jake's whistle signaled a successful ride.

Just as often, she was thrown to the frozen ground. Her legs ached, her hips were black and blue. Frustration filled her. Nettie fought back hot tears and pounded her gloved fists on her thighs. This would never do. She had to perform better before the trip and be able to graduate to bulls or Tex Austin wouldn't take her to London.

"Come on, little gal. Why don't you rest awhile?" Jake pleaded when she limped back to the fence.

"No." She gritted her teeth. "I gotta try it again."

Each night she went to bed surrounded by hot water bottles to ease her aches and bruises. But in spite of the bone-deep weariness, she looked back over her day in satisfaction with hard work well done. As she drifted off to sleep in Jake's arms, thoughts tickled through her mind. London. Travel. Rodeos. Maybe even fame.

The days ran together as she repeated the relentless practice. Each morning, Nettie arose with new determination. *Today I'll do better.* She lay back on the bed to button her denims. Strange how they seemed tighter despite the grueling work she was doing. She sucked in a breath. *Must be building lots of muscle.*

Finally, winter's snow and ice gave way to March's thaw. The corral's hard ground became a quagmire. Nettie fought to stay on the steers' backs if only to avoid one more mud-and-manure bath. But soon the spring winds sucked the moisture from the soil as April brought warm sun and new grass.

On one of those soft mornings, Nettie awoke with a groan. She snuggled farther into the covers. Lethargy weighed her down. Her head pounded and she felt every joint protest. What would it hurt if she skipped today? The temptation to stay in bed this morning was so great she couldn't even summon the excitement thoughts of London usually evoked. Maybe she'd been working too hard.

She heard Jake clattering pans in the kitchen downstairs and reluctantly swung her feet over the side of the bed. Smelling coffee brewing and bacon frying, she stood up. Nausea hit her with such a force she almost didn't reach the chamber pot before retching. The room swayed.

Kneeling on the cold hard floor, Nettie leaned against the side of the bed. A cold sweat had drenched her nightgown, and she shivered. She grabbed at the blankets to pull herself back into bed, but sank to the floor, weak as a newborn calf.

Jake clumped up the stairs. "Up 'n' at 'em, sunshine. Breakfast is ready." He burst into the room. "I brought you coff— " He put down the cup and knelt beside her. "Nettie, honey, what's the matter?"

"Sick." Nettie couldn't say more.

Jake helped her into bed and dabbed the sweat from her brow with his bandanna. He sat beside her on the bed, stroking her hand. "You've been working too hard. Maybe you'd better take a day or two off."

Nettie nodded, then drifted off to sleep. Later, she felt better and got up, ready to ride again, but Jake convinced her to stay inside. That afternoon, she sat in her rocking chair and sipped warm broth. Maybe she'd caught the influenza. But there was no cough, no congestion. Maybe it was something she'd eaten the night before. Was it the leftover venison she'd warmed up? But Jake wasn't sick.

She sighed. Oh, well, she felt okay now. But it was nice to just rest for a change. She reflected on the past weeks of bone-jarring work. Yes, it was hard, but doggone, she loved it. Every jar, every jounce. Even flying through the air to land on the hard ground. It gave her purpose. Charged her life with spark, like the battery in that old Model T Jake had bought when he courted her.

Nettie curled her hands around the warm cup. Nothing satisfied her more than knowing she could pit herself—all 102 pounds of her— against a 900-pound animal, and come out on top. She leaned back in the chair and dozed.

That evening, Jake went out to do chores, and Nettie got up to cook supper, but as soon as the pungent aroma of frying meat hit her nostrils, she ran for the slop bucket by the back door of the kitchen. Her stomach heaved until she thought it would come up too. Panting, wiping the sweat from her face, she slumped into a chair. What was this?

A chill came over her as she remembered the influenza that made her whole family so sick and took her baby sister three years before. She blinked back the grief that returned to overwhelm her.

Nettie covered her abdomen with her hands. The ache of that loss never quite went away. She gently massaged her belly. Something didn't feel quite right. A surge of adrenaline shot through her. Her head spun.

No. It couldn't be. Was she—?

Her thoughts jackrabbited. When had she last had her monthly? She'd been so busy training, she hadn't noticed. Nettie counted backward. This was April. No, she couldn't remember anything in March. February. Before Marie and Tom came with their news of London.

No. It couldn't be. The knowledge shook her and she buried her face in her hands. She was pregnant.

After a sleepless night, Nettie walked to the pasture with a halter, vaulted onto Tootsie's bare back, and dug her heels into the mare's sides. She wanted to scream. Had to get away, to think. Her stomach cramped. No. She wouldn't give in to the nausea.

Nettie grasped with her knees and urged Tootsie faster. The horse's great muscles bunched and smoothed as she galloped through the meadow toward the rims, the flat-topped hills that surrounded their valley. The power and speed of the ride calmed Nettie and allowed her mind to go blank. A cool spring breeze blew through her hair.

When they reached the small reservoir, Nettie slowed Tootsie to a trot, then stopped under the lonely cottonwood tree. She slipped from her horse's broad back, left the reins to dangle, and walked to the edge of the water, murky from the spring runoff.

Nettie scrubbed her fingers through her hair. It had never occurred to her that she would get pregnant. What an idiot. What had she been thinking? This was not a subject she could have comfortably broached with Jake, or even her mother and her sisters, although they had given plenty of hints in the form of ribald jokes. Of course she knew the breeding and calving cycles from watching the cows.

But this was different. This was her. Nettie kicked at a dirt clod. She hadn't planned on having kids. She was going to go to London and be a rodeo star, had been dreaming of something like this her whole life.

The blood drained from her face. Her ears buzzed. She would have to give it all up. Have a brood of kids like her mother. Cook and clean up after them. Listen to them scream. Change dirty diapers. Wipe noses.

Nettie doubled over, pounding her fists on her knees. No. No. No. What was she going to do? Maybe she wouldn't have to tell Jake. Not just yet. Maybe she'd just keep riding, go to London anyway, pretend this wasn't happening. She sank to the damp earth, groaning in her frustration.

A small black beetle climbed a stalk of grass. Nettie watched each painstaking step upward. Then a wind gust shook the stalk and the insect fell to the ground, only to begin the journey over. Again and again. What patience this bug had. Maybe it was just stupid. What was it aiming for, anyway? If it ever reached the top, its weight would just topple the whole thing.

The sun passed its midday peak and warmed her. She reached out, flicked her finger at the beetle, and watched it land at the base of a sagebrush. "If you're going to have a goal, might as well try for something worthwhile."

She stood. Time to get back and get on with her life. No use stewing about what couldn't be helped. Maybe she could work around the nausea, keep training. She pulled herself up onto Tootsie's back and rode slowly homeward in the lengthening afternoon shadows.

Jake looked up from the upturned horse's hoof he held between his knees and shoved his hat back from his forehead. "Have a nice ride?"

Nettie nodded, not trusting her voice. She crawled off the horse and removed Tootsie's halter. "Yeah, nice day for a jaunt." Her nerves humming at a raw pitch, she felt Jake's eyes on her and busied herself brushing the mare.

He finished his task, slapped the big draft horse on the rump to send him off, and came to stand beside her. For the first time, instead of comforting her, his big, warm presence felt intrusive. A chill ran through her. She mustn't let on how she was feeling. Nettie ducked under Tootsie's neck to brush her other side.

His low voice came softly across the horse's back. "Do you have something you want to tell me?"

An involuntary whimper escaped Nettie's throat. Did he know? Her breath caught. Her hands shaking, she dropped the brush. Dizziness came over her and she staggered backward, only to be caught in Jake's arms as he rounded the horse.

He grasped her tight against his chest, rocked her, and stroked her hair. Her pent-up breath finally released in jerky little sobs.

His voice rumbled in his chest. "You're going to have a baby. I thought maybe so when you got sick yesterday."

He knows. She looked up into his face, her eyes wide. "What're we going to do?"

His eyes bored into hers. "Well now. I just figured you had a handle on that stuff, with your mom and your sisters and all."

Sure, leave it to a man not to even consider it. A few minutes of pleasure and now look. Her whole life had changed. She gulped. "It's not something people talk about much. Sure, I know Mama raised seven kids, but I thought it was 'cause she wanted them. I don't know. I guess I just didn't think about it."

"Yeah, neither one of us did." Jake dropped his arms, reached into his shirt pocket for his tobacco, avoiding her gaze.

A cold hollow formed inside. He was angry with her. Maybe he didn't want this child, either.

She clenched her fists. "Why are you mad at me? This wasn't all my doing." Her voice rose. It sounded hysterical to her, but she didn't care. "We're supposed to be partners. In rodeo, in ranching. In this, too. I can't do this by myself. I just can't."

Nettie swallowed a sob, turned, and ran toward the house. She heard Jake call, "Wait," but she wouldn't look back.

CHAPTER FOUR

Friday, April 25, 1924

A baby. London out of the question. Jake's upset. Guess he wasn't planning on this either. What am I going to do now? What's he going to do, give me back?

Nettie lay in bed, spent from the deep, wracking sobs that had enveloped her after she left Jake in the barnyard. When he came upstairs, he molded his body to cradle hers. She pretended to be asleep, biting her lip to keep the tears back.

Long after his breathing settled into soft snores, she lay staring into the night. A cool grassy breeze wafted through the slightly opened window.

She really shouldn't have been so angry, or yelled at him. But darn it anyhow. She thought he would've been a little more sympathetic. And just when she needed it the most, too. She knew she was right. That feeling of partnership was missing. Jake suddenly seemed so far away.

Soon Marie would be on the boat to London: excitement, fame, and fortune. Why couldn't things work out for her? Just once. She should be sailing along with her friend, the cowboys, the costumes, the horses, the bulls.

Hot tears welled. Something always seemed to get in the way of her plans. Suddenly that silly beetle climbing the grass stalk over and over came to mind. She was no closer to her dreams than that bug.

She turned to lie on her back.

Jake stirred beside her. "You awake? Feelin' okay?"

"Fine. Can't sleep. I've been thinking."

He raised up on one elbow. "What about?"

"Oh, just how unexpected things happen. Well, it's like before we were married, the day we were out gathering horses and that hailstorm came up so sudden. We weren't expecting it. We weren't ready for it."

"Yeah. You were scared, weren't you?" He reached over and stroked her arm.

Nettie sat up and adjusted her nightgown. "I didn't think we were going to make it, there, for awhile."

"But we did. Thank God that ol' shack was out there. We made it, and with just a few bruises and sore spots. Learned us to be more watchful, didn't it?"

"Of the weather, anyway." She paused. "But Jake, my rodeo dreams. And now this. We never talked about having kids. I guess I just figured we'd go on riding and rodeoing together, just the two of us. Wasn't that your dream too?"

Jake swung his legs over the side of the bed and reached for his cigarette papers and tobacco pouch on the nightstand. "Yeah. It was." His voice was flat, expressionless.

Surely he cared more than this. She pulled her pillow up to prop against the headboard. "C'mon, Jake, what are we going to do?"

He poured tobacco into the paper held between his fingers and thumb, then pulled the pouch strings shut with his teeth. Sealing the edges of the paper with the point of his tongue, he twisted the ends and struck a match on the bed frame. "Well, I think we're gonna have a baby." He took a deep drag.

"B-but, I didn't want to have kids. I just wanted to ride, go to rodeos with you. And go to London. Please don't be mad at me." Darn it, she wasn't going to cry again.

Jake stood in front of the window, his long, lean frame silhouetted in the moonlight, his white sleeveless undershirt molded to his strong torso. He exhaled a long streamer of smoke. "Honey, I'm not mad at you. I know how important this trip was to you." He turned toward her. "Sorry I reacted so badly. I was just surprised too, is all. I wasn't thinking we'd have kids so soon either, but that's the way of the world. It's what happens."

A wisp of smoke curled around his blond head. "But right now, you—and the baby—are the most important things in the world to me. You'll ride again."

Nettie sniffed and reached for a hanky.

"Maybe there's even another London trip in your future. We can't know that. Look at Marie. She has kids, but she's rodeoing again now that they're older. Havin' kids is a natural part of life."

"I know. But somehow, I thought I was different, that we might not have any. Some women don't."

"But most do." He finished the cigarette, stubbed it out in an ashtray on the windowsill, and slid into bed beside her. His warm hand caressed her stomach. "And I'm glad we're going to be a family. Our dreams can still come true. We have a long life ahead of us." He cradled her in his arms.

Nettie couldn't stay mad at him for long. Darn it, he always knew just what to say. She gave in to the warm reassurance of his body close to hers and relaxed against him.

For some strange reason, she felt content.

CHAPTER FIVE

Thursday, July 17, 1924

Marie's in London. I'm home, getting fat. Jake seems okay with the idea now. Not sure I am, still. Mama's beside herself with joy. Everybody's trying to pamper me. Don't like it. Can't ride steers anymore, but finally won argument with Jake. I'm still riding Tootsie every day. Don't care what anybody says.

Nettie opened another letter with newspaper clippings Marie had sent from London, laughing at the reactions of the English to the "Wild West." The reporters called the troupe "the queer and romantic men and women from the west" and dubbed the rodeos "Hell on Hind Legs."

She read a clipping from the *London Evening News*.

The cowgirls surprised London. It is amazing to see these slips of girls take fearful tosses while fighting outlaw horses, and then half an hour later it is still more amazing to see these same girls strolling out to tea in their Parisian frocks.

Nettie could just picture Marie, first dressed like a man, involved in a man's sport, then dolled up like a princess. She stared out the window at the prairie, browning in the summer sun. In a heartbeat of yearning, she imagined herself in Marie's place, receiving accolades from an adoring crowd. Why a baby? Why right now?

The kitchen door thumped open. Jake came in and leaned down to kiss her forehead. "More news from London?"

Nettie reached for another clipping. "Listen to this. You're not going to believe it: 'Enormous crowds attended the opening performance at Wembly. As in the ordinary run of events during a roping contest, several steers broke their legs and had to be shot.'"

She looked up from reading. "Says here a group called the Animal Protective League put out a pamphlet denouncing rodeo as *'too dangerous.'* Tex Austin and the riders were arrested for injuring the animals."

Jake's eyes widened. He shook his head. "Well, I'll be darned."

"There's more. They had a trial, and Marie writes that the courtroom was packed, and it was front-page news every day. Isn't that something?"

Jake pursed his lips and let out a whistle. "How'd it end?"

"Case was dismissed. The judge ruled that rodeo was not a form of cruelty to animals, but all a part of working western life, and if an animal was injured it was quickly and humanely put out of pain. Here's a quote from the newspaper: 'When asked if rodeos were cruel, American trick rider Tad Lucas answered, "Yes! But only for the cowboys and cowgirls."' Ha!"

Jake chuckled. "Ain't that the truth. What's this modern world coming to?"

"It's outrageous. How could they do that?" Nettie folded her arms. "I suppose that's England for you. They wouldn't do that here, would they?"

"Yeah well, I heard ol' Buffalo Bill was getting checked out by the ASPCA in the late 1880s already."

"Really?" Nettie hadn't been aware of that.

"And you know the Calgary Stampede doesn't have steer-wrestlin' or ropin' anymore, don't you, 'cause it's too hard on the 'poor animals.'" His tone was mocking. "But, matter of fact, us riders've had a heckuva lot more broken bones than the steers ever did."

Jake got up from the table and muttered something about "goin' out to 'abuse' the animals."

Bemused, Nettie folded the letter and clippings back into the envelope. She longed to have seen this excitement and drama.

She felt Jake's frustration, though. Nettie couldn't see the sheriff in Sunburst enforcing some fool law like that. But, if the authorities had already started to outlaw some events as close as Calgary, it might be only a matter of time before it happened in the United States. Then, she could just foresee someone coming up with the idea that riding steers and broncs was too dangerous for women. She tucked the envelope into the back of her journal. What a time to get pregnant. She might never get to rodeo again.

❦

Nettie lifted her foot, barely hooking the toe of her boot in the stirrup before it slipped out again. "Drat." She wiped the sweat from her face with her shirtsleeve. The hot August sun beat down on the parched earth, and miniature dust devils swirled around her. All this trouble just to ride into town to get some groceries.

"What's that you say, dear?" Jake came around the side of the barn, his head cocked.

"I said drat. Drat and dagnabbit anyway. I can't lift my foot high enough to catch the stirrup anymore."

Jake chuckled. "Guess we'll have to get you a step stool."

Nettie made a face at him. "You're full of beans." She tried again. Her foot slipped out of the stirrup and she fell heavily against Tootsie's flank, her face perilously close to the saddle hardware.

"Wait. Wait! Are you all right?" Jake rushed to her side.

"I'm fine. Just mighty clumsy." Nettie ground her teeth.

"Here, let me help you." He cupped his hands. Nettie stepped into them with one foot and he lifted her high enough to swing her other leg up over the saddle.

24

Jake's brow furrowed and he patted her stomach. "You're gettin' too big for this saddle. I'm worried about that high horn."

"Well, I'm not going to quit riding. I've already had to give up rodeo." Her snappish tone surprised her, and she ducked her head. "Sorry. It's the heat, I guess. I promise I'll be careful."

Jake pushed his hat back and studied the saddle. "Hmm. While we're in town this afternoon, let's stop at the blacksmith's. I have an idea."

"What?"

He winked. "Just you wait and see."

"Okay." Nettie frowned. *Wonder what he's thinking up now?* But if he wouldn't tell her, she wasn't about to give him the satisfaction of asking again. She nudged the horse forward. She could be just as stubborn as he was. She gave him a sideways glance. He sure was being nice, though, worried about the saddle and all.

﹏

The little town of Sunburst squatted on the valley floor, the blue shadows of the Sweet Grass Hills to the north along the Canadian border. Nettie and Jake rode past the grain elevator on the east edge of town and up to the livery station and blacksmith shop, where Sven Jorgensen swung his hammer against the heated steel just outside the smithy door. His arm muscles bulged beneath his rolled-up shirtsleeves and sweat poured from his smoke-blackened brow. He looked up as she and Jake dismounted.

"Hallo there, Jake, and Mrs. Jake." He bobbed his head. "What can I do you for?"

Jake smiled and gestured toward Nettie's protruding belly. "We have a little problem. Nettie here's not about to stop riding just because she's expectin', but I'm concerned about that sharp saddle horn, if her horse should stumble."

"Ya. I see." Sven wiped his face with a gray towel. "Maybe she shouldn't ought to ride no more."

"No." Nettie squared her shoulders. "That's not an option."

Sven jerked his head around in surprise. "Okay. You want I should cut it off?"

Jake nodded. "That might work. That's what I was thinkin' at first, but I think the saddle's too deep and narrow front to back. She still has three months to go."

"Why are you talking like I'm not here?" Nettie scuffed her toe in the dust. "I could just ride bareback."

Sven stepped back, his eyes wide, and Jake moved closer to put an arm around her. "You're one terrific rider, little gal, but I'm afraid you might slip. Your center of gravity is a little off."

Nettie rolled her eyes.

Sven tapped a grimy finger on a front tooth. "Say, I just remember. You might check with the Johannsens. I think one o' their boarders mighta left a saddle with no horn."

"I knew you'd come up with somethin', Svenny." Jake clapped the blacksmith on the shoulder and turned to Nettie, his hands cupped to help her remount. "C'mon, let's go visit the Johannsens. I guess you haven't met them yet. Cleve's the county surveyor."

Nettie kept quiet, but inside felt like a teakettle about to boil. Why did women have to get so heavy and ungainly with pregnancy? She and Jake rode through town past the Sunburst Merc and the Stockman's Bar on one side of the main street. Nettie wiped sweat from her brow. *If I wasn't in this condition, we'd probably be stopping for a cold one at the Stockman's.*

On the other side of the street stood a two-story bank and the theater, advertising the silent movie *The Iron Horse*, directed by John Ford. Nettie felt her mouth droop. *Or maybe we'd take in the show.* Her carefree life had changed and she wasn't sure it was for the better.

As they approached a weathered clapboard house at the west edge of town, Nettie saw a toddler playing in the dust that was the front yard. *A dirty kid.* She swallowed. *A glimpse into my future?*

The little boy had somehow made a patch of mud. His diaper had been discarded nearby, his bottom firmly rooted in the mire. He slapped his hands and feet in it, chortling and singing an off-key baby tune. Suddenly a chuckle rose in Nettie's throat. Despite her reluctant thoughts, she couldn't help but feel drawn to this grinning little imp. Maybe she'd have a little boy like that. Or, a little girl.

A tall, angular blond woman came to the open door, wiping her hands on an apron that stretched across a bulging stomach.

Nettie stared.

"Hello? Well, hello there, Jake." She put out a hand. "And you must be Nettie. I'm Myra." The woman stopped, her eyes coming to rest on her young son. "Oh, goodness, Russ. What have you gotten into? Two-year-olds. They're always coming up with something new. Oh well, he's cool and happy." She laughed then. "Come on in out of that heat. I'll get you some iced tea, and then I'll dunk Mr. Mudpie in the horse trough."

Nettie smiled. Myra certainly was calm and cool with her messy little one. *Could I be like that?* She followed the woman inside.

Everything in Myra's cheerful kitchen was blue and white, from the checkered curtains on the window and covering the cupboard fronts, to the tablecloth. Even the floor was a blue linoleum with white splotches.

Nettie settled her bulk gratefully into a kitchen chair, massaged her belly, and stretched her stiff legs. Riding was getting more difficult, although she'd never admit that to Jake. She watched the woman chip ice from the block in the icebox. Myra put the chips into glasses, poured in the tea, and offered the drinks to Nettie and Jake. "Looks like you're due pretty soon."

Nettie took a sip and closed her eyes, savoring the cool drink. "Yeah, about three more months. And you?"

"Any day now." Myra chuckled. "Not soon enough, as far as I'm concerned."

"Are you going to the hospital in Cut Bank?" Nettie held the cold glass to her cheek.

"Naw. I'll have it at home, just like the first, Virginia, and with the muddy one out there. I drop 'em so easy, it's hardly worth going to bed for." Myra laughed, a merry tinkle.

Nettie gazed at her in wonder. "Birthing three kids and you're still so cheerful. What's your secret?"

Myra burst into guffaws this time. "Oh, you'll find out. I know you're scared, with the first one. But being a mother is just the most natural wonder God ever gave us. Kids are a delightful distraction from everyday life."

Nettie couldn't help but laugh with her. This woman she could get to like.

Cleve Johannsen arrived a little later. Jake told him of Nettie's predicament and Sven's suggestion.

The big man thought a moment. "Yeah. It's an English saddle of some kind, used for racing, I think. Got no horn. Let's go take a look."

Jake followed Cleve outside, and Nettie accompanied Myra to collect Russ. He protested mightily when she picked him out of the mud, holding him off to the side of her large belly. His wails turned to gasps as she plunged him into the watering trough and pumped cold water over him. He squealed with delight then and splashed in the water until his mother had the mud rinsed off his chubby body.

Nettie caressed her stomach and smiled. What a cute little towhead. Would her baby be so happy, so carefree? As if in answer, she felt a familiar flutter beneath her hands. She met Myra's gaze and her smile broadened. Maybe being a mother wouldn't be so bad after all.

Nettie sat in the shade the next day, fanning herself in the heat and watching Jake with increasing excitement. *I'll be able to ride again.*

He unlaced the short racing flaps and stirrups from the flat, hornless saddle and replaced them with longer gear so she could ride western-style. Then he hoisted it onto Tootsie's back and cinched it up snug. "Okay, it's ready to go. Wanna try it out?"

"Sure." Nettie stepped onto the huge log Jake had dragged into the corral so she could mount without help, and swung into the saddle. "Let's ride over to Papa's, pay them a visit. I can't wait to show them this saddle." She laughed. "It looks so funny without the pommel. I feel like I'm going to fall forward."

Jake put his hand on her tummy. "You'll get used to it. Now I don't have to worry about little Jake here gettin' hurt." He winked. "Can't wait till he can come ridin' with us."

"Little Nettie." Nettie teased back, warmth suffusing her face.

"We'll see. Betcha it's a boy." Jake mounted Alsanger.

They generated their own welcome breeze riding along in the stifling summer heat. Nettie swayed in the saddle, growing used to its feel. She closed her eyes, leaned forward, and drew her knees up along the horse's shoulders as far as she could before the stance put pressure on her middle. She pictured herself on a racehorse, galloping at breakneck speed around a track, leaving the other riders in the dust, just like Marie Gibson at the Miles City Roundup a couple of years ago.

Excitement coursed up Nettie's spine. Racing horses. That might be even more fun than riding steers or broncs.

She opened her eyes wide. "That's what we should do—breed racehorses."

Jake's head drew back in surprise. "Racehorses? Hmm." He rubbed his chin and rode in silence for awhile. "Interesting thought. Racing is gettin' to be more and more popular at the rodeos." He tipped his hat back and scratched his head. "I might know of a guy in Canada we could talk to, maybe buy a thoroughbred stallion and a mare or two."

"Yeah. I could ride in the races, and if we had a winner, we could raise colts to sell." Nettie returned Jake's grin and they rode on, her thoughts on the future.

The well-worn trail over the rim of hills to Nettie's family homestead had grown as familiar as her own kitchen. In the past two years she had ridden back and forth several times a week to visit Jake and help him with his herd of horses. Now that they were married, she and

Jake made the hour-long ride over the nine miles to visit only about once a month. They topped the last rise and she could see the little house on the knoll.

Mama straightened up from her garden as she saw them approach, lifted her red-checkered apron, and flapped it in greeting. She ran toward them, her face bathed in a broad smile, and raised her hand to help Nettie down from her horse. Her embrace was tight and warm. Nettie hugged Mama's shoulders in return.

Every time she saw her mother, a warm wave of relief washed over Nettie that Mama had forgiven her for eloping. She had missed her mother those months Mama shunned her.

Jake gave a quick wave and turned his horse toward the field where the men were working.

"What a nice surprise. I'm so glad you came today. I just put up a bunch of green beans, and Papa shot a young antelope yesterday. We'll have a celebration." Mama stepped back, her hands on her hips. "My, my. That baby's just growing like a melon in there. You're so pretty, my dear, just glowing. Come, come inside, we don't want you to get heat stroke." She picked up her basket of greens.

Nettie grinned wryly. Mama was like a hen with chicks ever since she found out Nettie was expecting. She would've thought her mother would be shaking her head, commiserating with her uncomfortable state, knowing the hardships, the pain, the work. But no, despite having birthed eight children of her own, one or more miscarriages, and three grandkids from Margie and Lola, she seemed to be happily looking forward to another grandchild. Nettie shook her head. *Some women just like having lots of kids around, I guess.*

"Does it hurt a lot, Mama, giving birth?"

Mama smoothed Nettie's hair from her forehead. "Well, yes. But when you see that precious little bundle, you won't even remember it."

Nettie raised her eyebrows. How could that be?

At suppertime Jake followed Papa, Ben, and Eddie in from the fields, and they sluiced the grime from their arms and faces in the water trough outside the kitchen door. Nettie's brothers greeted her with broad grins.

Eddie teased, "Hey, gettin' pretty fat, huh, sis?"

She stuck her tongue out at him.

Ben punched Jake's arm and winked as they trooped to the long pine table. Papa swung an arm around her shoulders and planted a kiss on the top of her head. "Good to see you lookin' so well."

"Thanks, Papa. After we eat, I want to show you my new saddle." Nettie smiled across at Jake and drew in the homey smell of roast antelope, new potatoes, and fresh green beans. Almost like old times.

CHAPTER SIX

Friday, November 7, 1924

Winter coming soon. I'm so big I can hardly stand it. Ready for this baby to be born.

Nettie paced the floor from kitchen to living room and back again, stopping occasionally to peer out at the leaden November clouds. Looked like it could snow any minute. The baby kicked violently.

"Calm down there, little one." She massaged her stomach. "I know you're ready to come into the world. But you've got a couple more weeks in there yet." On the other hand, *she* was ready for this to be over. She felt so heavy. So misshapen.

Maybe a short ride would calm the turmoil inside. Nettie groaned. She reached for her winter coat and patted her belly. "Enjoy this while you can. It's gonna be cold out here in the world."

Nettie led Tootsie alongside the big log and tried to hoist herself up onto the horse's bare back. Jake had been so sweet to get that flat saddle for her, but today she didn't want to bother with it. She wanted to feel the warmth of the mare's winter coat, the ripple of muscles as she rode. But without a stirrup, she was unable to lift herself up. She tried again and failed. With an exasperated grunt, she maneuvered the horse next to the corral fence, and climbed up the poles high enough to ease onto Tootsie's back.

This was only the first week in November. The baby wasn't due till around Thanksgiving, but she sure did feel uncomfortable. And so restless. Several times recently, Jake had come in from chores and expressed amazement to see her scrubbing, dusting, re-fluffing the tiny comforter in the wooden cradle he had made. Domestic busy work just wasn't her.

And the baby expressed discomfort as well, keeping her awake most of the night, kicking and moving around. She tried not to worry, but couldn't help feeling a twinge of fear when she thought about what it would be like, giving birth. Despite Mama's reassurances, it had to be terribly painful.

Then having the little one to take care of. Would it be a boy or a girl? She wondered how long she'd be tied down until the child was old enough to ride along with her. Four or five years, maybe. Drat. It seemed forever. What if she got pregnant again and had another kid, or several more? She'd never get to rodeo again. She heaved a great moaning sigh. Why, oh, why?

"No. I will *not* have a bunch of kids. That's just not acceptable. I won't do it." Tootsie's ears flicked back at Nettie's shouted words. *But how do I prevent it?*

She reined Tootsie toward the east pasture. The frozen grass crunched beneath the horse's feet, and she could see their breath hover on the frosty air. A wind gust tugged at her coat. It was getting colder. She hoped it wouldn't snow too much before the baby was due. The thirty miles to Cut Bank and the Purcell Maternity Home was a long way even in good weather. Sven, the blacksmith, had volunteered to drive them to town when the time came, but if the baby decided to come early, she wondered how they would coordinate all that.

Jake would stay with Snooky and Ruth O'Haire, the couple who'd stood up with them at their wedding in Great Falls. She hadn't seen them since they'd moved back to Cut Bank. Maybe she'd be able to become friends with Ruth now and learn more about fashions and town living. But no, probably not. The O'Haires didn't have children. Nettie was about to. The O'Haires were rich. She and Jake were not.

And what would Nettie do with the latest fashions now, anyway? She rolled her eyes.

The horse's gentle gait seemed to sooth the baby. Finally, no more kicking. The tightness in Nettie's back muscles relaxed. She turned the horse toward home and fought to stay awake herself, in spite of the cold.

"There you are." Jake's shout roused her. "I was just about to get worried." He hurried up to Tootsie's side and helped Nettie slide off. "Gosh, you're bareback. I wish you'd taken your saddle."

Nettie shot him a look from beneath lowered brows. "It's more comfortable this way."

He frowned. "I went to the trouble to find you that saddle, and now you've put yourself—and the baby—in danger."

"Jake." Nettie drew out his name in a warning tone and narrowed her eyes.

He ducked his head with a sigh. "I know, honey. I just worry about you." He took her into his embrace.

She smiled up at him and kissed him on the cheek. A lone snow-flake drifted between them. "What if it snows before we can get to Cut Bank?"

"Well, I've been thinkin' that same thing. So, when I was in Sun-burst this afternoon, I talked to Sven. He's coming out to get us first thing tomorrow morning in his Model T, and he'll come back to take care of the horses. We're gonna go to town early, just in case." He patted her shoulder and chuckled. "I don't want to have to deliver a baby myself in the middle of a snowstorm."

Jake's words soothed Nettie's worries. That suited her just fine. She and Jake had helped many a heifer and mare give birth, but this was a little different. She couldn't quite see Jake hooking her up to the calf-pulling gear.

Early the next morning, pain spasmed from her lower back through her abdomen. She grabbed her midsection with a sharp cry and pulled her knees up, curling forward.

Beside her, Jake jerked to a sitting position. "What? What is it?"

Nettie drew a long breath. The pain passed quickly, thank God, but she'd thought for a second there it was going to tear her in two. *Is this what it's going to be like? Oh, dear Lord, how am I going to get through this?* She exhaled through pursed lips. *No need to worry Jake.* "Just a momentary pain. I think going to town today is a very good idea."

By the time she was dressed and Jake had coffee made, they heard the putt-putt of Sven's Model T touring car outside. While the blacksmith arranged blankets and hot water bottles in the backseat, Jake picked up Nettie's suitcase, put his arm around her waist, and escorted her to the car. He tucked the blankets around her, climbed in, and rebuttoned the canvas curtains covering the windows. Sven ground the gears and they drove off in the heavy gray dawn.

Amber stalks of grass poked through the skiff of snow that covered the prairie. The temperature had risen, and Nettie saw a few big flakes hit the windshield. A contraction cramped her abdomen. She bit her lip to keep from crying out, forced herself to breathe deeply. She prayed the snow would hold off until they got to town. *Oh God, I don't want to do this. Please help me.* It was going to be a long thirty miles.

Sven flicked a lever on the steering column. "W-e-l-l, I'm sure glad I bought the electric windshield wipers on this here Tin Lizzy."

"Yeah, me too." Jake bent his head forward to peer at the back and forth movement of the wipers. "Even though it don't rain more'n once in a month of Sundays around here, those gadgets are sure earnin' their keep today."

Once Sven turned onto the hard-packed road leading south to Cut Bank, he shifted and accelerated. The sudden increase in speed pushed Nettie against the backseat and she gasped.

Jake turned to look at her. "You doin' all right back there, sweetheart? Are you having pains?"

"No, I'm fine." She lifted the corners of her mouth into a wan smile, just to reassure Jake. The speed of automobile travel still sent shivers up her spine. She longed for the nice, smooth back of a horse to hang on to. But then again, she imagined the long, slow, cold ride in their horse-drawn wagon. No, she was thankful for Sven's touring car. While not heated, it was sheltered from the wind, the seat was comfortable, and she appreciated the hot water bottles packed around her. Her middle stretched tight like the pig bladder her brothers had filled with air and played ball with as kids. *So uncomfortable. I want this to be over.* She stretched her legs along the length of the seat, tried to find a position of relief in the blankets, and closed her eyes. Maybe if she could fall asleep, they'd get there quicker.

Nettie's eyes popped open as the car swerved around a curve. To her horror, she saw another car coming straight at them. "No!" she yelled out. She braced her feet against the opposite side, covered her belly with one arm, and grabbed the hand-hold strap hanging from above the door with the other hand.

Sven yelled out a string of Norsk syllables and wrenched the wheel. The oncoming car veered by with only inches to spare. The Model T skidded to the right, fishtailing on the snow-packed road. Sven wrestled with the steering wheel and stomped on the brake. The car continued its slow-motion spiral across the road, turning, twisting, sliding.

Jake shouted.

Sven cursed.

Nettie screamed and held onto the strap with all her strength, her body rigid.

Then a loud thump vibrated through the entire car. The rear slid and hung onto the road for a split second before being wrenched to an abrupt stop in the shallow ditch.

Nettie sat in stunned silence. For a moment, the two men also were still. Sven's hands still had a death grip on the wheel. Jake's arms and legs were spread-eagled in a brace against the dashboard.

Then Jake jerked open the door and came around to the backseat. He put his arms around Nettie. "Are you all right? Honey? Talk to me. Are you hurt?"

Sven loosened his grip, grabbed the bulb that blew the horn, and pumped it furiously. The raucous claxon blared, accentuating his shouts. "That consarned son of a coyote!" More Swedish followed and he pounded the steering wheel.

Nettie did a quick scan of her body, wiggled her fingers and toes, and rotated her neck. Everything seemed to be working. "Uh." Her voice came out in a croak. She cleared her throat. "I'm okay. Are you?"

"Yeah. Me too." Jake grasped her hand tightly, peering into her face. "The baby?"

But the baby had gone quiet. Nettie held her breath, waiting. What had happened? Her throat closed. Why couldn't she feel the baby? She didn't think she'd hit her stomach anywhere.

"Honey, what's happening?" Jake's face was etched with worry.

Oh, dear God, no. Is the baby—? Then she felt it. A hard kick against her taut abdomen that felt like it would rip right through her. "Ahh." Nettie let out her breath in a gasp of pain and waved a hand. "Honest, we're just fine. The baby's kicking." For once she was glad to feel those blows.

"Oh, good." Jake blew out a pent-up breath and looked around at Sven. A curve of a smile began. "And I think Svenny is all right too, at least physically."

Sven turned to them, a flush rising up his neck and spreading to the roots of his white-blond hair. "Ah, Jake. Mrs. Jake. I'm so sorry. Please forgive my cussing, that I get so mad." He looked out the side window, down the road where the other car had disappeared. "But I like to shoot that son of—ah, excuse, please."

Jake opened the door. "Let's take a look at the situation. We've gotta get our little gal to the hospital." The men got out.

Sven kicked at the rear tire. "Dang, it's flat."

"And we're stuck pretty good in this snowdrift. Good thing this ditch isn't too deep." Jake shoved his hat back and scratched his forehead. "Well, we'd better get busy."

Nettie eased out of the backseat to watch the men. The breeze swept her with chilling fingers. Snowflakes landed on her lashes. Her nerves jangled as she remembered the number of times Jake changed flat tires on that trip to Browning when they were courting. A cramp gripped her middle. She held her hands to her abdomen to keep from crying out and leaned against the car. Would they make it in time? *What if the baby comes before we get there? If it starts snowing harder, we're in trouble.* She bit her lip and held herself tight.

Sven unfastened the spare from the rear of the car, then reached into the storage compartment for a jack. Jake shoveled snow from around the tire. Wading through the deep drift to the road, he kicked through the snow until he found a flat rock.

"Don't worry, honey, we'll be outta here in a jiffy." He placed it under the axle to brace the jack, and pumped until the wheel slowly lifted out of the compacted drift. The two men grunted, pulled, and pushed, Sven punctuating their efforts with Swedish curses. Finally they had the old tire and wheel unscrewed from the hub and mounted the spare.

"Okay. We got that done." Jake mopped his brow with his shirt-sleeve. "Now, how're we gonna get outta this ditch?"

Sven looked at him with a lopsided grin. "We gonna push." He turned to Nettie. "Can you sit in driver's seat and keep the wheel straight?"

Nettie felt the blood drain from her face. "Me? I don't know how to drive."

"You don't haffta. Just steer the wheel."

Nettie opened the door. "I don't know if I can fit in here." With a grunt, she heaved her awkward bulk up into the driver's seat, and gingerly squeezed into position, the steering wheel pressing her abdomen slightly. "I can barely breathe." She gripped the wheel tight with gloved hands. Her heart hammered. She looked back at the men with their hands positioned on the rear of the car. "Ready?"

Jake nodded and they gave a heave. The car rocked slightly and settled back into the snow. They tried again and yet again.

"She's stuck good." Sven came around to Nettie's window. "If I start 'er up and show you which pedals to push, can you help?"

Her heart galloped faster. "I don't know." Her stomach cramped again. *Oh, my gosh, is the baby coming now?* "Jake!" Her voice rose to a wail.

Jake's head loomed next to Sven's. "You can do it, little gal. Hang on. It's all right. If you can ride the toughest steers and the rangiest broncs, you can push a coupla pedals."

She looked into her husband's encouraging face and gulped. "Okay. I'll try."

"Good girl." Jake reached in and squeezed her shoulder.

Sven hunkered down in front to crank the Model T. The engine caught and chugged. He came to the window. "Now, hold down this pedal. When we yell, ease off and push the gas lever here on the steering column. If we yell again, push this pedal on the right and let up on the gas. Okay, got it?"

"Okay." Nettie grimaced. She wasn't so sure. At the signal, she pulled her foot slowly from the left pedal while pushing down on the gas lever. The engine roared, the wheels spun, but the car didn't move. The men yelled. She stopped.

Sven gave further instructions. "Now, we gonna do it again. But we want to get car to rocking back and forth. So give 'er some gas, then ease it off, then juice 'er again."

She gulped, gripped the wheel and the lever, and poised her feet. Back and forth, back and forth. The wheels spun. Snow flew high. Then in an instant, the back wheels bit solid ground and the car lurched forward onto the road. Nettie screamed.

Jake and Sven yelled.

"Stop."

"Push the brake."

"Let up on the gas." The men's voices came from behind as the auto swerved down the road. Nettie pushed the gas lever up and the brake pedal down. The car veered to a stop and the engine died.

"Aah!" Nettie rested her shaking hands on her heaving chest.

Jake helped her out of the car, holding her tight in his arms. "You did great. You drove the car and got us out." He rubbed her back gently and peered into her face. "Are you all right?'

A pain shot through her midsection and she doubled over with a cry. "I think we'd better get going."

Nettie's pains came more frequently as the miles seemed only to lengthen. Her back ached. She tried to stifle her moans. Jake turned from the front. She'd never seen him look so frightened. "Come back here and hold me."

"Can't you go any faster?" he urged Sven, climbing awkwardly over the seat. The Swede pulled down the gas lever and the car slid and swayed over the icy road.

Nettie felt a hot wetness gush from between her legs. Her water must have broken. She dug her fingers into her thighs. *It's going to be soon. Please hurry, Sven.*

By the time the Model T lurched to a stop outside the maternity hospital, Nettie was incoherent with pain. The two men pulled her from the backseat and Jake carried her inside. The nurse took one look at Nettie's sodden skirt and yelled, "Get Dr. Smith. She's hemorrhaging."

The nurse put Nettie into a bed, and bathed her face with a cool cloth. Jake held her hand. "It's all right, little gal. You're all right."

The last thing Nettie remembered was a bespectacled man leaning over her and putting some kind of mask over her nose and mouth.

CHAPTER SEVEN

November 9, 1924
Cut Bank Pioneer Press
Local Happenings

A seven-pound, 22½-inch boy was born to Mr. and Mrs. Jacob Moser of Sunburst at the Purcell Maternity Home. The happy parents have named him Neil Jacob Moser.

Nettie gazed at the bundle in her arms and pushed the rocking chair into a soothing rhythm with her toes. She couldn't help studying her sleeping son's face, his forehead as it wrinkled then smoothed, the whorls of his ears, his pursed mouth. The rosebud lips smacked, then settled into a smile. She watched his red-mottled hands open and close and wondered at fingernails so tiny and yet so perfect. She held her breath as he sighed, laughed when he yawned, and was surprised at his strong grasp on her thumb.

In the month since he'd been born, time held no meaning for her. She could not get her fill of looking at him. She sat, entranced, until her arm became numb. When Neil stirred, opened his eyes, and whimpered, she held him gratefully to her breast or changed his diaper. Then she put him into his cradle, rocked him back to sleep, and settled on the sofa for a welcome nap, if only for a few minutes.

A void she'd never noticed seemed to have been filled with the birth of this child, as though a piece of her had been missing and was now restored.

Although she didn't recall a thing about the birth, the doctor said she'd had such complications, even with emergency surgery, it was a miracle Neil had survived. But it meant she'd not be able to have any more children. That knowledge gave her a guilty sense of relief since she'd never actually wanted any kids at all, but it dampened the joy of having her perfect, miraculous baby. Her heart contracted. What if he got the influenza, like Essie?

She felt a frosty draft when Jake came in from doing the afternoon chores. He closed the door softly behind him and peeked from the kitchen into the living room where she sat with Neil. Nettie looked up at him and smiled.

"Oh, he's awake." He came in, kissed her, and dropped to one knee beside the chair, gently smoothing his son's dark hair.

"I'm glad you came in. I need to get up for awhile, make a trip to the outhouse, and cook supper."

Jake carefully took the bundle from her and they traded places. "You mean you've been sitting here all afternoon?"

Nettie nodded. "I just don't like to leave him for even a minute. You'd think I'd never seen a baby before."

Her husband's strong face softened as he looked at his son. "He's so small. It almost seems as if he'll break, doesn't it?"

She gazed down at Neil. "I know he won't. Babies aren't as fragile as they look. I helped care for my brothers and little sister. But it's so different when it's your own." She yawned and shuffled stiffly into the kitchen. "I am so tired, though."

"Well, I think it's time I go get your mother tomorrow. I think you're being stubborn, refusing her help," Jake scolded her with a smile.

"I should be able to do this myself. She did it, with eight kids."

"But she didn't have surgery and difficult births." His face softened. "I'm just glad my sister was here the first few days."

Nettie nodded. "That did help." She had to admit it had been pretty tough since Beulah left a week ago to care for her own sick child. Getting up every two or three hours during the night to feed

Neil. Washing diapers, hanging them outside in the freezing temperatures, bringing them in stiff as a board to finish drying around the coal stove. And on top of that, fixing hot meals for Jake when he came in, bone cold from feeding the horses and chopping ice in the reservoir.

"Maybe you're right. You'd better go get Mama." She grinned. "She's probably chomping at the bit, waiting to see her grandson."

Jake smoothed her hair. "Why don't you let me cook supper. You just sit and enjoy Neil some more."

❧

Bone-weary, Nettie sat in her rocker and watched her mother fold diapers, smooth each one into a perfect square, and line them up in the drawer, all facing the same direction. She closed her eyes against the sight. This was so Mama. Trying to show up Nettie's imperfections. She ground her teeth. *How am I ever going to measure up?*

Her mother went to the kitchen to put the big copper kettle on the stove to boil the next batch of diapers.

Neil whimpered. Nettie rushed to his cradle to pick him up. She kissed the dark downy fuzz on his head, murmured to him as she sat, and nestled him to her breast. The midafternoon sun dipped low over the white-capped hills and beamed a small patch of light on the shiny wood floor.

Mama bustled in from the kitchen, wiping her hands on her apron. "Now honey, you shouldn't be picking him up every time he cries. You're just going to be spoiling him."

"I know, Mama, but he's hungry. It's been three hours since I fed him last."

"Well, I'm just trying to help. I've had a bit of experience, you know."

Resentment boiled inside Nettie. "I know that. You cared for eight babies, but this one is mine. And if I want to hold him all day and watch him sleep, that's what I'm going to do."

43

Mama gave her a wide-eyed glance, grabbed a discarded blanket from the floor, rearranged a pillow on the sofa, and brushed a hand over the small end table.

Nettie frowned. Oh dear, she hadn't dusted for weeks. Would Mama think less of her? But what did she expect? Nettie'd just had a baby.

Mama took Nettie's empty teacup and walked away. Her words continued from the kitchen, where she stirred the pot full of simmering diapers. "Always remember, you want to be sure the water is boiling. Got to kill all the germs. Too bad it's winter. The sun does such a nice job of bleaching in the summer."

Nettie's patience had thinned to almost nothing. "I know all this, Mama." Neil tugged against her swollen breast, grunted, and swallowed noisily.

Mama grabbed a basket of clean, wet diapers. "I'm going out to hang these on the line. Be sure to wrap him up good now. Don't let him get cold."

"I know, Mama. I helped you with the young ones, you know!" Nettie's tight chest heaved. She couldn't help herself. "I can handle this much." Her shoulders slumped. *But can I? I still need her help.* She was so weak. And so tired. Maybe she wasn't cut out to be a mother, would never get it right.

It was all too much. Nettie knew she was acting like a petulant child. She should be grateful that her mother was here for a couple more weeks, at least until she could regain some of her strength. But how much more of this feeling inferior could she take?

Mama set down the basket and stood in the doorway. "I know, honey." She sighed. "Guess I'm trying too hard. Just want to spare you some of the mistakes I made."

Nettie looked up in surprise. Her mother looked tired, worn. Her shoulders slumped and she brushed back a stray tendril of hair. With so many kids, Nettie supposed Mama hadn't really had time to attend to every little whimper. Maybe she had with Margie, her first.

Of course later she had Lola and Joe, then Nettie, to help with the younger ones.

A hot lump of guilt choked her. "Did you ever feel so tired, so inadequate, after your babies were born?"

Mama came over and knelt beside the rocker. "Yes, honey, I did. After every one. But I know you're going to be a good mother." Tears glistened in her mother's eyes as she gazed at Neil. "I can't help thinking about little Essie."

Nettie put her hand on Mama's arm, reliving the helplessness they'd both felt when her baby sister died. "I'm sorry, Mama." She also remembered the time Mama had a miscarriage, how tired and sad she'd seemed. "I know you're trying to help."

Her mother nodded and brushed Neil's downy head. "Babies are so precious." She met Nettie's gaze. "Even when they're grown up."

Nettie brushed away a tear of her own and squeezed Mama's arm.

After awhile, she stood and laid Neil back in his cradle. "Time for your bath." She smiled down at him, went into the kitchen, grabbed a washbasin, and poured hot water into it from the kettle. Then she ladled in cold water from the drinking bucket, tested the temperature with her elbow, and set it on the table. She retrieved Neil and undressed him in the warm, steamy kitchen.

Mama rushed over to help. "Careful, now. Support his head in the crook of your arm so he doesn't slide underwater."

Nettie forced a smile. "Good advice, Mama. Thank you."

Mama looked blank for a moment. Then she smiled back.

When Neil's feet touched the water, he stiffened and scrunched up his face as if ready to let out a wail of protest. But as Nettie eased his body more fully into the basin, his features relaxed. He smiled and let out a happy sigh.

"You like that, don't you?" Nettie wet a washcloth and squeezed water gently over his tiny chest. Neil smiled and kicked. Finally, when the water began to cool, she lifted him onto a towel that had been warming by the stove. He fussed a bit at being taken out of the water, but quieted when Nettie powdered him with cornstarch and put on a clean diaper.

She peered out the window at the lengthening blue shadows that stretched from the snowy hills. Where was Jake? He should be coming in soon. Nettie needed his warm, comforting touch. She hugged the baby close before tucking him under the covers in his cradle. Then she leaned back in the rocker and closed her eyes, just for a moment.

The smell of roasting meat roused Nettie from a doze. The little sitting room was shrouded in darkness, but the lantern in the kitchen filled the doorway with cheery yellow light. She heard Mama say something in a low voice and Jake's rumbling laugh in reply. She must have been more tired than she'd thought to fall asleep and not even notice when Jake came in.

Neil stirred. She rose stiffly, lifted him to her shoulder, and shuffled into the kitchen.

Jake grinned. "Hi there, you sleepyheads. You were both snoring so loud I thought the rafters would shake loose."

Nettie gave a half-smile, waved his words away with a yawn, and went to the icebox to retrieve a jar filled with milk. She poured herself a big glassful, drank it all, and surveyed the cozy room.

Mama stood at the stove, checking a kettle and brushing a damp curl off her forehead. To Nettie's astonishment, she saw streaks of gray in her mother's hair, and the thought hit her that Mama's back was bent a little more than she remembered. How could she not have noticed that before, as much time as they'd spent together? Gosh, Mama must be in her mid-fifties now. Time, hard work, and many children had caught up with her energetic mother. In the hospital, one of her first thoughts had been the realization of how much pain her mother had endured, giving birth so many times. Her throat closed, as though a milk bubble had been caught there.

Nettie reached out and touched Mama's shoulder. "Thanks, Mama." Her mother turned with a smile and nodded.

"You want me to hold him awhile?" Jake set down his cup and stood up from the table, his arms outstretched. Neil whimpered and nuzzled her neck, making small sucking noises.

"Let me feed him first and then you can." Nettie thought she saw a quick flash of something cross his face. Disappointment? But she turned back to the dark room and nestled into the rocker with her son.

"We can eat as soon as you're done." Mama opened the squeaky oven door. "Here, Jake, would you carve the roast?"

Later that night, Nettie slid into bed next to Jake. As many naps as she'd taken during the day, she was amazed at how much she longed for a full night's sleep.

He turned on his side with a smile and reached for her. "I've missed you lately, my darlin'." He stroked her hair and leaned toward her mouth. She melted into his kiss, relieved to finally have a quiet moment with her husband.

As if on cue, Neil gave a squawk from the crib. Nettie's head snapped back as if stung by a bee. Drat. *Can't I have a few minutes of peace?* She flung back the covers.

Jake held on to her. "Let him cry a little."

"But—"

"It ain't gonna hurt him any." Jake enveloped her in his big, warm arms.

Nettie relaxed against him, but her mind was on the baby and his increasing wails.

Jake stroked her hair. "Shh, shh, now. He's okay."

Then Mama's voice came from the hall. "Is the baby all right? Do you need help?"

Nettie pushed out a forceful sigh, untangled from Jake's embrace, and rushed to her son's crib side. "I got him," she called out.

The baby's face wrinkled and turned an angry red. He let out another lusty cry, and she scooped him to her bosom. "Are you hungry again, my little sweet?"

Nettie heard Jake push air from between his teeth as she sat on the edge of the bed to nurse Neil. She ached for Jake's comforting arms, but the baby was hungry. This helpless little being needed her. What else could she do?

After Neil drank his fill, she put him over her shoulder to burp, and walked the hallway outside the bedroom until he finally went to sleep. She eased him back into the crib, tucked the blankets close around him, and leaned down to brush his head with her lips. Then she slipped quietly back into bed, where Jake lay with his back to her, already asleep. She molded her body against him and drifted off, wondering how long it would be before she was able to have a normal life again.

The next morning, before she was fully awake, Nettie groped for Jake, but felt only emptiness. Her eyes popped open. He was up and gone already. She yearned to feel his arms around her. Would they ever have a few minutes alone again, if only to cuddle? Even though he was around every day, same as always, she missed him. Missed his long embraces and sweet kisses, missed sitting by the fire in the evenings just holding hands. She pulled his slept-in undershirt close to breathe in his scent. *Is this all we get of each other?*

Neil let out a sudden wail, breaking the spell. With a groan, she slid from under the warm covers, and reached for her robe and slippers in the frosty bedroom. By the time she picked him up, he was in full concert, eyes screwed shut, his little face purple with rage.

"Oh, come on now. You didn't have to wait that long." Nettie changed his diaper and unbuttoned her nightgown. As quickly as it had begun, the crying stopped, replaced with happy grunts. She gazed down at the little bundle that was so much a part of her, and again felt that unaccustomed fullness inside. After he finished nursing, she sat for a long time, content just to rock with his warmth close to her heart.

When she finally dressed and ventured downstairs, Mama had the coffee boiling and pancakes sizzling. Nettie transferred Neil to his cradle near the stove and sat down to eat. The kitchen door banged open. Jake came in with a pail of fresh milk. He only glanced at her before he set up the strainer with its cheesecloth filter and poured the milk through into the large glass jar.

Nettie grimaced. *Oh, dear. He's upset about last night.* Mama looked at Nettie with an upraised eyebrow. Then she poured cups of coffee and set them on the table. "Breakfast is ready, Jake."

He set the milk bucket on the cupboard with the other dirty dishes and sat down across from Nettie. Cupping his hands around the steaming coffee mug, he stared into its ebony depths.

She looked at him, a tiny pang of fear icing its way through her. "Good morning, honey. Did you sleep well?"

He glanced out of the corner of one eye at Mama, flipping hot-cakes. "Good enough."

Breakfast continued in silence, punctuated only by sidelong glances at each other, eyes quickly averted. If only he'd say something, anything. Nettie wanted to ask him why he was upset, but Mama sat right next to them. No sense getting her involved.

As soon as he wolfed down the last of his hotcakes, Jake stood up. He smoothed the wisps of dark hair on Neil's head. "That's my boy." Without a word to Nettie, he grabbed his coat. "Gotta go feed the horses."

Nettie felt the door's thud echo off her chest. She got up to fill the dishpan with hot water.

"No, no, honey, I'll do the dishes. Listen, why don't you go out and help Jake this morning? I can watch Neil for a couple of hours, till he gets hungry again." Mama gave a little chuckle, reached out and squeezed Nettie's shoulder. "You go. Be with Jake for awhile. Being a new dad is hard on a man."

Nettie threw on her coat and overshoes and without buttoning up, raced headlong into the frosty morning toward the barn. She had to catch him before he left for the pasture. The icy air cut into her lungs. She coughed and stumbled. She wasn't sure quite what had happened between them, but whatever it was loomed over her like a dark cloud. And, whatever it was, she needed to put it right.

The moist air of the dusky barn welcomed her, and she drew comfort from the familiarity. She savored the musty smell of hay and horses, then stepped between the stalls. It was like coming home again. She'd missed this the past couple of months. Tootsie gave a welcoming nicker and Nettie caressed the chestnut's soft nose and ears.

"What're you doing out here in the cold? Did something happen?" Jake's voice came out of the dimness.

Nettie turned toward him. "No, I just wanted to be with you." She could see him now, her tall, muscular cowboy, with his pitchfork halted in mid-pitch. He leaned the fork against a stall and took a step in her direction. She moved forward, in a hurry now. Then she was in his arms, her face buried in his rough coat. They rocked together.

"Oh, Jake, I've missed you." Her words were muffled against his chest.

He tightened his embrace enough to take her breath away. "Yeah. Me too."

Nettie lifted her face to kiss him. The piercing cry of a hawk, a chicken's squawk, and frantic flapping of its wings startled them apart.

Jake ran to the barn door and tossed the pitchfork after the predator. "Dang them chicken hawks!"

The spell broken, he turned away to pick up the pitchfork again.

Nettie opened her mouth, but not a sound would come out. It still wasn't all right between them. She'd rushed out here for nothing. She had to try again. "Jake, will you talk to me?"

He jabbed a forkful of hay, paused, and looked at her. "Nothin' to talk about."

"But, last night—"

"You can sit with Neil all you want, but I have a ranch to run." Jake tossed the hay and the pitchfork over the stall.

Shoulders drooping, Nettie turned and trudged back to the house.

A few days later, with Mama gone, Nettie was left to cope with the mounds of dirty diapers, a baby who suddenly turned fussy, and a silent Jake.

CHAPTER EIGHT

Sunday, February 1, 1925

Does a baby have to cause so much trouble in a marriage?

Nettie pulled the chair close to the cook stove and adjusted the blanket to form a tent over Neil's head. His piercing squall ended in a barking cough. He wheezed as he struggled to inhale. His little face twisted and turned red with the effort. Perhaps more steam from the spouting teakettle would help.

The memory of her baby sister gnawed at her and left a familiar hollow ache. Although it had been five years ago, she could still hear little Essie's rattling breaths and then the silence of her death. Influenza. The thought was like a pair of hands had seized her stomach and twisted it.

Her son was only three months old. Could he have the influenza? Where would he have gotten it? Had Jake brought the germs back from town? She couldn't bear to lose her baby. A deep understanding spiraled through her. Mama must have felt that a part of her had died with Essie. Nettie's heart contracted, again feeling her own sadness from that time. But only now was she able to grasp the depths of her mother's despair, the long days she'd sat just rocking, staring at nothing.

Neil drew in a noisy breath and coughed again. Worn out from the effort to breathe, his eyes closed and he slept for a few minutes, only to repeat the exhausting process when he awoke. Nettie paced the kitchen floor. Condensation rivulets etched the frost on the windows. She struggled to breathe, too, in the steam-thickened air.

Jake tromped down the stairs, rubbing the sleep from his eyes, his sandy blond hair stuck up in several directions. He looked like a little boy. Then the furrow between his brows deepened as he looked at the little steam tent and back at her. "It's after midnight. You been up all this time, honey?"

She shot him a look from beneath lowered lashes, her eyes gritty. "The more he coughs, the more he cries, and that just makes the cough worse." Her shoulders sagged.

As if on cue, Neil stirred and cried, ending in a paroxysm of barking hacks.

In one fluid movement, Jake whipped his coat on, stuck his feet in his boots, bundled the blanket around the baby, and rushed him out the door.

"Jake!" The cold air from the open door fed the cold tongue of fear that licked at her. Frantic, Nettie ran through the crunchy snow, her house slippers flapping with every step. She grasped her sweater together in front with one hand and flailed the air with the other, as if that could make her run faster. Anger rose up in her like a hot wind and she screamed. "Stop. Jake. Come back here."

She followed Neil's barking cough. Jake had gone crazy. He could kill the baby.

Nettie's screams echoed off the side of the barn and seemed to thump back into her chest. Jake rounded the building, heading back toward her. She stopped, sobs now choking off her airway.

"Hey, hey, hey, little gal. It's okay. It's okay." Jake held the now-silent Neil against one shoulder and gathered her under his free arm.

She pounded his chest with her fists. "What've you done?" Sobs choked her. "You killed him!"

"Hold on there." He pulled her face into his chest. His familiar tobacco and horse scent filled her nostrils and his soft voice soothed. "Neil's all right. Listen. He's stopped coughing."

Nettie stepped back, still struggling for air through her hiccupping sobs, and looked at the wrapped bundle on Jake's arm. With freezing fingers, she lifted a flap of the blanket away from the baby's face. She gasped. It was true. His breathing was almost normal, his eyes closed in peaceful sleep. Tears welled. *Oh, thank you, Lord. He's breathing.* She looked up at Jake, forgiveness filling her heart with white light. "What did you do?"

He smiled back. "Cold air. Cures the croup. When one of my sisters had a cough like this, my mother bundled her up to take her to the doctor. As soon as she hit the cold air, the cough cleared up. Doc said that was the best remedy."

"Essie." Nettie's legs wobbled and she plopped onto the snowy ground. "I was so scared he was going to die like Essie." The tears spilled through her lashes and ran down her cheeks.

Jake put out his hand and pulled her up. "I'm sorry. There wasn't time to explain." He put his arm around her. "Let's go back inside. You should get some rest now or you'll be sick too."

Nettie leaned against him as they walked back to the house. She was chilled through, covered with a clammy sweat, and her arms and legs shook. She wasn't cut out to be a mother. What if Neil didn't get better? If she kept doing the wrong thing, like steaming him when he needed cold air . . . no, she couldn't even think of it. She wouldn't.

Inside, Jake laid their son in his crib near the window and opened it just a crack.

Nettie smoothed Neil's hair. She kissed his forehead, then slumped against the wall. These past weeks of feeling that Jake was angry with her because she spent too much time with the baby, and then, despite everything she tried to do, Neil got so sick. Could she do nothing right? Not motherhood. Not even being a wife. She closed her eyes against the pounding in her head.

Then she felt Jake slip his arms around her. She leaned into him, absorbing his strength. Fear and frustration ebbed. She could stay there forever. When he stepped back, she looked up at his face, so kind and warm. Her great love and longing caught in her throat.

Jake held her by the shoulders and gazed straight into her eyes. "Neil will be all right."

The tears came then, washing her with relief. "But I didn't know how to make him well." She blinked, looking up at him. "I feel like I've disappointed you, as a wife."

Jake's head jerked as if he'd been slapped. "No. No, little gal, you haven't."

"I know we just don't have any time alone together anymore. It's been so hard, with the baby. I'm so tired. I can't do everything the way Mama says I should." She tightened her arms around him.

"I've been selfish." Jake's voice was husky. "I want you, like we were before Neil. I thought when your mother was here, it'd be easier, you'd have more time."

Nettie lowered her forehead to his chest. "I'm sorry, Jake. I had no idea it would be like this. I love my—our—baby. And I love you. But I'm not just a carefree cowgirl anymore."

His big hand moved slowly up and down her back, creating heat where he touched. "I know, honey, I know. Trust me." He guided her to the sofa. Ever so slowly and tenderly, he undressed her, then himself. They nestled into the soft cushions, still a perfect fit.

For now she could forget everything but his strong, comforting arms around her and his warm murmurs of love in her ear. As long as she had him, and her baby was all right, she would be okay. *I'm doing the best I can. That has to be good enough.*

CHAPTER NINE

Sunday, April 26, 1925

Warm winds blowing. Snow all melted. Water running every-where. Jake in mud almost up to his kneecaps. Baby and I stuck in the house. Getting cabin fever.

Nettie stared out the window toward the barn where Jake scraped the mud and manure out of the corrals with a large blade pulled by a team. The hard edge of winter had finally softened with Chinook winds that erased the whiteness from the hills overnight.

Now water trickled, an almost eerie sound breaking the stillness of this arid land. Reminded of the old ditty "water, water everywhere, but not a drop to drink," Nettie smiled. Then she turned to watch Neil wave his feet in the air and chortle as he tried to catch his toes. At six months and two weeks, he delighted in entertaining himself.

Nettie smoothed a crocheted doily and straightened the pillows on the sofa. "Oh, no." She stopped short and laughed out loud. "I've turned into my mother." Arranging and straightening, indeed. She doubled over with laughter and sank into the cushions. *I must be going stir-crazy.* It had been a long four months, cocooned from the winter storms and caring for the baby, with no chance to ride.

She watched Neil gurgle in his nest of blankets. Her heart felt full to bursting. This new life had changed hers and there was no going back. Yet she yearned to feel the freedom of wind in her hair, the rippling of her horse's smooth, powerful muscles as they galloped over the prairie. That had been an essential part of her life for nearly twenty years, as long as she could remember anyway. She gazed out the window again. *It might as well have bars on it. I can't leave the baby.*

Nettie paced from living room to kitchen and back. How could she combine the two lives, the one with responsibilities she must now shoulder, and the one she longed for, ached for? She couldn't leave her baby alone while she went for a ride. Jake would probably watch him for a little while, but he couldn't feed him. Besides, she wanted to be out there alongside her husband again, to work the horses, to ride the range.

The house was so stuffy. The walls had grown closer over the winter. She couldn't stand it one minute more. Nettie bundled Neil up, put on her coat, buckled up her overshoes, and slogged through the mud to the corral.

Jake stopped the team and hopped down from the earth scraper. "Hello. How're my two sweeties?"

"Well, he's fine, but I needed some air. I just can't stay in the house any longer. Thought I'd take a little walk." She shifted Neil's weight to her other arm.

Jake pushed back his hat and scratched his forehead. "It's pretty soupy out here. Watch your step and don't fall in the mud. I'd be all day tryin' to find ya."

Nettie gave him a half-hearted smile. "I think I'll go in the barn, visit Tootsie and Alsanger."

The saddle horses whickered when she entered. She stopped to let her eyes adjust to the murky light, and rubbed her palm over Jake's angora chaps on the wall. An old twinge reminded her how much she'd missed Jake that winter he'd gone to Oregon, before they were married. Nettie brushed her cheek against the soft hair, smelling the warm summer evenings, feeling the zing of new love, the carefree rides with her cowboy.

Sighing, she reached toward her bridle, then withdrew her hand. No. There was no way she could go riding today. Jake was too busy. Just forget about it. Her shoulders slumped. *He can go whenever he wants. Men have it easy.*

Nettie walked to Tootsie's stall and scratched the mare's ears. The horse nodded its head as if saying she, too, wanted to go for a ride.

"Have you missed me, girl?" She settled Neil on one hip while she stroked the silky mane and smooth neck with her free hand. How could she carry him and ride too? Holding him with one arm? *I could ride real slow.* No, too dangerous. The horse could shy at something and she might drop Neil. Maybe she could strap him to her back with a blanket. *Stop it, Nettie Moser. Have patience.*

The baby reached toward the horse and cooed. Nettie swung him closer so he could touch Tootsie's soft nose. The mare flared her nostrils to take in Neil's scent then gently rubbed her face against his chubby little fist. He snatched his hand back, squealed in delight, then leaned forward to touch her again.

"You like the horsie, don't you?" With a smile, Nettie pictured her tiny cowboy on the back of a horse, riding as though he'd been born there.

"Is the little guy ready to ride?" Jake's entrance startled her and the picture faded.

"Almost, I think." She turned to look into her husband's eyes. "But I'm more than ready. I want to ride so bad I can taste it."

Jake put a hand on her shoulder. "I'd take Neil and let you go in a minute if it wasn't for this mud. Heck, I don't even want to go out in it."

Nettie squared her shoulders. "It's not the first time I've ever ridden. Even in the mud." She sent him a blazing glare. "You know that."

He chuckled. "I know, little gal. I know." He gazed out the barn door at the trickles of water zigzagging through the corral. "Just give this wind a few days, and it'll soon be dry enough. We'll get you back up on horseback."

Despite the defiant voice inside, anticipation zinged through her. Nettie squeezed her fists to dampen her excitement. "All right. I can wait a little longer, but not too long."

During the next few weeks, warm winds absorbed the extra moisture from the ground like a monstrous sponge. Nettie was finally able to push Neil's buggy as far as the barn without getting it stuck in the mud, then a little farther out into the pasture each day. The air smelled of warming earth, of new growth. The faint tinge of green on the rolling prairie and distant rims stirred her. Soon wildflowers would add a palette of color. Newborn calves and colts would frolic. She felt that itch to run, too. It truly was spring.

On a balmy May morning, Nettie let Tootsie into the corral from the pasture and positioned the baby buggy in a sunny corner. While Neil napped, she brushed out the remainder of the mare's shaggy winter coat. Wads of matted hair accumulated at her feet. Tootsie would be sleek and shiny again, ready to gallop over the prairie.

She heard Jake whistling in the barn. "Whatcha doing in there?"

"Just workin' on somethin'. Don't come in here just yet."

Nettie raised her eyebrows. What secret project was her husband up to now? She glanced at Neil napping in the sun. Pleasure swelled inside. Here, she had everything she loved most: her husband and partner, her baby, and her horse. Just one thing was lacking. The freedom to jump on Tootsie's back and ride any time she wanted to.

"Jake, honey?" She peered tentatively into the cavernlike darkness of the barn door.

"Uh-huh?"

"I was thinking I'd like to take Tootsie for a little ride. Could you watch Neil for awhile?"

Rustling noises came from the murkiness. "Uh, just wait for a few minutes."

Nettie frowned. That wasn't the answer she expected. He'd been more than willing to watch the baby a few times recently while she took a short ride. She threw down the currycomb and stared into the barn, hip cocked, her fists resting at her waist. "Why? He's asleep now. He won't be any bother." She knew her voice sounded petulant, but she couldn't contain the frustration that built within.

Jake poked his head around the doorjamb, a big grin on his face. "Okay, okay. Hold your horses, little gal. I just thought you might like to take our son along." He stepped out into the sunshine, holding a piece of saddle blanket stitched together with rawhide.

Nettie glared at the thing. "What is that? What are you talking about?"

"Here, let me show you." Jake lifted the now-alert Neil from the buggy, slipped his chubby little legs through openings left in the red-and-white-striped blanket. Then he fit leather straps, like a harness, around Nettie's shoulders. The baby fit perfectly next to her heart, facing outward so he could see. And her hands were left free.

She smiled up at Jake. "Why, you devil, you. It's like what the Blackfeet use to carry their papooses. What a great idea."

He grinned back at her. "Let's all go for a ride." He saddled Tootsie and Alsanger and helped Nettie mount. Just like old times, but with Neil gurgling and cooing in front of her.

Warmth spread through her. This was living. This was perfect.

Once again Nettie could let the dust collect inside the house while she enjoyed the out-of-doors. The days blended into a springtime mix of sunshine, laughter, sharing, and togetherness as Nettie rode with Jake by her side and Neil tucked into the blanket carrier. Even fixing fence became a pleasurable task. Nettie carried a picnic lunch for her and Jake, and whenever Neil was hungry, all she had to do was slip off the horse, sit in the fragrant new grass, and nurse him. And diapers fit just fine in her saddlebags.

The spring rains kept the countryside lush and green well into the summer. The days were warm and moist, the skies blue and clear. Every day when Nettie rode, the sage-scented breeze caressed her face and made Neil laugh with delight. Late afternoons often brought moisture-laden clouds. Piling up like feather pillows on the horizon, they moved lazily over the rims. This was a signal for Nettie and Jake to head for home. They stood in the maw of the barn door and watched as the sky and the land darkened. The wind stirred up miniature dirt devils just before the clouds spread their life-giving burden gently over the prairie.

Jake wrapped his arm around Nettie. "This one's a good soaker, keep us in grass this year."

Then they ran for the house and settled in for the evening, maybe even the whole next day. Nettie read, a rare luxury, while Jake repaired harness by lantern light. Neil in his crib nearby gurgled and banged an Indian gourd rattle against the rails. Nettie looked up from her book or newspaper every so often and smiled, her heart full, warm and snug with togetherness.

After the rain, she stood outside on the moist dirt, taking in gulps of sweet, clean air as satisfying as the aroma of fresh-baked bread. Everything was washed clean, the ground smooth, the prairie lush and healthy-looking.

"Sure nice to have a summer like this." Jake surveyed their herd of horses that remained fat and sleek on grass that grew to their knees.

Nettie nodded and reached for his hand. Life was good.

The year continued to yield rain and grass and contentment. Jake went to rodeos, sometimes winning a few dollars. Nettie usually stayed home, preferring not to watch the activity she'd had to give up, temporarily, she hoped. That was the only thing that marred their idyllic life, not being able to rodeo. *Oh well, give me just a few years, till Neil is older. Then watch out.* But she looked over at her little guy, playing so happily by himself. Rodeo was a dangerous business. Could she risk leaving her son without a mother?

In the fall, Jake sold several draft horse pairs, and he and Nettie laid in their winter supplies: hay for the horses, coal for the stove, flour, sugar and salt, oatmeal, and coffee. The root cellar, dug into a small hillock just outside the house, was full. Potatoes, jars of canned venison, and the berries and vegetables Mama had canned and given them, since Nettie still had no desire to garden. Nettie smiled. *Thank goodness for Mama.*

The winter winds came and played hide-and-seek around the house, looking for places to enter. But Jake had puttied around the windows, Nettie stuffed rags into cracks, and together they poured additional sawdust between the walls for insulation. So while the wind shrieked outside in fury, Nettie snuggled next to her baby and her husband, warm and cozy, reliving the soft, summer days and planning for next year.

CHAPTER TEN

Tuesday, November 9, 1926

Neil's birthday today. Two years old, already showing signs of the cowboy he'll be. Loves to "ride" on his pa's foot while Jake bounces it up and down. Chortled and sang when we put him on Alsanger's back. Cried when we took him off. Jake out hunting coyotes. This year not as good as last. A little drier, horses didn't bring as much. But we'll be fine. Plenty of food for winter. Looks like it's setting in early. But there's always next year.

Through the window, Nettie watched the snowdrifts change shape as lavender shadows lengthened. The last pinkish rays of the sun were about to sink behind the hills. Jake should be coming home soon from checking his trap line. She shivered a little. The stove must be low on coal. She grabbed the empty coal bucket. *Better get that fired up and start supper.*

She checked on Neil. He galloped carved wooden horses across the rag rug and made tongue-clicking noises against his teeth.

She smiled. "Mama's going out to get a bucket of coal. Want to come?"

He paused in his baby drama, looked up, and flashed her a toothy grin. "O-tay."

Nettie bundled him up, put on her coat and overshoes, and they walked out to the little coal shed behind the house. Digging in the pile of black lignite, she filled the bucket and headed back.

She searched the darkening horizon for Jake and Alsanger's familiar shape, but it was empty. "It's getting dark. Wonder where your pa is."

"Papa?" Neil popped his head up and looked over her shoulder.

"Not yet, honey. He'll be home soon." *I hope.* Nettie's imagination created pictures of Jake, his arm caught in a trap or his boot caught in a stirrup, dragged through the snow. She shook the images off, went inside, and filled the firebox on the stove. Then she picked up Neil again and went out to refill the coal bucket.

Hoofbeats crunched on the hard-packed snow. Tootsie's rumbling nicker came from the corral. Nettie caught her breath. "Jake?"

"Papa." Neil waved his chubby arm.

Jake touched his hat brim as he reined in, then dismounted and unsaddled. He hefted a burlap sack to shoulder height, grinning.

Nettie set Neil down, ran to her husband, tears streaming, and buried her face in his rough coat.

"Hey, I'm glad for the welcome-home hug, but what brought this on?"

She stepped back and smiled. "Nothing. Just a little worried, getting dark."

"Aw, don't worry 'bout me none. Traps yielded treasure today. Lookee here."

Nettie clapped his shoulder. "Good. That's great." Coyote pelts were prized back east for wall hangings and trim on coats, caps, and gloves. "All right. Come in. I'll fix supper."

Jake thumped inside. "Got five rabbits, two coyotes, and a weasel, too." He shed his overcoat and sat at the table. Picking up a pencil, he stuck it in his mouth to moisten it, then scratched numbers on a piece of paper. "Let's see. Got twenty rabbit hides curing, and along with the fifteen coyotes, at about five dollars apiece. . . . This keeps up, next time Sven ships a train car of hides back to St. Louee, we'll have us a pretty little nest egg."

CHAPTER ELEVEN

Sunday, May 22, 1927

Where are our nice gentle spring rains? Didn't have much snow last winter. Seems like it's been hot since February this year. Grass will be burned up if we don't get rain by June. Jake's hunting coyotes again.

Spring was usually Nettie's favorite time of year. Spring was rebirth. It meant release from the long winter months of imprisonment inside the house and the endless, repetitive chores of keeping the fire going, cooking, heating water, and cleaning, all the while keeping track of her fast-growing son.

Spring was the moist, loamy smell of the soil releasing its first shoots of delicate green grass. Gentle, soaking showers. The softness of the air, warmed by a smiling sun. Breezes that stirred the spirit. Spring was freedom.

But this year was different. The sparse coat of snow melted early. The usual muddy weeks were cut to mere days by steady winds that blew in constant discontent. The early greening of the prairie had been arrested, the short grasses already turning yellow. Nettie felt an unexplainable restlessness in Jake and in herself too. Even the horses seemed agitated. They stood by the fence as if looking for food, then one would turn suddenly and nip another's rump. At that, they'd all take off running across the pasture, manes and tails flying in the wind.

She meandered out to the corral where Neil watched Jake saddle Alsanger. His new foxhound, Kewpie, circled, her ears perked.

Nettie rested her foot on the bottom pole of the corral. "Going out after coyotes again?"

Jake fastened a gunnysack to the saddle on one side. "Yup. If it don't rain this summer, we'll need all the hides I can get to see us through."

"Ride, Papa?" Neil lifted his two-year-old arms high. Jake picked him up and swung him around. "Not this time, pardner. You stay here, take care of your ma."

He handed Neil to Nettie, gave her a peck on the cheek, then lifted Kewpie into the sack—only her head sticking out now—and swung up onto the big horse.

"She loves the chase. When I get close, I let her out of the sack and away she goes. Best trackin' and huntin' dog I ever seen." He grinned, touched the brim of his Stetson, and wheeled the horse away.

"C'mon, son, let's go feed the chickens." Nettie took Neil's hand. In the barn, Nettie picked up a bucket and filled it with grain. They had lots of eggs. And the milk cow gave plenty of milk. She still had canned goods in the root cellar. Even if Mama's garden wouldn't produce much this year, they'd be okay. Jake's hunting brought in meat, and the hides he shipped would probably be enough to buy coal. Surely they'd be able to sell enough draft horse pairs this fall to buy hay for the rest of the herd. She told herself not to worry, yet a sense of disquiet kept her contentment at bay. What if they couldn't buy hay? What would the horses eat?

The resilience of the prairie lay just beneath the dusty surface. Sporadic warm showers brought hopeful color to the hillsides and returned smiles to Jake's face. Summer passed as nature teased them, sending just enough rain showers to keep up the façade before the wind drove it away again.

Nettie's worries also hid just below the surface. How long could they last without good rains? She dumped her dishwater at the base of a spindly cottonwood. At least she had Neil and Jake. She delighted in watching her son grow and develop, looking forward to a time when she could get back to rodeo riding.

⌘

The next year was a mirror image of the hopes that rose and fell. That winter the small amount of snow brought little relief to the parched earth, and each month that passed without rain brought stark reality to an unnamed fear. Drought.

CHAPTER TWELVE

Sunday, July 14, 1929

Spring rains never came this year. The little bit of grass that came up is nearly gone. Used up rest of the hay already. Jake's not himself. I'm really worried.

When they watched the skies now, it was with a tingling sense of hope and dread. The clouds built up over the rims, dark and angry, then dispersed as the hot winds blew them to nothing.

In June, Jake had only shrugged when the thunderheads passed over and splattered just a few hard raindrops like bullets into the dust. There was always a chance that the next storm would dump its load and the grass would come back, resurrected from its hardpan grave.

Each time the sky grew dark, Nettie ran to gather clothes from the line, shut the windows in the house, and bring four-year-old Neil in from riding his stick horse. While their son played cowboy on a saddle in the kitchen, she and Jake prepared themselves, anticipating the long, drowsy afternoons of gentle rain when they could rest without guilt, and just be together as the earth replenished itself. But disappointment always followed one brief, hopeful interlude after another.

As summer wore on, the clouds produced nothing more than a frightening display of heat lightning, the air so charged with electricity that the hair on Nettie's arms stood up. She thirsted for a view of something green, the smell of new grass. A silent vigilance overtook their lives.

She watched the tension pull at Jake, his hopeful expectation as the sky darkened, the half-smile when he heard the first clap of thunder, and then the slump of his shoulders when the storm again passed them by. Her heart ached for him, and fear built inside like the thunderheads on the hills.

He no longer whistled in the mornings as he put the coffee on to brew. It had been weeks since she had seen him joke and wrestle playfully with Neil. He rode out every morning, with Kewpie in the gunnysack, but more and more often he returned with nothing. The drought had killed or driven off the coyote's food supply, too.

Disappointment pooled inside Nettie like the rain puddles she craved. One evening as she fixed supper, Nettie saw Jake ride in. She stirred the biscuit batter and plopped it by spoonfuls on a baking sheet. After she put it into the hot oven, she straightened and peered out the window again. What was taking him so long to put away the horse? She dipped pieces of sage hen in flour and put them in a pan to fry. Half an hour passed, the biscuits and meat were done, and he still hadn't come in. She wiped her hands on the dishtowel tied around her waist, then checked on Neil, playing in the living room with his wooden farm animals, and stepped outside to holler that supper was ready.

In the deepening shadows of dusk, she saw him sitting on the rock by the corral, his face buried in his hands. Cold fear swept her, stopped her from calling out. Her feet felt too heavy to move. Her strong, invincible cowboy seemed beaten. If he had no hope, what was left?

She moved toward the rock as though walking through molasses, sank down at his feet, and reached up to take his big hands in her small ones. "What's wrong, honey?"

"No more coyotes. Don't have enough hides." He shook his head. "Runnin' out of grass. Where'll we get money to buy hay?"

Nettie dredged deep inside herself for the right words, some spark that would kindle his fire again. "We've been through droughts before. We still have food to eat." She paused, but got no response. "Your son is growing and happy. And you'll find enough hay somewhere."

He sighed. "I dunno."

Nettie reached out and rubbed his shoulder. "Come in now. Have something to eat. Get a good night's sleep. You'll feel better in the morning."

Late that night a low rumble woke her. As she sat upright in the darkness, she heard a plop-plop on the roof. A moment of silence. Then it came again. Steady now, raindrops drummed softly on the shingles. A giggle rose in her throat. She shook Jake's shoulder. "Jake. Wake up. It's raining."

He rose up on one elbow to listen. "Hallelujah." He threw off the sheet and strode to the window. Lighting a cigarette, he took a deep drag and stared out at the dark wetness through swirled smoke. Then he turned to her, a grin in his voice. "By George, I think this might be the break we've been waiting for." He stubbed out the cigarette and bounded onto the bed, gathering her tightly in his arms.

But when they awoke the next morning the parched earth steamed, already drying in the heat of the bright sun.

Drat! Nettie's shoulders slumped. *I had so hoped this was it.*

Jake rode off again, his mouth set in a grim line.

Neil followed Nettie, his chubby legs stretching to keep up as she went about her chores. A taut nervousness strummed her body. She couldn't relax, with Jake in such a state of mind. But he knew lots of people all over the country. Surely he would find someone who could help, or something he could do. She saddled Tootsie and hoisted Neil up behind the saddle. "Upsy-daisy. There you go."

"Yippee. We get to go ridin'." He grinned, and his little arms hugged her waist as they rode out to the pasture.

The horses switched their tails at the flies, unaware of the human drama taking place over their future. Nettie got down and peered at the short, dry grass. Jake was right; it didn't look like enough to last until winter. They'd fed the last of their hay in early spring, while they waited for the grass to green up. And even if they could find some to buy, what would they buy it with?

She squinted up at the cloudless sky, wishing she could do a rain dance. Anything to pull Jake out of his worry. Anything to feed the horses. Anything to ease her own anxiety.

When Nettie and Neil rode home, Jake was leaning against a dilapidated Ford pickup. What on earth? She helped Neil down and dismounted. "What'd you do, buy a truck? To haul hay? Where's Alsanger? You didn't trade him off?"

His shook his head, his face still grim. "Naw. Al's at Sven's. Borrowed the truck from a guy in town. Just came to tell ya, him and I gonna take a quick trip up to Canada. He's maybe got a line on somethin' that could make us a little money."

Nettie scrunched her forehead into a frown. Thoughts and questions swooped through her head like a hawk after mice. "What's up in Canada?"

Jake took her in his arms and gave her a quick kiss. "Can't go into detail right now. I'll be home in a coupla days."

"Is it a rodeo?" Nettie persisted. "A buyer for draft pairs?"

Without a word, Jake patted Neil on the head and jumped into the pickup.

Nettie strode toward the vehicle. "Jake! Answer me. Right now. Why are you going to Canada?" The truck started with a roar and a loud bang, making Neil jump beside her.

"Gotta go." With a wave, Jake ground it into gear and drove off in a cloud of dust and oily-smelling exhaust.

Nettie stared after her husband. What was he up to now? And why wouldn't he tell her?

"Where'd Pa go?" Neil looked up at her, his hazel eyes wide.

Dadgummit. He'd left her to try to explain something to a child that she didn't understand herself. "Uh. He just has to take a short trip. He'll be back in a couple days. C'mon, let's go in the house, have some supper."

Fury, mixed with fear, whirled inside like a dust devil. She couldn't eat. Worry punctuated her sleeplessness. What was in Canada? Jake wasn't all that good a driver. Who was this man he went with? She punched her pillow and turned on her side. Why hadn't he answered her?

Nettie got out of bed, stared out at the moonlit night, and clenched her fists till the nails dug into her palms. She stared at Jake's cigarette fixings on the bed table and almost wished she'd taken up smoking. It would at least give her hands something to do.

By the next evening Jake still hadn't returned. Nettie tried to put on a cheerful face for Neil, read to him, told him jokes just to hear his childish giggle. But after she put him to bed, she sat by the window, waiting to hear the pop and roar of an engine or hoofbeats, anything to let her know that Jake was all right. Why was this trip a secret? Maybe it was something dangerous.

Just as dawn gave its first golden hints of sunrise, the sound of a galloping horse roused Nettie from a neck-cricking doze in her chair. She leapt to the window. Jake approached on a puffing horse, something—an animal?—draped across the front of his saddle.

Why is he running a horse that hard? Nettie ran outside. Jake's face was swollen, bloody. An unconscious man lay belly-down over the horse. "Are you all right? What's happened? Who is this?"

"Help me get him down." With panted grunts, Jake tugged at the man's legs. "He's hurt."

She helped Jake ease the man off the horse and carry him into the house, where they laid him on the sofa. Jake lit the lantern. Nettie recoiled at the sight of the man's bloody head. A huge gash on his forehead still oozed. His white shirt was soaked with blood.

"Need hot water. Bandages." Jake's voice startled her out of her shock.

An icy finger of fear ran through her. "Jake, tell me. What happened?"

"Had a little accident."

"Take him to a doctor?"

"Had t'get him outta town."

Nettie ran to get the old sheet she kept for rags and bandages. An accident. Just what she'd been afraid of. She dipped hot water from the reservoir in the stove, wet a washcloth, and bathed the stranger's face. With Jake's help, she dug a hunk of glass from the wound, cleaned the gash with hydrogen peroxide, and bound his head with strips of sheeting. Then she turned her ministrations to Jake.

He tried to wave off her attentions. "I'm okay."

Nettie pushed him into a kitchen chair. "Hold still." She cupped his chin firmly in her hand and looked him straight in the eyes. "What have you gotten yourself into?"

He rolled his eyes. "We were just goin' a little too fast, is all."

Nettie thinned her lips, anger rising. "Why?"

Jake shrugged. "Cuz we were being chased."

"By who?" Nettie dabbed hard at a cut on his cheek. "What did you do?"

He winced. "We had a load of whiskey."

Nettie stopped in mid-swipe. "You what?"

He ignored her silent stare. "We were doin' fine. Spud knew Coots was a safe spot to come across the border." He grimaced again as Nettie cleaned another cut. "A revenue cop parked at that all-night diner. Came out just as we drove through, stopped us for a burned-out taillight. Then he wanted to see what we had in the back. That's when Spud stepped on the gas. He couldn't afford to get caught. He's already wanted in Canada."

Nettie waited, incredulity building, while Jake stopped to catch his breath.

"He came on across the border after us for several miles, and Spud thought he knew this shortcut across the hills. Well, about the time we lost the cop, we hit a big coulee." He looked as though he might cry. "Rolled the pickup. Bottles all broke. Had to walk to a nearby ranch and borrow a horse. And that's all she wrote."

A nearly blinding anger spread through Nettie's body, like something boiling out from her core. "You got tied up with a criminal.

You lost what money you had. You risked your life. All for a load of booze?"

Jake ducked his head. "I'm sorry, honey. I was just trying to—"

Nettie snorted. "Sorry? It's dangerous, it's stupid, and it's illegal. I thought you knew better than this. That you cared about us. What has gotten into your head?" The heat of her anger seared through her mind. She pummeled him with her fists.

Jake grabbed her hands. "Dadgummit, Nettie. You don't understand. I did this for you and Neil." He stood up and looked into her eyes, still holding her at bay. "Should I let you guys and the horses starve to death?"

Spud groaned from the sofa and stirred. "You go see to him." Nettie turned on her heel and stomped away from the injured man who had gotten her husband into this mess.

The rest of the day, Nettie and Jake tiptoed around each other in palpable silence. Jake kept his gaze lowered. Nettie refused to look into his face. Spud awoke, recovered enough to sit up. She handed the unwanted guest a bowl of broth.

Neil stared with curiosity at the man on the sofa. "Who's that?"

"A 'friend' of your pa's." She glanced sideways at Jake. "He's just about ready to leave."

Spud left at dawn on the borrowed horse. Nettie seethed with anger and fear. "What's going to happen now? Is the law coming after you?"

Jake avoided her fierce gaze.

When Sheriff Ingram rode in, the noon sun burned with an intensity that Nettie's anger rivaled. Jake stepped up beside Nettie and tightened an arm around her shoulder.

Ingram tipped his hat to Nettie, got down from his horse, and shook Jake's hand.

"How do, Sheriff?" Jake lowered his hat brim slightly.

Trying to hide his bruises. Nettie stood in silence.

The lawman shuffled his boots in the dust. "Just out doin' a little visitin'."

"Good to see ya, Al. C'mon in. It's about dinnertime." Jake glanced at Nettie.

"Naw. Thanks, anyhow. Gotta keep movin'. Lotsa ground to cover." He turned as if to leave, then stopped. "Say, you heard anything about a rum-runner getting in a bad accident? Name's Spud Hartman?"

Nettie kept a smile frozen on her face, willing herself not to scream. *Oh my gosh. Now Jake's going to be arrested.*

Jake shook his head. "No. Can't say I've *heard* anything about it."

She smiled innocently.

The sheriff nodded. "Okay, then. Had a telegraph from a Canadian officer. Thought I'd check around. Thanks for your time." He heaved himself onto his horse and reined it to turn. Then he stopped again. "By the way, what happened to your face?"

Jake laughed. "Oh, just came up against the wrong side of some horsepower."

The sheriff laughed, too. "Well, you be careful now." With that, he rode away.

Nettie stared at Jake, hardly able to breathe. She jabbed her finger into his chest. "Don't you *ever* do that again!"

Jake ducked his head and put his big hand over hers. "Yes, ma'am."

CHAPTER THIRTEEN

Saturday, August 17, 1929

Something terrible is happening to us. Don't know what to do. Jake's brush with the law has me so scared. Don't know if I can forgive him.

Silence hung between Nettie and Jake like a thick burlap curtain. She went through the motions of cooking, cleaning, doing chores as if in a dull, lifeless body, while her brain beat a tattoo of recrimination. "What ifs" skittered through her mind. What if Jake had been killed? What if he'd been arrested? How would she and Neil live? What could she do to help?

Most days, Jake mounted Alsanger and disappeared in the direction of town. He came back late in the evenings, smelling of whiskey and cigarette smoke. Sometimes he gave her a few dollars he'd won at poker to put in the cookie jar. Most of the time, he came back empty-handed.

Nettie kept hearing her mother's voice, reminding her of "the evils of strong drink and gambling." She'd never thought anything of Jake playing cards for money. It was just something men did, to entertain themselves. And she had never minded Jake having a few drinks while he played, or at post-rodeo celebrations. After all, Papa kept his moonshine jug in the barn.

The Prohibition law was stupid, anyhow. Nobody paid it any mind, not even the sheriffs. But, now that Jake had broken the law and put himself in danger . . . Nettie rubbed her hands over her face. On the other hand, he was just trying to find a way to take care of his family. And gosh, they sure could've used the money. Was she being too hard on him?

Her stomach roiled with fiery acid. She could hardly eat, barely sleep. She couldn't bring herself to speak of it to him.

Late one afternoon, as she and Neil came back from checking the horses, Jake was back from town already. He leaned on the corral fence, one boot resting on the lower pole, his hat pushed back, a far-away look on his face. Nettie dismounted, lifted Neil down, and unsaddled her horse.

Neil ran to his father. "Pa, we saw the horses."

Jake picked up his son and swung him to sit on top of the fence. "You did, huh? Were they all there?"

Neil's eyes shone big and earnest. "Yeah. We counted fifty."

Jake raised his eyebrows at Nettie. "That's a lotta horses to feed, ain't it, little gal?"

Nettie frowned, wondering what he was getting at. "It sure is." She scuffed the toe of her boot in the dust, waiting for a clue.

"W-e-l-l." He took off his sweat-stained hat and rubbed his fingers through his damp hair. "The farmers aren't gonna get much of a crop, so they aren't in the market to buy any draft horses."

Icy sweat trickled down her back despite the August heat. Was he going to make another whiskey run to Canada? *Please, Lord, don't let it be that.* "Jake, you know how I feel about—"

"It's okay, little gal. I'm not going to Canada again. I promise." He had an earnest look on his face.

Nettie stared at him, still ready to lash out, until she comprehended what he'd said. Her anger melted into a puddle of love. She felt the weight of his responsibility for them. *He's really trying.* She put a soft hand on his arm and smiled. "Good."

"But there was a fellow in town today who's been loggin' in the western part, down around Evaro, and he says there's jobs to be had in the woods."

Nettie's shoulders tightened, thinking of trees falling, axes slipping, logs rolling down mountains. "Which is more dangerous, logging or revenue agents?"

With a wry smile, Jake put his hat back on and reached out to take her hand. She let her hand lie in his. "I'm thinkin' on checkin' it out. But, my idea is to take a draft pair along and see if that loggin' outfit wants to buy horses. And, there might be a coupla rodeos on the reservation or around Missoula I could take in. Maybe win a few dollars."

"How long do you think you'll be gone?" Nettie's grip on his hand tightened.

"Oh, a month, maybe."

A month. Maybe. Maybe longer. They hadn't been apart since that winter he'd gone to Oregon to work. That was a long, lonely, uncertain time. And that was before they were married. Before she knew she loved him. She wrapped her arms around him. Even though she was still incredibly angry with him, she did love him. And she didn't want to lose him. "All right. Come in the house. I'll fix us some supper."

Jake kissed her and they clung to each other as if for the last time.

Nettie fixed breakfast in slow motion the next morning, drawing out the moments she and Neil had left with Jake. Jake, too, seemed to move as through quicksand, as if picking up one foot and putting it in front of the other was an impossible task. But the time came when he could delay no longer.

He saddled Alsanger, tied the rope of one draft horse to his saddle horn, and tethered the other behind the first. Then he turned to Nettie and gathered her in his arms with a fierce hug. She clasped him back as hard as she could, to squeeze out the ache that had formed in her heart.

"Can I have a hug, Pa?" Neil's small voice broke their hold.

Jake held Nettie's shoulders and gazed into her eyes before he turned to Neil and picked him up in a bear hug. "You be good, li'l pardner. Take care of yer ma for me."

Nettie fought back the urge to jump on the horse and go with him.

He rode off, the ever-present dust swirling around the horses' hooves. When he reached the gate to the road, he turned in his saddle and waved his Stetson. Nettie stood in the doorway with Neil who clutched her hand, so small and forlorn.

"Bye-bye, Pa." His voice, high-pitched with unshed tears, made her bite her lip to keep from letting her own tears go.

She knelt down and gave her little man a long, hard hug. It would be tough, but they could do this. Neil's tear-filled eyes gazed into hers. "Don't worry, Ma. Pa'll be back soon."

Setting about her chores with a ferocious determination, Nettie worked at top speed from early morning until she could fall asleep from sheer exhaustion. She raked the barn clean of straw and manure. She swept and mopped the floors in the entire house. And she rode out to check on the horses every day.

Nettie refused to think about what had happened to Jake on his Canadian whiskey run or what could happen to him while he was gone this time. Or even the emptiness she felt. Every time he came to mind during the next few weeks, she found something to keep busy, or tried to capture a wisp of joy by playing with Neil.

One afternoon when she and Neil arrived at the horse pasture, they found the herd pressed against the far fence. Their heads reached through the barbed wire to snatch at the wizened grass on the other side. Nettie surveyed the dry ground on her side of the fence. She could practically count the blades of grass. On the other side, the grass was short, coarse, and brown. But at least there was some. The man who owned this section had left his homestead last winter, trailing his cows to better pasture somewhere. *Maybe we should've done that too.*

She dismounted. "Neil, honey, can you reach inside the saddlebag and find the wire cutters?"

What would it hurt? Nobody used this pasture. Their horses needed to eat. The poor things' ribs were starting to show. She looked around as if someone might be watching, then strode to the fence and snipped the wires. Pulling them back, she wrapped them around the posts on either side, making a wide gate.

"All right, you ol' nags, go on in there." Nettie stepped back, and the herd surged through to the feast.

"One, two, three," Neil counted. "Four, five, six."

She smiled at him and rumpled his hair. Somehow, she and Jake had to find a way to take care of this little guy, to make sure he had some kind of future. Their own ranch. That would ensure a good life for Neil.

As they rode back home, she thought about going into town to see if there was any mail. It had been three weeks since Jake had left, but she remembered how she had longed for a letter from him when he had been in Oregon that winter six years ago, before they were married. He just wasn't much of a letter writer.

Maybe tomorrow. They could get their chores done early, check on the horses, and then ride on into Sunburst to get the mail. Her heartbeat quickened at the thought of seeing people, Sven at the smithy, maybe stop by for lemonade at Myra Johannsen's. Yes, that's what they'd do tomorrow. She kicked Tootsie into a trot. Anticipation lifted the heavy loneliness.

As they rode within sight of the barn, Tootsie lifted her head and whickered, low and rumbly in her throat. An answer came from the corral.

"Pa."

"It's Alsanger." She and Neil yelled at the same time. Her heart beat faster, and without any urging, Nettie's horse picked up its pace. Neil clung to her waist behind her, whooping as the horse galloped home.

Jake opened the corral gate with a flourish and a bow. Neil slid to the ground and leaped into his father's arms. Nettie followed right behind. She flung her arms around them both. Her head bumped Jake's when he leaned around their wriggly son to kiss her. She laughed.

Finally Neil was ready to be set down, and he ran to Alsanger to pat the horse's sweaty neck.

"You're back early." Nettie couldn't help but smile. "I'm glad to see you."

Jake tucked his arm around her and squeezed her to him. "Not half as glad as I am to see you, little gal. Forgive me?"

She nodded. *For better or for worse.* For some strange reason, she remembered the minister's words at their wedding. Whatever Jake had done was for them. Whatever it was, they were in it together. Yes, during these past few weeks she had felt incomplete without him.

"So, you must have sold the horses." Nettie looked up into his tan face with those piercing blue eyes.

"Yup. Shore did. Didn't have to go work in the woods. And I won Top Hand at the Arlee Rodeo." His grin was bigger than ever. "We got us enough money now, and I got a shipment of hay comin' by train from the west."

Relief rose from deep within her. "A winter without worry." She leaped into his arms, and he swung her around, both laughing in the descending lavender dusk.

CHAPTER FOURTEEN

Sunday, August 10, 1930

Dust still blowing. Will it ever stop? So long since we've had even a drop of rain. Don't know what to do about the horses. Not much grass left. Jake's beside himself with worry.

Nettie stopped writing. What was that noise? A low, clicking hum. The wind? No. She'd never heard it like that. The sound grew louder. She stood and went to the window.

At first she didn't see anything. The air hung hot and still. Her mind filled with confusion. Then a movement down by the corral caught her eye. A dark river of motion, flowing, clicking, humming.

Grasshoppers.

Nettie sprinted for the door. "Neil! Where are you?" Frantic, she ran toward the barn. "Neil!"

"Here I am, Ma." His small voice came from the hayloft. He pointed to the mass off to one side. "What's that?"

She climbed up the ladder inside the barn and sat beside him. "Grasshoppers, honey. They won't hurt you." The whirring, low-flying cloud clung to the ground, slowly moving through small patches of withered grass, leaving the ground as bare as a table-top, swarming over the corral fence. What was left of the posts stood like skeleton bones, stark and fragile.

Her son's eyes were wide, pools of gray-green in the dim light. "What are they doing?"

"They're eating." Revulsion fought her calm words.

"Why did they eat the corral poles?"

"Because there aren't any crops and not much grass left." She tried to still the fluttering fear inside her stomach. *Now there won't be any grass left for our horses.*

Nettie and Neil watched until darkness settled around the path of destruction left in the insects' wake. Jake rode in from town and found them still sitting in the open door of the hayloft.

⌒⌒

Nettie leaned back in her saddle to survey the prairie from her vantage point atop the rimrock hills. Not a hint of color showed itself in the miles of parched ground, not even the usual late summer amber of prairie grasses. Hot wind swirled around her, the sky filled with brown haze from dust that had burdened the air for weeks. Her sinuses burned. Even Tootsie snorted and bobbed her head as if to clear her nostrils.

Their band of horses stood bunched in the lee of a shallow coulee, tails switching as the grit-filled wind peppered their behinds. Nettie chewed on her lower lip. *What are we going to feed them?* Horse prices had dropped, but hay prices were sky high. She blinked, trying to clear her eyes, but the inside of her lids felt like the sandstone of these brown hills. *If this is what hell is like . . .*

Her back tightened. A bleak future blurred her vision. How much worse could it get? An image came unbidden, of bleached bones scattered around a dry reservoir. She closed her eyes and shook her head to clear it of the grim vision. To contrast that thought, she tried to conjure a memory of a green prairie and horses grazing in contentment.

From beside her, a small voice interrupted her thoughts. "There's Pa." Neil kicked his little pinto forward. "C'mon, Ma."

Nettie followed her son down the path that led to their ranch house. She squared her shoulders. Had Jake's visit to the landowner given him some answers?

Neil waved his hand in the air and whooped as he urged his horse forward. She watched her five-year-old son ride so sure and confident, as though he were one with the horse. Her heart expanded with pride. Riding with such ease was something the three of them shared. As long as they had horses and a place to live, they would be all right. She urged Tootsie into a trot to keep up with her little cowboy.

Jake rode toward the barn from the road, his wide shoulders slumped, his head downcast. Her insides tightened. More bad news. This drought had aged him. Lately she'd noticed new worry lines on his forehead and the crinkles around his eyes had deepened from squinting against the merciless sun.

She and Neil reached the corral. Not much left of it after the grasshoppers.

Nettie waved at Jake, who straightened when he saw them. He slid off his horse and grabbed Tootsie's reins as Nettie dismounted. Neil took off in one last mad gallop around the barn.

Nettie forced a chuckle. "Just like his mother, can't get him off his horse."

Not hearing a response, she turned to peer anxiously into Jake's face. The nerves in the ends of her fingers twitched. "What did you find out?"

"Well, there ain't enough grass on this whole ranch for a bird to build a nest." Jake curled the corners of his mouth upward in an attempt to smile, but it died as quickly as it had begun.

"What did Ol' Man Davis say?" Nettie's hands felt cold despite the relentless heat.

Jake shook his head. "He won't renew the lease. Gonna let the bank have it."

Nettie doubled over as if she'd been kicked in the midsection by an angry steer. "No."

They had no money. Their herd of draft and draft-crossbred horses, raised for farming and for rodeos, were worthless. Farmers had nothing to farm. Nobody had money to spend on rodeo stock.

There was no way they could buy the ranch now. Was this what always happened to dreams? First, her dream trip to London with Tex Austin had vanished when she found she was pregnant. Then, she'd had to continue to put her rodeo dream on hold while raising Neil. So she and Jake conjured a new dream of owning a ranch.

And now this dream was shattered too.

Nettie lowered herself onto the big rock by the corral. "What are we going to do?" She looked up at Jake, tears stinging her sun- and wind-burned face.

He sighed deeply and sank to the stone beside her. "I don't know, honey. I just don't know."

Cold fear prickled the back of Nettie's neck.

The next morning Nettie awoke in the eerie haze-filled dawn to find Jake's side of the bed empty. Had he gone to Canada again? She sat up and hugged her bare arms to her chest. With eyes squeezed shut, she sought to draw strength from somewhere deep inside. It seemed as if he'd tossed and turned all night. Untangling herself from the sweat-dampened sheets, she dressed slowly. For a few more minutes she pretended it was a bright morning six years ago when the grass was green, she was still a newlywed with dreams of rodeos and fame, and she wouldn't have to face another scorched and hopeless day. This must be what "for worse" had meant.

Downstairs she found Jake hunched over a cup of coffee at the kitchen table. She rubbed his stiff shoulders. He didn't move. Nettie sat beside him, her hand still on his arm. He lifted his eyes to meet hers and licked his wind-cracked lips. "I'm going into town today, see what I can find out about grazing land. Maybe there's something in the western part of the state."

Nettie's lips trembled. "How long did Davis give us?"

"Oh, whatever we need." Jake stared across the kitchen through the dusty window. "But there's nothing to feed the horses, so it doesn't really matter. Nobody's got any hay left either." He scrubbed his hands through his hair and stood abruptly, knocking the chair over. Nettie jumped.

"Gotta go." He gave her a quick peck on the cheek.

She grabbed his hand and stood. "You'll find something. I know you will."

He gave her more of a grimace than a smile, and then he was gone, dust boiling up to his horse's withers as he rode away.

Nettie stood by the window, cradling Jake's half-empty cup, until the dust cloud vanished over the top of the hills. Selling the horses probably wouldn't bring much money, even if Jake could find a buyer. But if he couldn't find grass for them, the animals would surely die. And they soon would have no place to live.

Her mind flickered to her childhood homestead, kids gathered around a table laden with food. But her parents weren't that much better off now. They had all her brothers to support on that place. If they had any crops left at all. Besides, she couldn't go back, begging for a handout.

She took a sip of the cold coffee. The bitter liquid trickled down her throat to meet the bile that rose up from her stomach. Ranchers all around had abandoned their land, letting the banks have it, their cattle left to forage where they could. As hard as Nettie tried, she couldn't think of a single solution. But her man would somehow find one. *I know he will.*

She turned to see Neil standing by the table, rubbing the sleep from his eyes. She smiled at him. "Are you hungry?"

He nodded. "Why didn't Pa take me with him?"

Nettie set the coffee cup into the dishpan. "He had to go talk to some people about finding grass for the horses. I don't know how long he'll be gone. Here, have some oatmeal and then we'll go out and do chores."

"Could I give Paint some of my oatmeal?"

Nettie smiled, her heart aching. "That's really nice of you, sweetheart, but you just eat now."

She watched as Neil ate hungrily, twice extending his milk glass for a refill. It wouldn't be long before the milk cow dried up. Again, blankness blotted her vision as she tried to imagine the future for her son. Would there be a ranch for him?

How naïve she had been to resent the months of her pregnancy, when she was afraid she might be restricted to a life caring for a large brood of kids. *That* certainly had not been her dream. But now Neil was as much a part of her future and dreams as Jake and their horses. Especially since she wasn't able to have any more children.

Guilt zinged through her. How were her parents, her sisters and brothers coping? If she wasn't so worn out, she should go visit. *I will. Soon.*

Neil followed her to the windmill to pump a little water for the saddle horses. She pulled the lever, allowing the big steel blades to catch the wind. At first nothing came, then finally a small trickle of water splashed into the trough. Neil cupped his hands at the end of the pipe and played in the water. The shallow well yielded less each day. At least the incessant wind was good for something.

They continued the chores, feeding a few bites from the last small mound of hay to the saddle horses and the milk cow. Nettie tried to ignore the eager looks the animals gave her when those bites were gone, and with a twinge of guilt, sat on the three-legged stool to milk the gaunt old Guernsey, Bessie. She would be drying up soon from lack of feed.

After sampling the first few squirts of milk in a tin cup, Neil went to gather eggs, one by one, from the chicken coop before running out to hunt for nests the hens built outside.

The afternoon shadows had lengthened when she sat down in the barn to soap her saddle. When she heard hoofbeats, she peered out of the barn door to see Jake ride in from the road. This time he sat erect. Even Alsanger seemed to have a spring in his trot. As she watched, the sky behind them appeared clearer than it had been in weeks. Nettie's heart beat faster. She ran out to meet him at the same time Neil rounded the corner, galloping on a stick horse.

Jake grinned and waved his hat. "I found out where there's some grass."

Nettie gave a whoop. "Great. Where?"

Jake dismounted and loosened the cinch. Alsanger blew through flared nostrils. "Yeah." He gave her a sidelong glance as he swept the saddle and blanket off his horse. "It's in Idaho."

Nettie jerked her head back. "Idaho?" Was he just teasing her?

Jake pressed his lips into a thin line. "Yup. We'll have to trail 'em down to Salmon."

"Yippee." Neil goaded his stick horse into action. "We're goin' on a trail ride. Giddyup."

Nettie stood still, feeling the hard-packed soil beneath her boots. "To Idaho?" Her mind raced. It must be three hundred miles away. She looked at Jake, her brow furrowed. "Neil can't ride horseback all that way. He's not six years old yet."

"Now, little gal," Jake sputtered. "We—"

"No. We can't go." The icy fingers of fear clutched at her. This wasn't part of her plan for the future. Her family lived here. So did Jake's sisters.

She turned away, but Jake put a gentle hand on her arm. "Just a minute, sweetheart. Let's talk about this."

Dizzy now with the turmoil that churned inside, Nettie stopped and leaned against a still-intact fence post. "This is our home. How can we just up and leave it?"

"We don't have a choice." Jake bent his head closer to her. "Davis won't let us stay here. Besides, we don't have anything to feed our horses."

"I know." Cold guilt joined the fear. *How can I question him? He's found a solution.* She shivered.

"This'll be temporary. We won't be gone forever." Jake stroked her arms. "When it rains here, we'll be back so fast you'll hardly know we've been gone."

Nettie tried to smile. "How're the two of us going to trail fifty head of horses? Through towns. And over mountains?"

"We'll have a crew."

"We don't have any money."

Jake squeezed her hands. "I already talked to a couple guys in town who are willing to help, for grub, until we can sell a few horses."

A crew. Food. Nettie looked up at Jake. "I don't want to be stuck cooking for a crew. I want to ride, help out."

Jake grinned. "Of course. One o' the guys I talked to—Shorty— he's a cook. I can build a chuck wagon, easy."

Neil rode by on his stick horse again.

"And Neil can ride on the wagon."

Nettie shook her head. "You have all the answers, don't you?" *How could I have doubted him? He really is trying to take care of us.* She took a deep breath. "Okay. But there's so much I'll need to pack up."

"I'll help you get ready." Jake drew her to his chest, and she leaned against his warmth, drawing strength from his embrace.

In the kitchen, Nettie rummaged through the cupboards. There wasn't enough flour left to last that long. They'd have to make a supply run to town. What would they use to pay for it? They'd probably have to barter something. Eggs? Milk? What else to take? She frowned. Clothes. They'd have to pack light, but it might be cold in the moun- tains, and they'd probably have to spend the winter.

She dashed up the stairs and came to an abrupt halt at the top. *We won't be coming back to this house.* Everything would have to be packed up to store at Papa and Mama's. Or leave it behind.

Knees wobbly, she sank down on the step. She never thought she would attach any sentiment to a place. When they'd married, she fig- ured they would move around, travel to rodeos. That was their dream then. But this was their first house together. Despite her avowed dis- like of such things, she was actually proud of the feminine touches she'd added, a crocheted doily on the back of the sofa, a vase for spring flowers on the windowsill.

With the arrival of their son, their little valley had become a safe haven for them and their horses. She loved the buttes that rimmed this place, purple in twilight, almost gold in sunlight, tinged with green in spring, now a desolate grayish brown in this drought. She'd grown content staying here.

The steps creaked as Jake climbed up to sit beside her. He stared into her eyes. "How are you feeling? Are you ready?"

She stared down at her hands, fighting tears. "It's going to be hard to leave this place." But when she looked back into Jake's eyes, she caught a twinkle in their blue depths. For the first time in months, she could see hope there. Excitement built slowly, down low in her gut, then rose through her body until she tingled with anticipation. This would be a challenge. An adventure. She'd be riding, working with the horses.

"Yes." Nettie broke into a grin. "We can do this together. Let's finish getting ready."

CHAPTER FIFTEEN

Sunday, August 17, 1930

Finally ready. A whirlwind week of packing, finding cowboys to ride trail, saying good-bye. Leaving tomorrow.

The last of the fifty horses filed out through the opening in the fence. Nettie reined Tootsie in and turned in her saddle to look back. The house looked forlorn, its coat of whitewash scoured gray by the wind. The once-cheerful Caragana bushes drooped, brown and dust-covered.

A thickness threatened to close her throat. No telling when they'd be back. Or even if. She blinked hard and wheeled her horse back onto the track churned up by many large hooves.

"Haw. Get up now." Nettie yelled and clucked her tongue to move a couple of stragglers along. She and the men kept the horse herd moving with piercing whistles and shouts as they drove them south toward Cut Bank, the first town they'd pass through.

The chuck wagon, pulled by their team of Percheron crossbreds, creaked and bumped along on its rubber tires. Jake had built it on the chassis of an old Star car. A pole tongue reached from the team's neck yoke to a pivot on the center of the axle and connected to the tie-rod. As the team turned, so did the wagon. It carried their bedrolls and supplies and led the way. Neil perched on the wooden seat beside Shorty, the scowling cook, and whooped, waving his small hat.

Her brother Ben, Jake, and two cowboys from Sunburst flanked the seething mass of horseflesh. They'd been happy to sign on to the trail ride just for the grub and a hope of a little money at the end. Nettie rode behind to make sure no horse dropped out of the procession. She pulled her bandanna up over her mouth and nose to protect her from the choking clouds of dust.

After a few miles, Jake rode back to relieve her of mop-up duty. "Go on up front. Get out of this dust awhile."

She rubbed irritated eyes and reached out to touch his hand. Typical of him to think of her comfort, but this was just part of the job. They'd all take turns at the rear. "Okay, I guess I'll go up and see how Neil's doing."

Neil clutched the bench seat of the bouncing chuck wagon with one hand and his hat with the other. His serious face broke into a grin when he saw her. "Hi, Ma! Can I ride for awhile?"

Shorty frowned and growled behind his graying mustache, something about "not gonna stop every coupla miles to let the kid play."

Nettie nudged Tootsie alongside and stuck out a hand. "Grab on." Neil stood, reached up, and she pulled him behind her on the horse. She flashed Shorty a grin. "There, you didn't even need to stop."

Neil's happy chuckle and his arms clutched around her middle thrilled her. Her little boy riding with her was all she needed to make her happy.

That night they set up camp about halfway to Cut Bank. Nettie helped Shorty unpack the chuck wagon. She dug out salt pork and beans while he built a fire and hung a heavy cast-iron pot from an iron rod scaffold.

Then Nettie found the coffee pot and measured a handful of grounds into it. Without a word, Shorty dipped water from a barrel and grabbed the coffeepot from her. He poured water over the grounds and stuck it onto the coals at the outer edge of the fire. Then he turned to the folded-down hatch at the back of the wagon that served as a table and mixed up a batch of biscuits.

With a smile, Nettie moved aside. She fastened a canvas tarp to the side of the wagon for a tent and watched the old cowboy. His mouth was set in a grim line in a leathery face. His sinewy arms flexed as he stirred the batter. He was one of those closemouthed ol' cusses who'd never known a softer side of life. She had no idea how this long and lanky cowboy, nothing but bone and muscle, his legs bowed by years on horseback, came by the name Shorty.

The smell of coffee and fresh biscuits soon brought the rest of the crew. They crowded around the campfire and wolfed down their food as if they hadn't eaten in a week. Forks clanking on tin plates and an occasional grunt of satisfaction were the only sounds in the quiet night.

Nettie savored the salty beans and pork. "Mmm, this is just as good as the fancy restaurant food we ate on our wedding trip to Great Falls."

Shorty stopped in mid-chew and gave her a quick glance. But as he turned silently back to his plate, Nettie saw a faint twitch at the corner of his mouth. *Ha. He's not immune to a compliment.*

When Neil finished eating, he hugged Jake goodnight, and Nettie settled him into his bedroll in the tent. "Did you have a good day, honey?"

Though he was on the verge of falling asleep, she could see a twinkle from beneath half-closed lids. Just like his dad's. He grinned. "Yeah, Ma. 'Specially when I got to ride. Can I again tomorrow?"

Her heart full, she smoothed his dark hair and kissed his forehead. "I don't see why not."

Neil gave her a quick hug and snuggled into his blankets, undoubtedly already riding his pinto into his dreams.

Nettie joined Jake by the dying fire. The stars seemed to reflect its embers in the indigo sky. The evening light faded over the silhouette of the Sweet Grass Hills they'd left that morning. Although she'd traveled a mere twelve miles behind the slow-moving horses, she was bone weary from the long day in the saddle.

She watched her husband smoke silently for awhile. "What's it like, where we're going?"

"Green, I hope. Grassy."

Nettie circled her hands around her steaming coffee cup. *I hope so. Green would be nice.* "Will we have a house to live in?"

He shrugged. "Dunno. We'll find out when we get there."

"Feeling good about this?"

He nodded. "Yeah. I think it'll be all right."

She leaned against Jake's shoulder with a long, tension-easing sigh. House or not, they'd taken a positive step toward saving their herd and their dream of someday having their own ranch. This was the beginning of a new chapter in their lives.

A faint pink tinge washed the edge of the horizon when Nettie opened her eyes to the sounds of Shorty clanging pots at other end of the chuck wagon. Another day in the saddle. Another day closer to survival for their herd.

Jake yawned and stretched in his bedroll beside her, then leaned over to give her a quick kiss before he reached for his clothes. He pulled his shirt and denim pants on over the wool long johns that he, like all the other cowboys, including Nettie, wore to absorb and dissipate the sweat that built up on these hot August days.

Awakened by their movements, Neil sat up and flung off his blankets. "Are we ready to go? Where's Paint?"

Nettie smiled at his eagerness. "We'll go in a little bit. First, let's get your face washed." She reached for the tin basin and poured water from a canvas bag that hung from the side of the wagon. Neil screwed up his face in protest, but held still for a few moments as she scrubbed.

"Okay. I'm clean enough. Let's go." He wriggled out from under her arm and headed for the campfire.

Nettie chuckled, and then splashed the cold water on her own face.

After a quick breakfast of biscuits and bacon, the cowboys gathered the herd. On the move once again, the horses ambled along at a comfortable pace, stopping now and then to graze on whatever grass they could find. With luck, they'd make the ten miles to the outskirts of

Cut Bank before nightfall. Nettie wiped her forehead with her handkerchief and lifted the itchy wool away from her skin. They wouldn't be able to afford a room in town tonight, but maybe they'd find a hotel where they could buy a bath. She glanced over at Jake on the far side of the herd. Maybe they could even share one.

She hid her half smile.

Neil rode up beside her. "I'm tired, Ma. Can I go back to the wagon now?"

"Hold up a minute," Nettie called to Shorty.

The cook scowled as he pulled on the reins. "Never get there at this rate," he grumbled. As he reached for Neil, one of the draft horses started forward, jerking the wagon. "Whoa!" Shorty yelled, pulling on the reins with one hand. Neil's foot slipped from the side and he hung precariously for an eternal second.

Nettie didn't even have time to scream. Shorty dropped the reins and grabbed Neil with both arms, yanking him onto the wooden bench. Then he pulled the team up sharply and turned back to Neil. "You all right, young feller?"

Neil nodded and grinned. "Yup."

Shorty looked up at Nettie. "He's okay. Don't worry. I'll take good care of 'im." With that, he clucked to the team and off they went.

Nettie sat, stunned, on the back of her horse. It had all happened so fast. But thank God for Shorty's quick reactions. Finally she grinned. Yes, Neil would be all right in the cook's care.

She urged Tootsie forward to catch up. What she would have given to go on a trail ride like this when she was a young girl. She smiled, remembering how many times she'd sneaked off to ride, only to meet Mama's disapproving look and even more chores than usual as penance. If Neil had been a daughter instead of a son, Nettie would certainly let her ride as much as she wanted to.

She gazed out over the herd, plodding along with dust boiling up over their backs, tails switching at the pesky end-of-summer flies. She hoped Jake was right about the grass in Idaho. If he was, the horses had a chance to survive, and so would her family. They no longer had a home, but they were together. She urged Tootsie forward to ride alongside her son.

"Look, Ma. A hawk." Neil pointed. Gracefully it soared in the cloudless azure sky, swooped and dove to the ground, and just as quickly rose again with something clutched in its talons. "What'd he get?" Neil's bright face was full of wonder.

"Probably a mouse or a prairie dog. How would you like to have to get your dinner that way?"

Her son's delighted laughter warmed her heart. "That'd be fun, Ma."

A week later, they set up camp at East Glacier on the outskirts of Glacier National Park. The cooler air from the craggy, snow-capped peaks to the north perked Nettie's spirits. For the longest time she rested her drought-seared gaze on the mountain serenity. What a contrast from the prairie where she'd lived her entire life.

After their supper of beans and potatoes, she stood and stretched. "Let's take a stroll into town and check it out. It's been several years since we've been here."

Jake frowned. "I dunno. What about Neil?"

"He'll be just fine with Shorty." She winked at him.

Hand in hand, Nettie and Jake walked into the tiny town. On one side of the road stood the livery stable, with a single gas pump outside. Several Blackfeet Indians leaned on the rail, smoking.

Drawn to the music that blared from the Two Medicine Saloon, they walked across the street. Inside, patrons hunched over red and white checkered tables, intent on supper. Because of Prohibition, alcoholic drinks were not served at the huge maple bar. Jake started for the room in the back.

"But, Jake—" Nettie knew he was heading for a shot of home-distilled or bootleg whiskey.

Jake turned and planted a big kiss on her mouth, stopping her protest. "Relax, little gal."

"Okay." Nettie nodded. *I'll just have to trust him.* She sat at a table up front and ordered a frothy root beer.

Nettie studied the photographs that lined the walls. In one, the cowboy artist Charles Russell and the actor Gary Cooper posed at the dedication of the Teddy Roosevelt Highway. This was the road they'd followed all the way from Cut Bank.

Jake came out to join her a few minutes later, a coffee cup partly filled with pungent amber liquid in one hand, the worry lines on his forehead relaxed. He peered closely at the picture. "Hey, there's Charlie Russell. I met the ol' coot in Great Falls at the Mint Bar where he traded his drawings for drinks." He chuckled. "I didn't think they could be worth all that much at the time, but he seems to have done all right for himself."

After they finished their drinks and exchanged pleasantries with some of the diners, Nettie and Jake walked up the road to the Glacier Park Lodge. Just inside the door, Nettie stopped to stare at the gigantic pillars that lined the lobby. "I never dreamed there were trees that big." She felt like a child, so small, so in awe. The few cottonwoods that grew back home were spindly in comparison. "I wish Neil could see this. He'd be amazed."

Jake slapped one of the logs. "Yeah, Douglas fir. I heard the Indians call it 'Big Tree Lodge.'"

A photograph above the fireplace depicted the opening of the Great Northern Railway through the town in 1891. "We came through here when my folks moved us from Coeur d'Alene. I was six. I remember stopping at the station." Nettie laughed. "Mama was afraid of the Indians, but I wasn't."

Trains had brought good things into her life. She thought of their wedding trip to Great Falls. For just a moment, she wished they could transport their horses, so she could experience the luxury of the dining car once again. She sighed. As if they could afford to ship fifty head of horses that far. They didn't even have enough money to buy supper at the Two Medicine Saloon.

She looked across the room at Jake and a warm glow washed away her wishful thoughts. All that didn't matter, as long as she was here with him.

"Heeya!"

"Git up there!" The cowboys yelled and whistled to push the horses toward the bridge spanning the wide Flathead River. Despite the long drought, blue-green water raced over jutting boulders and formed deep, eddying pools along steep, tree-lined banks.

Nettie looked across the long wooden bridge. *Must be a good five hundred feet.* Those side rails didn't look like they'd hold back a calf, much less a herd of horses. And it was a good ten feet to the rock-strewn river below.

Jake rode up front, leading a draft pair on a rope. They would cross first and the rest of the herd would follow. At least that's what Nettie hoped. She reached over and slapped a straggler on the rump with her hat.

The men closed ranks on either side of the horses. Nettie pushed from behind, her nerves strung tight. "Go on, git, git."

Jake's pair stepped onto the structure but halted as their hooves thumped on wooden planks. They snorted and pawed at this new footing, then tried to back off. Jake tugged on the lead rope. "C'mon now."

First one, then the other horse thrust a leg forward, hesitated, then made another step, and another. Jake coaxed them toward the other side. The next several horses followed, then more. Nettie reined Tootsie to the left then back again, urging the group to keep moving. Ah, maybe this wouldn't be too bad after all.

Hooves thundered and planks rattled. The entire structure swayed. Nettie gripped her reins. The bridge might not hold up under all that weight. Maybe they should have taken them across one at a time so the horses wouldn't crowd each other until the railings gave way.

Jake made it across with his lead pair. He called and clucked at the horses on the bridge. Those who reached the other end bolted off. The structure shook in their wake. The horses still on solid ground on Nettie's side balked at the entrance. They milled around in confusion, flailed the air with their hooves, and whinnied with fear. Anything to avoid stepping onto that swaying, noisy bridge.

Dust swirled. The horses' fear and sweat was sharp in Nettie's nose. She saw confusion in the great mass of horseflesh. Animals turned every which way. Some came back toward her. Teeth gritted, she urged Tootsie into a fast trot, criss-crossing the rear of the herd. The men riding the flank did the same, whooping and slapping at the stubborn horses with their lariats.

Someone motioned to Shorty to help and he pulled the chuck wagon up on the left, just before the bridge entrance, to form a barrier.

Nettie caught a breath. *Neil's still inside.* "Get him outta there!" She tried to catch Shorty's attention, to no avail.

Shorty, on foot now beside the chuck wagon, waved his arms and shouted. A big roan brushed against the side. Shorty jumped up onto the seat just as the sea of horses flowed around the wagon, pushing and jostling it from all sides. It rocked up on two wheels and balanced for a moment as if deciding whether to tumble down the embankment.

Nettie screamed, a useless gesture against the noisy chaos of snorting, whinnying, stomping horses. *Lord, keep it upright.* Then the wagon tilted back, the wheels landing with a jolting crash.

Nettie caught a glimpse of Jake astride Alsanger on the other side of the river, keeping those horses from wandering off. He looked back at the confusion.

"Jake, do something!" She yelled again and threw up her arms in a helpless gesture, knowing he couldn't hear her. "C'mon, git up, git up!" Nettie continued her push at the rear, all the while angling her horse toward the chuck wagon and sending thoughts toward her son. *Neil, stay in the wagon.* She could just see him trying to get out and help.

As if he had heard her, Jake gathered his rope in one hand and rode back onto the bridge. When he came close to the first of the balky horses, he swung the loop. It settled neatly around a gray Percheron's neck. Jake tugged hard and talked calmly. At first the horse stood its ground. Finally the animal gave in to its training and followed, head down, nostrils flared, snorting at the creaky boards.

Behind the big gray, another horse clopped onto the bridge. Then another followed and another. Finally, the rest calmed. In single file, the horses crossed.

Nettie galloped back to the chuck wagon and slid off her horse even before it came to a complete stop. She whipped back the tarp covering and gathered Neil into her arms. Her heart pounded. "Are you all right, honey? Were you scared?"

Her little boy looked up at her with his hazel eyes big and round. "No, Ma. I watched through that hole. I wanted to help, but Shorty wouldn't let me."

Nettie's hug on Neil tightened. *Thank you, Lord.* She forced herself to breathe deeply and relaxed her grip to smooth his dark hair back from his forehead. "That's good, honey. I'm glad you stayed in the wagon. After we get the horses settled down, would you like to ride with me for awhile?"

Neil's gap-toothed grin beamed up at her. "Yeah, Ma."

As Jake and the men set up camp that evening, hobbled the saddle horses, and divided up the night watch, Nettie walked to the chuck wagon. "Thanks for keeping Neil safe today."

Shorty ducked his head. "It's okay."

"Can I help you with supper?"

He pointed to the kettle on the fire. Nettie grabbed a long spoon and stirred the stew while Shorty put a big pot of rice on to boil. After it had cooked, he added a couple cans of condensed milk and a pound of raisins, sprinkled cinnamon and nutmeg on top, and let it simmer a little longer.

He glanced at Nettie's questioning face and grunted. "Spotted pup."

Her stomach growled. Hmm. A sweet treat sounded good for a change.

After everyone had eaten their fill, they all sprawled by the fire, smoking and drinking coffee from tin cups. Nettie's brother Ben took out a deck of cards, and soon he and the other two cowhands were engaged in a spirited game of poker with wooden matches for chips. Neil watched for awhile, then wandered aimlessly from the chuck wagon to the fire and back again to the wagon.

Nettie leaned against a log, watching her son stand next to the wiry cook, who washed dishes, asking questions and nodding at Shorty's curt answers.

Perhaps she should distract Neil. Wouldn't want him to get on the old man's nerves. Maybe just put him to bed.

Then Shorty dried his hands on the dishtowel tied around his waist. Pulling out his pocketknife, he reached for a willow branch lying nearby.

She sat bolt upright. Was he cutting a switch to paddle Neil? She didn't think her son had bothered him that much. But before she could get to her feet, the cook sank down on his haunches and began whittling, cutting the stick into small pieces. As the pile grew, Neil began stacking them, building a little log cabin.

Nettie smiled. The old man had a heart after all.

The last horse crossed the Buckhouse Bridge south of Missoula. Nettie let her taut muscles relax. The herd had gotten the hang of these bridges at last. No trouble on this one. Just a few more miles today on this dusty gravel road that followed the winding Bitterroot River, and they'd be able to camp alongside the water. Even though it was mid-September and the days were growing shorter, it was just as hot as August. Another 150 miles or so to go.

She took off her hat to fan a breeze over her flushed face, then used the neckerchief to mop her brow, pushing wisps of wet, matted hair back. *Sure will be nice to finally get to Idaho.* She gazed at the cool green of the willow and cottonwood trees that grew along the river, already imagining herself in the shade, drinking from its cool depths, listening to its soothing ripple. She pictured herself slipping into a shallow pool, soaping the sweat and grime from her body. That water would sure feel good tonight, if she could find a secluded place away from the men.

The insistent bray of a car horn startled her. They hadn't met with much traffic on this trip. Just ahead, where the herd blocked the road, a touring car had stopped. A large older woman sat in the driver's seat, squeezing the bulb of the claxon as if hoping it would miraculously part the sea of horses. Her angry mouth moved soundlessly, while the feathers on her purple hat bounced in emphasis.

Nettie urged Tootsie into a trot around one side of the herd. Out of the corner of her eye she saw Jake headed around the other side. Maybe they could talk some sense into this mad matriarch before the horses scattered to kingdom come.

The horn squawked again. And again. The woman's fist pumped out of the window at the stalled beasts.

A big brown mare stood directly in front of the car, head held high, and ears back. With the next blare of the horn, the horse turned. With her backside square to the car, her rear legs lashed out like a strike of lightning. One. Two. With the precision of a crack shot, each kick smashed a headlight. Then the mare wheeled around and calmly trotted around the car. The rest of the herd followed.

The woman's face was a picture of shock, nearly pure white. Her red slash of a mouth became a wide O, her hat askew. She pulled on the gas lever and with a spurt of gravel, drove off.

A giggle bubbled up from Nettie's throat. She clamped her hand over her mouth, but couldn't contain herself. Laughter erupted full bore. Across the backs of the now-moving horses she saw Jake slap his leg, his head thrown back in brazen delight. And on the chuck wagon seat, Neil and Shorty joined in, whooping and waving their hats.

CHAPTER SIXTEEN

Sunday, September 21, 1930

Trail ride going well. Sure seeing some beautiful new country. Different from home. Neil enjoys riding, camping. I do too.

Nettie sat on a windfall log, pencil poised above her journal, embraced by a bubble of peace. The low-slung valley stretched itself for miles, cradling the river, captured by the Bitterroot mountain range to the west. Even though the water ran slow and brackish through the months of drought, she was drawn to the narrow swath of green willows and cottonwood trees that meandered alongside. An oasis in this moisture-starved land. Hope filled Nettie with warmth. *That's what Idaho will be, an oasis.* The fir-clad slopes rising into the cloudless sky soothed her sun-seared eyes. What a difference a few hundred miles could make, from brown treeless prairie to this cool green haven.

Mere yards away, Shorty's voice broke through the idyll as he cleaned up from supper preparations. "Thought you better know, we're gettin' low on grub. Flour. Coffee, too."

Jake shoved his sweat-stained hat back from his forehead. He worked a hand-whittled toothpick from one side of his mouth to the other. "Yeah, I know. We'll take care of 'er in Darby tomorrow." He caught Nettie's eye as he walked away from the chuck wagon, shrugged one shoulder, and winked.

They'd been scraping the bottom of their supply barrel for several days. Her brother Ben had left the trail at Missoula, since he needed to take on a paying job. But it still took a lot of food to feed the remaining six of them after long, hard days in the saddle.

The warm, peaceful moment punctured, Nettie pursed her lips and closed her journal, leaving it perched on the log as she strode to catch up with Jake. "We're out of money, too, aren't we?" Money-making ideas skittered uselessly through her mind as she watched him build his smoke. No time to hunt for pelts on the trail. Nothing to barter with.

Jake dug into his shirt pocket for his sack of Bull Durham. "We'll figure somethin' out." He dished the thin paper lengthwise between thumb and forefinger, pulled the drawstring of the bag open with his teeth, and tapped out tobacco. Jake closed the bag again and wet one edge of the paper with his tongue. Spitting a few stray bits of tobacco, he rolled the paper into a cigarette, twisting one end shut.

"Big logging operations around here." He struck a match on the heel of one boot, lit up, and drew on the cigarette. The tip glowed red in the evening dusk. "I'll ride up first thing in the mornin', see if they need a couple horses."

Nettie squeezed his arm. "That's a good idea." Her man would prevail.

The next day after Jake left, Nettie lingered over a cup of coffee. The sun rose, hot and penetrating, as if laughing at her enjoyment of the cool green. Neil played in the shade of the wagon, building and rebuilding his log structures.

Midmorning, Jake rode back into camp. Even though he whistled around a stalk of grass hanging from his lip, there was that barely perceptible slump only she could detect. No luck. Dejection slumped Nettie's shoulders too. She chewed on her lower lip. *Now what'll we do?*

Shorty leaned his bowed and bent body against the chuck wagon, a questioning look on his face. Jake dismounted and poured the dregs of coffee from the pot. "Get 'er packed up. We'll be goin' on into Darby now." He came over to sit beside her on the log.

She looked into his eyes. "No sale, huh?"

He shook his head, mouth a grim line. "Got all the horses they need. Switching to steam skidders, and shipping on rails they built right by the logging cuts."

Nettie closed her eyes, the familiar chill of fear filling her chest. If they couldn't feed the men, they wouldn't be able to keep a crew long enough to get the horses over the mountains.

Their future livelihood looked doubtful.

She opened her eyes and tried to find words to comfort her husband.

Jake rubbed his palm over the stubble on his cheeks. "Farmers have switched to tractors. Now the loggers too. Nobody wants our horses anymore."

Nettie forced a cheerful voice. "Well, they can't all be switching over. Maybe the next place will still be using horses."

Jake shook his head. "Some days I wonder if this is all worth doin'."

She reached for his hand. "Yeah, it's worth it. Horses aren't going away entirely. We just have to get through this rough patch."

He squeezed her hand and smiled. "You're right, little gal."

Late that afternoon, they straggled with their herd through the sleepy little town of Darby. No one paid them any mind. They passed by two weathered livery stables, a gas station, and a blacksmith shop where the smithy was working under the hood of a Model T. Nettie winced at the irony. Even the blacksmith had to change his way of life.

Nettie saw two churches and a small one-room school. "This looks like a nice place."

Jake grinned. "Think this is a place you might like to live?"

She shrugged. "If we found our ranch here." *Maybe lots of rodeos nearby.*

Next came a large pool hall and combination watch-repair and barber shop, where Jake stopped a minute to ask where to camp.

Nettie chuckled as she counted six saloons before riding by the jail and one bank. "They do have their priorities in this town."

Jake laughed. "Yeah, I just might like it here."

Nettie leaned over and punched his arm. "Not a chance."

He grinned and winked.

She caught Shorty staring at the general store as they passed it by. *Yeah, Shorty, I'm wondering if we'll be able to buy food too.* Following the herd, she rode with the rest of them to set up camp in an abandoned apple orchard just outside town.

As the men hurried about their settling-in chores, Jake pawed through his saddlebags. He took out his Colt revolver, opened the cylinder, spun it, and inspected the barrel. "I'll run back into town, see if I can hock this. Wanna come?"

Nettie raised her eyebrows. That Colt had belonged to his dad. *Surely, he doesn't want to give it up.* Besides, they might need it on this trip. "Sure. I'll ride along."

Once in town, Jake tied their horses to the rail. Nettie waited while he stepped into the pool hall. In a minute, he came back out and cocked his head toward the lone gas station across the street. Nettie followed him inside. As the man behind the counter stood, rolls of fat seemed to uncoil. He braced himself against the wooden structure. "He'p ya?"

Jake placed the pistol on the scarred counter. "What'll you give me for this?"

The man took the gun and turned it over in his massive paws, sausage fingers rubbing the barrel.

"Like new." Jake rocked back on his heels.

The proprietor scratched his bristly jaw, his chins shaking. "Coupla bucks."

Nettie's breath caught in her chest. Surely it was worth more than that. They might as well take the gun and go rob the bank. "No, Jake," she whispered her protest.

He pointed at the barrel. "No sign of wear."

No response.

"We're trailin' a herd of horses down to Salmon City. Be back next spring. Betcha could get ten, twelve bucks for it, easy."

Fat jiggled again as the man shifted from one foot to the other. He cleared his throat. "Five." He set the Colt on the counter. "Take 'er or leave 'er."

Nettie frowned. That still wasn't much. *Better than nothing, I guess.* Jake nodded.

"No." Nettie couldn't help herself. She took out the silver cigarette case she'd won in Miles City and plunked it on the counter. "How about this? Six bucks."

"Honey, you can't—" Jake protested, but Nettie put a finger on his lips.

"I don't need it. Too fancy. And I don't smoke anyway," she whispered behind her hand.

The fat man picked it up, a sudden smile on his face. He studied it for a moment, turning it over and back again. "Five."

Nettie leaned closer, narrowing her eyes at him. "Six."

He took a half step back and stared at her. Then he nodded. "Done."

Nettie swallowed the regret that rose momentarily like bile. A pretty big prize. But, they couldn't feed it to their men, or the horses. It was the right thing to do.

Out on the boardwalk, Jake jingled the six silver coins in his pocket and gave Nettie a lopsided grin. "Shall we go buy some grub?"

She smiled back. Shorty would be happy to get a sack of flour, coffee, beans, and maybe even some beef. Nettie linked her arm with Jake's. "Let's."

The next morning Nettie scraped the last film of slightly rancid butter from the bottom of the battered lard can. *We should've bought some milk in town.* The cream from the milk they'd gotten in Missoula had jiggled and jounced enough along the road that it had coagulated into chunks of butter, a treat the men enjoyed on their pancakes. And Neil liked to drink the buttermilk she drained off. At least she didn't need to churn.

"We'll have to see if we can stop at a ranch house today and get you some more milk." She turned to Neil, who wolfed down the last of his hotcake and washed it down with weak tea.

He swallowed. "I'll go with you."

That afternoon they stopped to let the horses water at a clear trickling stream and sat in the shade to eat cold biscuits. The men lay back to catch a short nap, hats covering their faces.

Nettie grabbed the pail. "C'mon, Neil, honey. Let's go for a walk. It looks like this trail might head down to that ranch over there."

They'd climbed slowly and steadily since leaving Missoula, and the cooler air at the foot of the Bitterroots caressed her skin, especially in the shade of the dense copse of trees. Nettie ambled along the dusty, rutted track and lifted her eyes to the majestic mountain called Trapper Peak that rose over the others to the west. Its jagged outcroppings, still white-capped despite the summer heat, jutted above the velvet green forest. She stopped to watch a small crested blue jay flit from the branches of one pine to another. It squawked. Its mate answered. A low hum of insects in the white-tufted bear grass lulled her. She reached down, took Neil's hand, and they walked on together, reveling in the peacefulness.

Passing a weathered barn where a couple of horses stood switching their tails against the flies, they turned toward a gray clapboard house. Clothes fluttered on the line in a slight gust of breeze.

"Helloo," Nettie called out.

"Rrrrwwff." A streak of gray and black fur sprang from beneath the raised porch floorboards. Long yellow fangs bared in an angry red grimace. Growls emanated deep from the bowels of hell.

No. As if in slow motion, she reached around Neil with one arm and pulled him behind her. Her other arm came up to shield them. She lifted her boot to kick out, knowing all the while it would be useless.

A shout. A scream. Was it hers?

She made a slow spiral. Turned just as the dog leaped past. Hot saliva stung her cheek.

Down on her knees. Huddled around Neil. Her back arched, expecting another attack. Eternal seconds. No crushing weight. No searing pain.

"Brutus. Down." The shout came again.

Hardly daring to move, she raised her eyes. She saw scuffed boots first. Then the tall, lumberjack figure of a man on the porch. Relief poured over her like cool water.

His brow was drawn into a deep frown. His hand shot out and he pointed a finger down. The scruffy German shepherd slunk beneath the porch with one last grumble, tail between its legs.

Nettie hugged her son's shaking body and shivered. Sweat cascaded down her sides. She looked down at Neil's white face and quivering mouth. Taking a long, deep breath, she let it out slowly to steady her voice. "It's all right, honey. The dog won't hurt you now."

"Don't mind ol' Brute here. He's just not used to strangers. You okay, ma'am?"

She stroked Neil's back, then stood to face the man. "You have no business keeping a monster like that." Nettie jabbed a finger in the air to accentuate her words. "Don't you ever let that happen to anybody again." Her knees felt like warm custard.

The man's face reddened. "I'm sorry, ma'am. We don't get many strangers hereabouts." He knelt by Neil. "Let me bring the dog out and let you meet him. Would you like that?"

Neil burst into tears and buried his face in Nettie's pant leg.

"No! You keep that dog away from my son." She reached out and gave the man's shoulder a shove.

He rocked back on his heels, nearly losing his balance. He stood. "I really am sorry, little feller. He won't hurt you. Ma'am, what can I do to make it up to you?"

With a shaky hand, Nettie lifted her bucket. "We came to see if we could buy some milk from you."

"No charge. Happy to give it to you." He stuck out his hand. "Name's Duncan. Charley Duncan. Come in, wait inside while I get the milk from the root cellar."

Nettie stepped forward to mount the steps to the porch, but Neil whimpered and clung to her waist.

"If it's all the same to you, Mr. Duncan, I think we'll wait here."

Charley reached a hand toward Neil. "Say, why don't you come along? Wanna ride on my shoulders? I can't go as fast as a horse, but you'll be really tall."

Neil glanced at Nettie, wiped the tear tracks from his face with the back of his hand, and nodded.

Charley squatted down to let Neil climb on his back. He picked up the pail and pretended to trot down the path toward the root cellar. Neil laughed and kicked his heels, as if on horseback.

Nettie released a trembling breath and followed.

Charley set Neil down, opened the wooden door in the side of a hill, and went down the steps. He returned with the pail full. "Where you headed?"

Nettie told him.

"Salmon, huh? Well, I got me a cabin in Salmon. You guys can stay there, get rested up before you take your horses on up the mountain. It's the least I can do."

A cabin. That sounded so appealing right then. Nettie nodded. "That's right nice of you, Mr. Duncan. Why don't you come back to camp with us and tell my husband about it?"

"Be glad to. But call me Charley."

Nettie's insides still quaked as she and Neil trudged back up the hill, Charley carrying the bucket. Neil grasped her hand with a vise-like grip. The idyllic afternoon stroll had been shattered. She took deep gulps of fresh mountain air and gradually calmed herself.

Nettie watched Jake's eyes narrow and his fists clench and unclench as Charley unfolded the afternoon's story. "What the Sam Hill? My son could've been k—" Jake stopped. "—could've been badly hurt." He reached out, drew Neil close to his side with one arm, and patted his head.

The man apologized profusely and offered Jake a bottle of his best home-distilled whiskey. After an initial wariness, Jake relaxed, and the men sat around the fire to swap drought stories, Neil sitting at his dad's knee, listening intently. Every so often, Jake reached down and tousled his son's hair.

Nettie's fright gave way to relief and she collapsed by the fire, next to her husband and Neil.

"You lookin' for pasture for them horses? There's good grazing up on Leesburg Mountain about fifteen, sixteen miles west of Salmon City." Charley gestured upward. "It's an old abandoned gold mining town. Not much left up there now but grass. The summit's about ten thousand feet, but the meadow's sheltered from the wind, so you oughta be able to winter real good. Besides, they haven't had a lot of snow the last few years, with the drought."

Jake nodded. "Sounds good."

The man unwound his long frame from the ground, poured himself another cup of coffee, and looked at the chuck wagon built on the automobile chassis. "Pretty ingenious invention here. I had an old Star car I drove the last time I was over there. But the brakes didn't work so good. It run off the road somewheres on the Idaho side of the pass. Barely had time to jump out 'fore it flew over the side. Maybe you can find it, salvage the tires or some other parts for your wagon."

Jake took a sip of his coffee. "Thanks. We could sure use extra parts."

"Say, just word of advice. Lost Trail Pass is likely too steep for that wagon, but fine for the horses. There's another, Gibbons Pass, that's a little wider." Charley grabbed a stick and drew a crude map in the dirt.

Jake studied the dusty scratches. "Couldn't we just take the horses over Gibbons too?"

"Naw, I wouldn't. Ya might meet up with another wagon coming the other way. I done it both ways. Easier to go single file over Lost Trail."

Neil looked up at Charley. "If it's a lost trail, how will we find it?"

The big man chuckled. "Well, Lewis and Clark couldn't find it, but we know where it is."

Nettie remembered reading about the explorers in school. "I guess somebody eventually blazed the trail."

Charley nodded. "Yup. Traders finally made it over, but they had to lock up the wheels and just let 'em slide down the mountain."

Neil jumped up from the log by the fire. "Hey, that's sounds like fun."

"No, it doesn't." Nettie grinned at her son.

Late that night after Charley had gone, Jake and Nettie watched the dying embers of the campfire. Nettie sagged against Jake's shoulder, letting the day's events wash over her. The peacefulness of her walk, the fear from the dog attack, Charley's friendly generosity. She sighed, suddenly weary.

Jake tossed the dregs of his coffee onto the coals with a sizzle. "Well, if what Charley says is right about how narrow the pass is, looks like it's gonna be a rough trip. Wonder if we can lighten the load and take the wagon over."

"Why don't Neil and Shorty and I take the chuck wagon over the longer, wider trail?"

"Split up?" Jake massaged her wrist. "Won't you miss me?"

Nettie snuggled closer. "Of course I will. I don't like the idea, but it sounds like the only choice."

"I know. I don't either." Jake drew her to his chest. "I reckon with the time the herd takes to cross the divide single file, the wagon oughta be able to travel faster over the other route and we'll meet up about the same time. Won't be but a couple days."

Lonesome already, she nodded. It was the only way, but she hated to be apart for even one or two nights.

CHAPTER SEVENTEEN

Friday, September 26, 1930

These mountains sure are huge. I wish I hadn't suggested splitting up on this trip over the pass. Hate the thought of being away from Jake.

The road narrowed as Nettie followed the band of horses higher into the foothills. She gazed in awe at mountain peaks piled one upon the other, as though they reached right into heaven. The pass cut a magnificent V-shape between the high tree-tufted slopes. Gray cliffs loomed far above the tree line, their violet shadows chased by the early morning sun. A red-tailed hawk soared across the blue.

Almost breathless from the beauty, Nettie pointed to one jagged, snowcapped peak lit by the sun, shimmering in the distance. "Isn't that splendid?"

Neil looked upward, his mouth wide open.

"Better be careful, a bird'll fly in there and build a nest," Jake teased.

"Aw, Pa." Neil rolled his eyes and grinned back up at his dad.

"These mountains sure are grand." Nettie's own mouth may have hung open in awe just a bit, too. As many days as they'd been traveling in sight of these mountains, she still couldn't believe their vastness, the ever-changing color and light as the sun progressed across the cloudless sky.

A cottony softness filled her chest. How insignificant she was in the shadow of this majestic creation. This must be just a small taste of heaven.

Jake pushed his hat back from his forehead. "Well, gotta split up, I guess." Before she could say a word, he hugged her hard, gave her a quick kiss, and clapped Neil on the shoulder. "See ya in a coupla days."

She clasped her hands over her breast, an empty spot forming already. *Wish I hadn't suggested this.* But it was too late to change her mind now.

Nettie lingered as long as she could. She watched Jake and the cowboys push the herd, walking single file now, strung out along the steep, narrow trail. Finally, she and Neil mounted their horses and turned away. Following Duncan's advice, they rode behind the chuck wagon to cross Gibbons Pass, which looped just a few miles to the east. Nettie, Neil, and Shorty would meet up two nights later at Gibbonsville with the cowboys and the horses.

Nettie leaned forward in the saddle and gripped tight with her knees as Tootsie labored up the mountain pass. She called out to Neil, "Hang on tight now. This trail is pretty steep, and narrow too."

Up ahead, the big blue steamer trunk strapped to the chuck wagon's side literally stuck out from the narrow path over the abyss. Nettie grimaced. So much for a wider trail.

Neil, who followed the wagon, reined his pinto close to the edge and leaned over to peer down. Nettie gasped. "Neil! Get away from the edge. You could fall." Her stomach churned. How could she keep her son safe if he insisted on being a daredevil?

"I won't fall," he called back. "Look at the water down there. It's wild."

She looked over the side. The river snaked far below. The water tumbled through its bouldered channel. A wave of dizziness made her sway in her saddle. *Almost like when I was pregnant. Thank goodness, that can't be it.* Had she had too much coffee this morning? Best not look at the scenery down there.

"Sure hope we don't meet anybody coming down from the other side," she muttered to no one in particular.

Several more times she called ahead to Neil. "Be sure not to get too far ahead of me. Hang on tight, honey."

His voice drifted back to her, filled with bravado. "I'm just fine, Ma. Stop worryin'."

She tightened her hold on the reins. *How can I not worry?*

The journey to the top seemed endless. Tootsie plodded upward. The great muscles in her shoulders bunched and rippled with each step. Nettie tried to shake the empty, nauseating feeling that she would fall any second, that her body was toppling over the sharp edge, swooping down, down, down in an unstoppable arc. This was nothing like riding over the rims of the hills back home. And she'd thought they were steep.

Hunkered down in her saddle, she clung with uncharacteristic ferocity to the saddle horn, and willed herself to stay upright. Each step was a jolting blow to her now-aching head, and the narrow canyon loomed ever closer. Would they never get to the top? Weariness possessed her.

Finally, as golden light faded into a dusky purple, she and Neil rode into a small clearing where the chuck wagon stood by a large boulder. Shorty sat unmoving on the seat, still grasping the reins with white-knuckled tenacity. As Nettie rode up, he pushed a gusty breath through pursed lips.

"Whew. Thought I was a-goin' ta meet my maker there a few times." He relaxed his grip, dropped the reins, and eased himself from the high wagon. Taking off his battered, dusty hat, he mopped his brow with his bandanna. "S'pose you want somethin' ta eat now."

Nettie swung her leg over the saddle and nearly fell to the ground. The scene spun before her. Her head felt as though it were detached from her body and throbbed with the beat of a tom-tom. She smiled gamely and tried to take a step. Her legs buckled. "Don't feel so well."

Shorty reached out to steady her. "Altitude sickness. Seen it b'fore." He gestured to Neil. "Get yer ma's bedroll. Be better layin' down."

Neil ran to comply. He helped her spread out the bedding and pulled a blanket up to her chin when she lay down. "Feelin' better, Ma?"

Nettie nodded, touched by his concern. Neil sat beside her and held her hand until she fell asleep.

Sure enough, the dizziness and nausea subsided after a night's sleep. The morning dawned clear and frosty. Nettie rose and stretched, stiff from sleeping on the cold ground. She still felt a little shaky, but the pounding headache was gone. After a quick cup of coffee and bowl of warm oatmeal, she mounted and followed Neil, Shorty, and the wagon down the west side of the mountain. Relief buoyed her and she could enjoy the scenery once again.

Two days later, the little party topped a hill overlooking Gibbonsville. Their herd of wide-backed horses grazed in a meadow near the mining town where the men had set up camp. For the first time in several days, Nettie felt like her equilibrium had returned. Tonight she'd be with Jake again. Happiness rose like the early morning sun.

She beckoned to Neil. "C'mon. I'll race you." Whooping, she kicked Tootsie into a gallop toward the camp.

That night as Nettie snuggled into her bedroll next to Jake, he turned to her and cradled her face in his hands. "Shorty told me how sick you got on the pass. Doggone it, why didn't you tell me?"

Nettie shook her head. "Aw, it wasn't anything. A little dizzy is all."

His concerned, piercing gaze searched her face. "I shoulda been there to take care of you."

Nettie huffed. "You don't have to take care of me every minute. I'm perfectly capable of doing that myself."

"Oh, little gal, I know you are." He reached out to smooth her hair, then took her into his embrace.

Despite her brave face to Jake, she couldn't shake the helpless feeling she'd experienced on the pass. But a good night's sleep, cradled in Jake's arms, wiped away the residue of her illness.

The next day was clear and sunny as usual, but the temperature remained noticeably cooler as the band of horses descended toward the Salmon River. Nettie had felt too sick on the trail to care, but now she noticed how much less her long, woolen underwear itched, and how she didn't need to wipe the perspiration from her face as often.

She rode along in the fresh morning air, reveling in the thought of a hot, sudsy bath and clean clothes when she reached Salmon City. It had been six weeks since they'd left home, and other than a rented bath in Cut Bank and another in Missoula, she'd bathed in rivers and streams since. Refreshing when it was hot, but she never quite felt clean. And, it would be nice to give her legs and backside a rest. After this long in the saddle, she felt as bowlegged as Shorty.

A shout from the cook brought her focus back to the chuck wagon. He pulled the team to a stop, jumped down from the high seat, and kicked the tire, cursing.

Jake turned from his position at the flank of the herd and rode up. "What's the matter, Shorty?"

"Dagnabbit. 'Nother flat." The cook kicked the offending tire again. It was the third blow-out in as many days. He looked up at Jake. "Didn't find Charley's Star car?"

Jake slid from his saddle. "We found it all right. It was stuck in the top of a tree, over the side of the pass. But somebody crazy enough to climb down there already took the tires."

Shorty grunted and his face crumpled into disappointment.

Nettie laughed, dismounted, and rummaged in the back of the wagon for a snack for Neil.

With a grimace, Jake took the wheel off the axle, removed the flat tire, and took out the punctured inner tube. He stored it in the first available space he could find, the camp stove oven. Shorty, meanwhile, pulled cotton from a mattress, which they then stuffed into the tire.

Jake looked at another, fixed the same way. He chuckled. "This one's looking a little square on the bottom, too." He added more cotton to round it out. Then he sat back on his haunches, pushed his hat back, and looked up at the sun straight overhead. "Might as well break for dinner. It's only another twenty-five miles. Just a couple more days. These tires'll make it."

Nettie grinned. Excitement stirred like butterflies. So close to the end of the trail.

CHAPTER EIGHTEEN

Wednesday, October 1, 1930

Salmon City. A place to stop and rest at last.

Charley Duncan's cabin was a one-room affair on the north side of the mining town of Salmon City. A musty, mousy smell assailed her nostrils when Nettie opened the door. Definitely a man's abode. No privacy for bathing either. Oh, well, at least they'd have a roof over their heads for a few days until they moved on to the mountain pasture.

Neil stayed outside to explore. Inside, Jake set up the camp stove, lit a fire in its firebox, and put on the coffee pot first thing, while Shorty brought in the chuck box. Nettie grabbed a broom to brush dust from a rickety table and cobwebs from the lone window. Then she squatted to rummage through the box, looking for coffee cups, and listened for the pot to bubble. It was nice to be able to use the little stove for a change instead of cooking over a campfire.

Blam!

The men hit the floor. Nettie rocked back on her heels. She stared through the smoke billowing from the little oven. What on earth?

"Dadgummit." Jake was the first to recover. He grabbed the coffee pot with one hand, opened the oven door with the other, and threw the liquid onto a smoking, gummy mess. Shorty and Nettie covered their noses with their shirttails and scooted out the door.

Neil rounded the corner of the house, mouth open and eyes wide. The other men came running from tending the horses. "What the heck happened?"

Jake emerged from the smoky interior, shaking his head, a sheepish look on his face. "Now I remember what I did with that inner tube."

Shorty stared at him for a moment, then burst into guffaws. Nettie joined in and soon they were all whooping with mirth.

That evening, with the men gone to check on the horses, Neil helped Nettie finish the supper dishes. "Ma, I saw a whole bunch of rabbits out back. Can I take the .22 out tomorrow and shoot some?"

The thought of fresh meat made Nettie's mouth water. "Sure, honey, we'll both go out." She wiped the last tin plate and turned to put it in the box.

Blam!

She dropped the dish and stared at the stove, expecting to see smoke erupt again.

Blam! Blam! Something thudded into the stovepipe on the roof.

Nettie grabbed Neil and pushed him to the floor. "Stay down. Somebody's shooting at us." Her heart pounded. What kind of a wild town was this Salmon City anyway?

"Hey, Charley. You in there?" A shout came from outside. The door opened with a loud squeal. A man took one step into the room and stopped, his mouth agape. He holstered the still-smoking .44 and snatched his hat from his head. "Ah, ma'am. Ah, I thought you was Charley come back. I'm truly sorry, ma'am."

Nettie got to her feet, knees wobbly, heart pounding like hooves on a hard-packed road. Neil peeked out from behind her. She planted her fists firmly on her hips. "Who are you? Why in tarnation were you shooting at us?"

The man, red-faced now, stammered and scuffed his boot on the floor. "Ah, ma'am. I'm a buddy o' Charley's. It's just our way of greeting each other. Brought him over a little moonshine to celebrate him being back." He held out a jug. "Here. You take this. I'll be goin' now. Sorry."

He turned on his heel, ran out to his horse, leapt on its back, and spurred it into a mad gallop, in a hurry to get away from his mistake.

Nettie took a shaky breath. Then the absurdity of the whole situation caught up with her and she giggled. What would they run into next in this adventure of theirs? She set the jug on the table, grabbed Neil by the hands, and swung him into a dance.

❧

Nettie pulled Tootsie to a stop and turned to look back down on Salmon. How puzzled she'd been on arriving and seeing all the roofs covered with small whitish discs. Turned out to be apples drying in the sun. This former gold-mining city had felt like paradise the past couple of weeks. Tall corn grew in the fields. Huge squash plants crowded the side of the cabin. The river brimmed with fish and the pastures with numerous rabbits. They ate their fill and rested up from the long weeks on the trail. She could've stayed there happily, had there been just another room or two in Charley's cabin. But the horses needed pasture, so now they were on their way to Leesburg Mountain, another sixteen miles to the west.

With a small murmur of regret, she spurred the mare forward to catch up with the chuck wagon. Neil and Jake rode just ahead, swapped gleeful jokes, sang, and teased each other. A pang of realization flashed through Nettie as she watched them. Her little boy was growing up so fast, his arms sinewy and strong, as brown as an Indian. He seemed to be having the time of his life on this trail ride.

But it was already October, and he would turn six next month. She wouldn't be able to get him to a school if they were going to be stuck on the top of a mountain all winter. She supposed she could help him read and practice his letters while they were snowed in. But she hadn't even gone to high school, so how much and how long would she be able to teach him? Oh, well, they'd cross that bridge when they came to it. It probably wouldn't hurt him to delay starting school for another year.

The road steepened until the horses pulling the wagon labored at the climb. Their large muscles bunched with each step, and their breaths came in great snorts as they dug in with their hind feet and lunged forward, then stopped and tried again. Nettie leaned forward in her saddle, her breath held. *Gosh, they're not going to make it.*

Shorty brought the wagon to a halt. "Can't go no more," he shouted.

Jake rode alongside, pushed his hat back, and scratched his head as he surveyed the teetering load and the precipitous trail yet ahead. He dismounted and rolled tobacco into a cigarette paper.

When Nettie caught up to him, Tootsie's withers were lathered. "What now?"

Jake took a drag and pushed the smoke out between his teeth. "Guess we'll have to unload some."

Nettie studied his face. *He's frustrated.* "I'll help."

She and Shorty separated the items and lashed them onto the backs of several horses from the herd. They stopped to wipe the sweat from their flushed faces.

Then Jake tied one end of his lariat to the wagon and looped the other around his saddle horn. He and Alsanger, with the team, pulled the wagon easily to the top, where the men reloaded it.

Nettie's shoulders relaxed. "Hey, that worked just dandy." *What a resourceful guy.* With a smile, she mounted her horse. Neil followed her up the hill on Paint.

As dusk brushed the mountain with blue shadows, the herd arrived at the Leesburg camp. Nettie swayed with fatigue in the saddle. A wave of dizziness overcame her and her head pounded. Oh, no, not that again. Brushing a sweaty tendril of hair out of her face, she closed her eyes, willing the pain away.

In the valley at the mountaintop, one dingy tent stood amidst dilapidated cabins along the creek. And only one cooking fire sent hazy smoke signals heavenward. Suddenly Nettie felt a lonely ache for her mother and sisters. They would probably be getting together to make cider soon. If they were here, they would help each other make their tents homey and comfortable.

Normally she didn't miss being around other women, but after so many weeks on the trail, it would have been nice to share the time with one or two here. It might be a long winter without female companionship.

As they approached, a man rose from a squat beside the creek, holding a gold pan. A sweat-stained hat shadowed his eyes and his weathered face sported a grizzled beard. His clothes hung from his stooped, thin frame. He waved at the newcomers. "Howdy, folks. Come to pasture your horses?"

Jake touched the brim of his hat. "Yep. Friends of Charley Duncan's. Didn't know there was still prospectin' going on here."

The old miner chuckled. "Oh, yeah. Long's I can get a couple bucks worth to keep me in grub. Welcome to pitch your tents anywhere."

Their herd already grazing on the lush high mountain grass, the cowboys unsaddled and prepared to set up for the night.

Jake rode up to the wagon, swung down from his horse, and clapped Shorty on the back. "Need a pair of pliers to pry your fingers loose?"

The old cook snorted and jumped down from the high seat.

A white-hot rod of pain pierced Nettie's temple. She heard their bantering as if from a great distance. All she wanted to do was lie down. She slumped in her saddle, afraid she would fall. *What a weakling. How am I going to take care of Neil?*

Still chuckling, Jake turned to Nettie. His grin faded as he looked up into her face. "Gosh a-mighty, you're white as a ghost." He helped her dismount and settled her into the bedroll that Shorty had already thrown down from the wagon.

The gentle whickers from the contented horses, the rattle of tin cups and plates, the rustle of bedrolls gradually faded as Nettie burrowed into the blankets and allowed sleep to overtake her.

Frost sparkled on the ground in the crisp October mornings. For the first week Nettie arose each day, ready and eager to take on the new adventure of living in this once-thriving gold mining camp.

She and Neil explored the ramshackle Opera House. They peeked through the slats of the boarded-up saloons. Nettie checked the few decaying cabins to find one they might fix up for their winter home, while Neil pretended to pan for gold in the creek. They studied the rings of stone where miners once had their cooking fires outside their tents, all apparently too busy "striking it rich" to build more permanent shelters.

A few head of stray sheep, abandoned when the rich vein gave out, served as a source of meat for the new residents. That, along with a cache of dried apples from Salmon, rounded out their larder. The old prospector came by occasionally with "a poke of candy" for Neil, a homemade sweet the man enfolded in candy wrappers he'd saved from more prosperous days.

But on too many occasions, dizziness or headaches drove Nettie back to bed by the middle of the day. She ignored them as long as she could, busying herself with daily chores. The pain was a fierce presence that lurked in the background at all times. Worry churned inside as she wondered how she would care for Neil and help Jake with the horses. The cowboys would be leaving for home any day now.

One morning after the second week, Nettie and Jake lingered over coffee in the warmth of the rising sun. Jake watched her with a pinched look around his eyes. Finally he cleared his throat. "This altitude sickness, or whatever this is, along with your headaches." He pushed his hat back. "It ain't good." Searching her face, he took her small hands in his. "I think you and Neil ought to go back to Salmon for the winter."

A hot shiver leapt up Nettie's spine. No, she couldn't leave. "But—"

Jake shushed her with a gentle finger on her lips. "It's for the best. You're so sick here. We have no place else to take the horses. You need to see a doctor. Besides, Neil can go to school."

Nettie closed her eyes. It would mean spending the winter without Jake. But as much as that thought pierced her heart, the excruciating spear of pain filled her mind more. Headaches ruled her days, interrupted her nights. She had to agree. She was no help to him this way.

She opened her eyes. "I think you may be right. And Neil does need to go to school."

Jake pulled her tight against his chest. "Aw, little gal, I'm gonna miss you like crazy."

Nettie gulped back the rise of tears.

Before noon, Shorty had Nettie and Neil's few belongings loaded onto the chuck wagon. One of the cowboys would stay in Leesburg to help Jake, but the other would accompany them to Salmon on his way back home. At the top of the steep road, the cook stopped the wagon. He and Jake unhitched the team to drag a large log from the side of the road and lash it to the back of the wagon.

"Why're you doin' that, Pa?" Neil asked.

"That'll give it some drag, so it won't crash down the mountain and run over the horses," Jake explained.

Shorty checked that the team was hooked up securely, climbed onto the seat, and snapped the reins. At the last second, the other cowboy jumped onto the log and rode it down the hill as it bucked like a mad bronc, raising dust and debris. Nettie held her breath, watching. The wagon could still crash after all. And the cowboy on the log, well, he was just plain crazy. The wagon jounced and swayed, barely keeping upright on its insane course.

Jake rode behind. His rope held the trailing end of the log so it wouldn't turn sideways and roll. Nettie could see no way he'd be able to help if it broke loose. Finally, a half a mile below, the whole entourage reached the bottom. Still in one piece. The cowboy still perched atop the log. He looked back up and waved his hat.

Nettie looked into Neil's round eyes, shrugged, and urged Tootsie downward. As the horse pitched nearly vertical on the steep path, she leaned back in the saddle until she lay almost flat against the horse's straining rump. Neil followed, adopting the same posture.

Once again Nettie said goodbye to Jake, feeling like a forlorn waif watching him ride back up the mountain, without her and Neil. She squared her shoulders, turned Tootsie, and rode on toward their new adventure.

Nettie and Neil settled into Charley's cabin in Salmon City and she enrolled Neil in first grade. He came home every afternoon, excited that he was learning to read.

Although the winter temperatures were slightly milder than Montana, Nettie spent her days sitting in the little two-room cabin, drinking coffee, staring out at the gray snowy landscape, and wishing she were up on the mountain with Jake. She had fewer headaches and the dizzy nausea didn't plague her here. *Maybe it was just my imagination. I should've stayed.* She got up to pace from the front room to the bedroom and back again. *He needed my help. I let him down.*

The winter dragged its heels through a dreary Christmas alone and into a bleak, blustery January and February. Although some of the neighbor women stopped a few times and invited Nettie to come join them for coffee or shopping or lunch in town, she declined. Even though she missed her sisters and Mama, she couldn't drum up much interest in becoming social. Not without Jake.

One April afternoon, Nettie took her coffee outside to sit in the sunshine. She breathed in the scent of new green grass in the warm air. Spots of spring flowers colored the meadow behind the cabin and the rhubarb plants showed their dark green curls above ground. A meadowlark trilled. Tootsie snorted in the pasture nearby, then raised her head and whinnied.

An answer came from the hillside. Nettie shaded her eyes and peered into the shadows. A horse cantered in her direction, its rider whooping and waving his hat.

"Jake!" Nettie yelled and ran toward him. He was out of the saddle before Alsanger came to a complete stop. He threw his arms around her and spun her around.

As giddy as a teenager, Nettie lifted her face to his and drank in his long kiss as though she'd been stranded in the desert for the past few months.

They finally broke apart, laughing. "Hey, little gal. I sure did miss you." Jake looked deep into her eyes.

"I can't believe you're here. Neil's going to be so surprised when he gets home from school." Nettie pressed herself against his chest again, blotting her tears on his shirt. "I've missed you terribly. I don't like this being apart, not one little bit."

Nettie and Neil went back up the mountain with Jake for the summer. But as soon as she arrived, Nettie was overcome with the same dizziness and pain as the summer before. She tried to ignore it, to hide it from Jake, but it became impossible. So once again, she and Neil rode down the mountain to spend the winter in Salmon.

"Next spring we'll go home," Jake promised as he settled them in the little cabin and left, just ahead of a snowstorm.

CHAPTER NINETEEN

Sunday, June 26, 1932

Back home, after almost two years! To Montana, anyway. With Jake and the horses again. Thankfully, the trail ride home much easier than the trip down. Camping in a tent on Margie and Glen's place. Somebody else living in our house on the old Davis ranch. Jake looking for work. Heading for Browning for 4th of July rodeo. Can't wait. Been too long.

Nettie approached the reservation town with Jake, Neil, and her four brothers. During the last few miles of the trip she rode as if suspended on a cloud instead of a saddle. She reined up on the rise overlooking the tent city that sprouted and doubled the population each year on this occasion.

The bubble of excitement that had been building all morning rose inside her and burst forth in a yell. "Yippee." She whipped off her hat, waving it at the scene below. "Race ya!" Nettie dug her heels into Tootsie's flanks and galloped down the hill to the rodeo grounds, Neil and the men pounding behind her.

"Beat ya," Nettie chortled as the men reined up beside her.

Cowboys, dressed in high-brimmed hats, bright colored shirts, and fanciful dyed angora chaps, greeted them with good-natured ribbing.

"Hiya, Jake, you back on the suicide circuit?"

"Hey, Nettie, Fannie Steele and Marie Gibson are here. You gonna give 'em a run for their money today?"

Exhilaration zinged through her at that news. She couldn't wait to see her friend, Marie. It had been so long.

Bob Askin clapped Jake on the back. "Welcome back, buddy. Where ya been all year?"

Running the gauntlet of well wishers, they finally reached the makeshift rodeo office where they signed up for their events, bronc riding and steer roping for Jake and steer riding for Nettie. As she signed her name, butterflies took flight in her midsection. A fleeting thought crossed her mind. She might be a little rusty at this.

Behind her, Jake talked to a cowboy with his arm in a cast. "Naw, don't want the shot," Nettie heard the cowboy say. "The pain makes me dad-burned mad, and I wanna be a little mad. A man always rides better that way."

"Yeah," another cowboy put in. "You can't stop something like that from hurtin', but you can durn well not let it bother you."

Nettie chuckled. Then she heard a familiar voice. "Antoinette."

She turned to see Marie, with whom she shared that highfalutin first name, standing by the corral, hip cocked, arms spread wide.

She grinned. "Antoinette, yourself." She adjusted the red neck scarf that matched Marie's, strode forward, and embraced her friend in a warm rush of happiness.

"And who do we have here?" Marie spied Neil standing nearby and disengaged from their hug.

"This is our number one cowboy, Neil." Nettie pushed him forward.

Marie stuck out a hand. "I haven't seen you since you were just a tadpole. You're getting all grown up already."

Neil ducked his head, and Nettie smiled inwardly at his shyness. He'd get over it sooner or later.

Nettie studied her friend, dressed as she was in a white shirt, denims, and boots. She looked as slim and energetic as ever. "Gosh, it's so good to see you."

Marie grinned. "You too. What's it been, two years? How've you been?"

Nettie, Neil, and Marie walked around the grounds, stopping now and then to watch a particular rider or roping event. Neil eagerly peered through the corral fence at the riders. "When can I do this, Ma?"

She stopped short. *Never.* She grinned at her son. "You'll have to wait a few years, honey."

Marie laughed. "Seems I remember your ma saying something like that."

Nettie remembered her first rodeo here eleven years ago, when she first met Marie, and her friend had changed Mama's mind about women riders being "loose women."

A whistle blew after eight seconds and the pickup man swooped in to grab the rider off his bucking bronc. "Rodeos sure are more organized these days," Nettie mused. "Not like we used to do, ride until thrown or the animal quits."

Marie shook her head. "Yeah, the 'big boys' in the Rodeo Association of America decided we needed help."

Nettie huffed a laugh. "Some of those old timers probably consider that being a sissy." A faint glow of pride warmed the memory of her very first ride when she stayed on until the steer quit bucking. Nothing could ever take that feeling of accomplishment from her.

Nettie and Jake spent the next two days catching up with old friends, reliving the "old days," and cheering on fellow riders. Jake's ride went well, but the prize was awarded to the cowboy in the cast.

Jake just laughed. "I guess there's something to be said about ridin' mad with pain."

Then it was Nettie's turn. She climbed the pole fence of the chute and looked down at the massive steer.

"Are you sure you should be doin' this?" Jake's voice came from behind her.

She suddenly felt faint and realized she wasn't breathing. This was crazy. What *was* she doing? Nettie swallowed hard. "Yes, I want to do this."

"You haven't competed for several years, or even practiced. You could get hurt."

Neil's face flashed before her. Was she being irresponsible? But this was her dream, put on hold these past eight years.

"C'mon, lady. Climb aboard. You can't chicken out now. Get this show on the road." The harsh words startled her. The cowboy manning the gate stared at her.

Nettie drew in a few big gulps of air and exhaled slowly. "I won't give this up, Jake. I'm going to ride." She settled onto the wide back, gripped the rigging with one gloved hand, and looked up into the grandstands. The crowd was hushed.

She nodded. The chute opened and the dance was on.

As if in a dream, the ride unfolded in slow motion. Every jump, every jolt, her every spur happened as if she were riding through molasses. Muscle memory took over. It was as though she'd never been away. Everything around her faded into a shimmery haze. Her body and mind caught up in the rhythm. She soared with each leap. Absorbed each landing. A primitive sashay with a steer.

The whistle sliced into the dream. Arms encircled her waist. She slid from the steer's back and the pickup man carried her on his horse back to the fence, where Neil whooped. Jake wrapped an arm around her shoulders. "You did it, little gal. Sorry I doubted you. Good ride. I think you've nailed down the ten-dollar prize."

The crowd cheered. Nettie waved her hat.

She was home. It felt so good.

~~~

The potato peeling spiraled from Nettie's knife, adding height to the pile. Funny how life was like that peel, never a straight line, always curving. Usually breaking off when she thought she'd be able to peel the whole spud in one piece. She arched her head back to stretch out the kinks.

The warm midmorning sun reflected off the side of the wall tent. Their temporary home, just a short distance from her sister's house. Jake had put down a plank floor and shelves for storage, and she kept it swept out every day. The canvas formed the walls, just like a one-room house. It was cozy enough, a bit romantic too. Their bedrolls rested on camp cots along one wall, a lantern sat on her big steamer trunk, which served as a wardrobe, and a fire pit outside was her cook stove, although they ate the noon meal at her sister's.

It was a good life. She enjoyed camping. It gave her a sense of freedom. More important, her little family was back together again. No more living apart from Jake. No matter where it might be.

Playful, high-pitched sounds came from Neil and his eleven-year-old cousin in the corral, where they were "breaking" a colt. More like playing with it, but at least it would be tame and used to kids by the time it was ready to be ridden. She smiled. It was good for Neil to get to know his cousins and have some fun. He was much too serious for a little boy.

Margie stepped out the door of her house just beyond the knoll where the tent sat, dumped her dishwater, and strolled toward her. Nettie smiled. The most fun was living next to her sister and getting to know each other all over again. She hadn't realized how much she'd missed their camaraderie.

"Good morning. Got some coffee left?" Margie picked up the pot from the fire and sloshed its contents.

"Help yourself. There's a clean cup on the shelf in the tent."

Margie poured two cups and offered her one. "Jake out looking for work again?" She plopped down on a rock next to Nettie.

Nettie set down her knife and took the cup. "Yeah. He went to Cut Bank to talk to Hugo Aronson today. Figures the man might have some construction work for him to do."

Margie sipped her coffee. "That'd be good. Get yourself a house. Living in a tent ain't no place for a woman."

"I love camping, especially being here near you. Sure, we'd like to find a place of our own before winter, but I'm having fun." Nettie grinned. "This enough potatoes for dinner?"

Shortly before noon, Nettie tended to the boiling potatoes in her sister's kitchen. Over the sound of Margie's teenage daughter setting the table, she heard men's voices. Nettie glanced out the window. Jake rode up the same time as Glen and his fourteen-year-old son, Gary—her favorite nephew—arrived from the field where they'd been plowing. Her husband laughed and joked with his brother-in-law as they washed up in the water trough just outside the house. *Must be good news. I hope.* She went to the door, anxious to find out.

Jake splashed water over his face, then looked up at her with a wide grin. "I got the job."

A weight she hadn't known existed suddenly lifted from her shoulders. She threw herself into his embrace, feeling the security of his strong arms around her. "That's great. What are you going to be doing?"

"Aronson has a contract with the International Oil Company at Sunburst. They need dirt work done at new drilling sites. That's one place we can still put our draft horses to use."

She smiled back at him, lost in his twinkling blue eyes. Maybe they could find a place of their own.

A week later, Nettie and Neil settled atop earth berms overlooking the field where Jake worked his team of four horses. A dip of his head told her he'd seen them arrive, but he kept going, making several more swaths through the prairie sod. The noon sun shone hot overhead, no shade anywhere, even from the tall oil derrick that men were erecting in the background.

Jake walked behind the fresno, a huge curved scoop that scraped large furrows of earth from the ground. He had discarded his shirt, but wore his straw hat. A tingle of admiration raced through Nettie as she watched his tanned arm and shoulder muscles bunch and ripple while he drove the team with one hand, operating the handle of the scoop with the other. Her strong, capable man. He made the work look so easy.

No sooner had that thought run through her head when the scoop bit into the earth and stopped abruptly. At the same time, the handle sprang toward Jake's head.

"Jake!" Nettie gasped and propelled herself to her feet, prepared to run and help. The pit of her stomach rose to meet her throat.

But his biceps bulged, the veins stood out in his neck, and he powered the handle down, just inches from his face, to lift the scoop out of the dirt.

"Ma, did you see that? Pa sure is strong." Neil's admiring tone brought her back.

She expelled her pent-up breath, forced her voice to be calm and cheerful so as not to alarm her son. "Yeah. He sure is, isn't he?" She stepped forward. "I think this would be a good time to take him his dinner."

They scrambled down from the dike. Jake pulled the scoop out of the dirt, unhitched it, and drove the team to the edge of the hollow area he had carved out. After the horses drank from a water tank nearby, he strapped feedbags of oats on them. Then he walked over to the base of the berm, where Nettie had spread a blanket and laid out a feast of fried chicken and boiled potatoes. "Next time I'll have to bring a tarp or something." Not even the pile of dirt provided shade as the hot midday sun beat down on the treeless prairie.

"You two sure are a sight for sore eyes." Jake plopped down on the blanket and ruffled Neil's hair.

"Oh, I know you. You're just happy to see food." Nettie tried to keep her tone light-hearted, but the near miss she had just seen still had her shaking inside. Sure, the pay for this job was most welcome, but she'd had no idea it could be so hazardous.

When they finished eating and Neil ran off to explore the dirt piles, she broached the subject. "Isn't this dangerous work to do by yourself? I thought I saw two men working that fresno down at the other site."

Jake shrugged. "Naw, it's not that bad. Just takes a sharp eye and a bit of brute strength." He flexed his biceps and winked. "Besides, I'd have to split my pay with another guy."

"Oh, honey, I know you're strong." Nettie shook a finger at him. "Just be careful, okay?"

He leaned forward and kissed her hard. "I am. I just have to think about you, waiting at home for me. I'll be careful."

Neil raced up and threw himself down next to his father. "What're you digging, Pa?"

"It's going to be a shallow reservoir." Jake reclined back on his elbows. "See, the oil rigs use water to drill with, so they need one area to hold the water and one for all the sludge that comes back up."

"Why are they drilling for oil?" Neil asked.

"Well, for all the gas engines everybody's usin' now." Jake stared off into the distance.

"But this oil discovery is good for our state, isn't it?" Nettie packed up the chicken bones and leftovers.

"Yeah, I guess. But best of all, it's puttin' silver in our pocket." He grabbed his hat and stood up. "Guess I'd better be gettin' back to work. Thanks for bringing dinner."

CHAPTER TWENTY

Sunday, August 21, 1932

Well, we're in a house now. Sort of a house anyway. Two old tar paper shacks butted together near Santa Rita. But there's pasture for the horses. Jake working the oil fields. Hot summer.

Nettie grabbed at the strand of rusted barbed wire partially buried in the dirt and under clumps of grass. Neil helped her pull at it until it was free. In the midafternoon heat, sweat slithered down her forehead into her eyes as she found the end and rolled it up. She added the roll to the pile they'd collected, took off one leather glove, and wiped her face with her bandanna. Neil had already found the next piece of wire and was pulling at it, his thin arms working furiously.

"Better stop and rest a bit. Want to go get some water?" Nettie fanned her face with her hat. "Your face is a little red."

"In a minute. Gotta get this clear." He whipped at the wire.

"Here, let me help with that." Nettie put her hat and glove back on. Together they tugged and rolled until they had a long stretch of fence cleared and ready for new wire.

"Why are we doing this, Ma? We're not going to live here that long, are we?"

"Probably just until fall. But if we leave all this old wire lying around, the horses could get cut up pretty bad. And we need to fix the fence to keep them from running all over the country." She rolled the wire. There were countless places like this around, homesteads abandoned during the drought, everything in ruins.

"Will Pa help us tomorrow?"

"No, honey. He has to work for the oil company, so it's up to you and me to get the repairs done." She missed the days when she and Jake did this kind of thing together. But to work outside and see the accomplishments of each day made her feel alive and useful.

She tossed another roll on the pile and turned to see where Neil was now. He stood motionless, one hand over his eyes. She strode forward with a frown. "What's wrong, honey?"

"Dizzy. Head hurts."

Nettie reached out and pushed his hat back to touch his forehead. It was hot and dry. "You'd better drink some water. And let's go to the house and sit in the shade." She reached for the canteen on her belt. It wasn't there.

Without warning, Neil bent forward and vomited. His legs buckled and he sank to the ground.

Nettie fell to her knees beside him. His eyes rolled back in his flushed face. Fear ran icy fingers up her spine. Heat stroke. She picked him up and ran toward the shack a quarter-mile away, panting and sobbing. A water barrel stood just outside the door. Tipping him upside down, she plunged him headfirst into the tepid water. Then she placed him gently on the ground in the shade. With shaking hands, she took off his long-sleeved shirt, poured a dipper full of water on his chest and neck, and fanned him with her hat. "C'mon, honey. Wake up. Neil? C'mon."

Finally his eyes fluttered. She lifted his shoulders so he could take a drink. He stared up at her with a vacant gaze.

She gulped. "Honey, are you all right?"

At the sound of her voice, his eyes focused and he nodded. "All right." He tried to sit up, but slumped back onto her arm. "Dizzy, Ma."

Nettie urged him to take another drink. "It's okay, honey. Just lie here and rest awhile." She felt his forehead again. He had broken a sweat. Good. She kept fanning him with her hat and dribbling water into his mouth. Darn. Why didn't she notice she'd lost the canteen? She should've insisted they take a break sooner. It must have been over a hundred degrees, and here they were, working out in the heat like madmen. How stupid of her. Would she ever get this motherhood stuff right? She hung her head and cradled him.

After supper when Jake came home, Neil was up, still a little shaky, but playing quietly. "I got heat stroked," he announced to his dad.

"What? How did that happen?" Jake's eyebrows drew together. He looked at Nettie with a frown.

She shook her head to stop Jake from saying anything more and turned to Neil. "Let's get you to bed now, honey." With a protective hand on his shoulder, she took him into the shack they used as a bedroom, tucked him into his bedroll, and kissed his forehead. "Sleep tight."

Jake sat at the table, his forehead resting in one hand. Nettie poured two cups of coffee and sat next to him.

Nettie looked into his solemn face. "I'm to blame for what happened. We stayed out in the heat too long without water. I just wasn't thinking."

He expelled a long sigh.

Nettie squeezed her eyes shut. "I did take a canteen, but I lost it."

Jake grunted and reached into his shirt pocket for his cigarette papers and tobacco.

Nettie drew circles on the oilcloth with her finger. "He's such a strong little man, such a hard worker. Sometimes I forget he's just a little boy."

Jake lit his cigarette and took a deep drag. "No. It's my fault for not being here to help you. Making my wife and seven-year-old kid do such hard work."

"It's not that difficult. I don't mind doing it. I want to do it. I just have to be more careful." Nettie's stomach contracted as Jake nodded.

"Things like this make me realize that I'm not very good at motherhood."

"Now, little gal. Don't you be sayin' that." Jake encircled her shoulders with his arm and drew her head to his cheek. "You're a fine mother. And a wonderful wife."

A tear slid from Nettie's eye and she leaned into his chest with a sigh. They sat in silence as the night closed in around them.

The late summer sun continued its fiery journey across the sky, toasted the grasses, and baked the earth brown. Its warmth lasted well into October. Jake had fixed the strap on the canteen so Nettie made sure they always had water along as she and Neil finished picking up old wire, fixed the fence, and left the horses to graze through the pasture. But the first arctic winds ghosted in with Halloween and sent tumbleweeds skittering across the frostbitten prairie.

Nettie awoke one morning, shivering, their blankets covered with a white rime. Looking around the room, she saw daylight through the cracks in the board walls where the exterior tar paper had blown off. Still half asleep, she snuggled closer to Jake, who snorted in his sleep and moved to mold his body against her back.

"Ma." The quiet little voice came from the corner. "Ma, you awake?"

"Hmm?" Nettie wasn't quite ready to face the day.

"Ma. I'm cold. Can I come in bed with you?"

She smiled to herself. No such thing as a private moment in this shack. "Okay, honey. Come on."

Neil slid in next to her. His feet were icy and his thin body shuddered. *Poor little guy. I should've put more blankets on.*

Nettie put her arms around him and held him until his shivering stopped and his breathing evened into sleep once again. She dozed. After awhile she felt Jake stir. When he propped himself up on one arm to kiss her on the cheek, he chuckled to see Neil there. He slipped from the covers, pulled on his warm clothes and boots, and clomped into the next room to build a fire in their only stove.

Nettie joined him when she smelled the coffee. She huddled next to the stove, cradling the steaming cup in her hands.

"I hate to bring this up, but we've gotta get you and Neil to a warmer place for the winter." Jake cut a slab of salt pork into slices and placed them into the frying pan. "Talked to Snooky O'Haire yesterday. Remember him and Ruth from our wedding? Anyhow, he says since the oil boom, houses and apartments are pretty scarce, but nobody's traveling 'cause of the hard times. So, they'll rent us a room at the Metropolitan Hotel in Cut Bank with cooking facilities."

Nettie frowned. "But that's going to be quite a ride for you every day to the oil fields. Didn't you say they want you to keep working all winter?"

Jake turned the bacon. "Yeah. Well, I figure I'll just stay on here during the week and come into town Saturday nights."

"No, Jake." That old empty space yawned inside Nettie once more. "That means living apart. I wasn't going to let that happen again." She sighed. "We need to be together, as a family. For Neil's sake."

She looked at her husband, shoulders slumped wearily, his weathered face creased in a frown. "Maybe we could fix this place up a little. Make it warmer."

He heaped bacon on two plates, cut thick slices of bread, and slathered them with butter. "It ain't ours. It'd take a lot of work. And I don't have time to do it. It's gonna snow any day now. This's the only thing I can come up with. Besides, I need to keep an eye on the horses out here. And, Neil needs to be in school."

Her mind in a swirl, Nettie sat at the table and stared into space. Jake was right, of course. But living in town. Away from Jake. Away from her horses.

Nettie got up from the table and looked out the small window. She'd been half afraid this would happen. "How much longer are we going to have to live this way?" She bit her lower lip. "When are we going to have a place of our own?"

Jake set his fork down with deliberate slowness. "I'm working on that, honey. It'll be worth it someday. Give me some time."

"How much time?"

He shrugged and gazed out the window.

Well, at least they didn't have a lot of possessions to move these days. That part would be easy. She turned back to Jake. "All right then. Settling in town will be better for Neil."

CHAPTER TWENTY-ONE

Monday, November 14, 1932

I never imagined in a million years I'd be living in a hotel. A long way from the rodeo life, even a ranch of our own.

Nettie stood at the second-floor window of the weathered clapboard hotel, gazing at the frozen ruts in the street below. The sky was as heavy as an old horse blanket. The November wind howled plaintively and spit a few snowflakes at the thin glass windowpane. She turned to Neil at the small table, where he ate his after-school snack of milk and cookies and read a book. Although it was only 4 p.m., it was already getting dark. She glanced around their narrow room, two cots at one end, a hotplate on a desk, and the table, just big enough for the three of them to crowd around when Jake came to town.

She and Neil had been there only a week and it already seemed like a month. The tiny room closed in around her.

The steam radiators alternated stifling hot air or freezing nothingness. She had no place to go, nothing to do during the day. No horses to tend. And no Jake. What could she do, get a job of some kind here at the hotel? Maybe she could. Surprise Jake.

"I'm going down to the office for a minute, honey. I'll be right back."

Neil grunted and reached for another cookie.

Downstairs, the hotel manager chewed on an unlit cigar as Nettie outlined her proposal to clean for hotel guests. He stared at the empty guest book on the desk in front of him. "Well, that'd be great. If we had guests." He looked up at her. "The only people here are residents, like yourself. And they clean their own rooms, cook their own meals. I'm the only employee right now. Sorry."

Back in their quarters, Nettie paced the length of the room and back. So much for that idea. She picked up a pair of Neil's socks from the floor and discovered a hole in one of them. Absentmindedly, she dug out her darning egg, needle, and thread and began to mend the hole. Nettie stopped in midstitch as a memory surfaced. As a kid, she'd gotten into big trouble with Mama by sneaking out to a rodeo and avoiding her darning job. A chuckle rose. Mama would get a kick out of seeing her daughter now.

Nettie finished the sock, pulled the chain on the bare bulb hanging from the ceiling. Dim electric light flickered and hummed. She sat at the table with Neil. "What are you reading?"

He looked up from his book. "*Wild Horse Mesa* by Zane Grey." He took a gulp of his milk. "Hey, the Rialto's showing the movie now, with Randolph Scott. Can we go see it?"

Nettie blinked in surprise. "I suppose so. Maybe on a Sunday when your pa comes to town." That might be fun. It had been a long time since they'd gone to a moving picture show. A long time since they'd had any money to do anything slightly frivolous. But with Jake's job, maybe they could, this once.

She got up to put a kettle on the hotplate to warm some soup for supper. "Do you like your teacher this year?"

"Yeah. Mrs. Haynes is really nice. Not like Mrs. Jones last year." He grabbed another cookie. "She just walked around the room all day with her ruler, whacking kids for talking." Neil hit the back of his hand with the cookie.

Nettie reached over and tousled his hair. "Anything would be better than a year of nothing but coloring."

Neil grinned. "Yeah. But I miss seeing who could fart the loudest."

"Young man. Watch your language." She rolled her eyes, trying not to laugh. "Well, I'm just glad you like reading so well. At least you learned something from all those library books."

Neil was already reabsorbed in his book. He continued to read as they ate their soup. Pride buoyed her heart like a balloon. He had taken to books like an eagle to the sky and was already reading at a fifth- or sixth-grade level, even though he was only a third-grader.

She cleaned up the supper dishes and glanced at the clock. "Time for bed now."

"Just a minute, Ma. I'm almost done with this chapter."

Nettie swept the bare floor and tidied the small room. "Okay, you must be finished by now."

Neil held up one finger. "Uh . . . not yet."

"Come on. You need to get your rest. You'll be too tired to get up for school tomorrow."

Neil stood up, still reading as he walked toward the little cot in the corner. He sat and continued to read.

Nettie put her hands on her hips. "Neil. Now!"

"Okay, Ma. Okay." Reluctantly, he set down the book, took off his shoes and pants, and crawled into bed.

"Good night, my little scholar." Nettie kissed him and drew the makeshift curtain around his cot.

Not that she could blame him. She loved to read too, even though she hadn't gone past the eighth grade. Mama had encouraged her to read schoolbooks and cookbooks, but considered novels scandalous and a waste of time. Now, with nothing to do, Nettie could just pick up a book any time she wanted.

Nettie fixed a cup of tea and sat at the table. She picked up Neil's book sack and took out another novel by Grey, *The Roaring U.P. Trail*. She riffled through the pages and soon was entranced in a story about building the transcontinental railroad.

She awoke with a start, dropping the book on the floor. The mournful sound of a violin came from the hallway. Nettie sat up straight, listening to the lilting music soar and dip. Her heart swelled with joy and then crushed with sadness as the instrument wove its musical story. She'd heard the fiddlers play dance music and cowboy songs many times. But she'd never heard anything like this. It seemed to reach inside her and pluck her soul bare.

She got up and walked toward the door, glancing at Neil's bed to see if the music had awakened him too. The bed was empty.

Her heart thudding like a bass drum, Nettie jerked open the door and stepped into the darkened hallway. The music stopped. *Where is it coming from? Where is Neil?* Then a long plaintive note pierced her heart. She looked up and down the hall. There. Light shone like a beacon from an open door two rooms down. She strode toward it. Shadows danced. Nettie peeked around the doorframe, and saw Neil standing beside an old man dressed all in black with a funny-looking flat cap on his head. The man sat on a chair, his face shining and serene, a violin tucked under his chin, now playing a simple tune, "Pop Goes the Weasel."

When he plucked the string on "Pop," Neil giggled. "Do it again!"

Relief left Nettie's knees shaky. The old man popped the string again, and she almost giggled along with Neil.

Lowering the violin, the old fellow rested his bow hand on his knee and smiled at Neil. "You like *musik, ja?*" His accent reminded Nettie of her own Swedish grandmother.

Neil peered into the man's gray-bearded face. "Can you show me how?"

He placed the instrument under Neil's chin, gently guided his small fingers onto the neck, and with his other arm helped Neil draw the bow across the strings. "*Das ist* 'A.' Now you do."

Neil pulled the bow, creating a squawking note. He looked up, his face beaming, and saw Nettie just outside the doorway.

"Look, Ma." He drew the bow again, making a somewhat more melodious sound.

"*Gut, ja, gut.*" The old man's face lit up with his smile.

Nettie stepped into the room. "I'm sorry my son bothered you." She gestured to Neil. "Come back to the room now. It's very late."

The man stood and put out a hand to shake. "Herr Blumberg. Is okay. Your son learn. I teach, *ja?*"

"Nettie Moser." She shook his hand. "Um, I don't know. We don't have money for lessons."

Blumberg shook his head. "*Nein.* No money. I happy to teach."

"Let me think about this. I'll talk to you tomorrow." Nettie pulled Neil up by the hand. "Come on, now. It's way past your bedtime."

All the way down the hall, Neil chattered. "Did you hear that, Ma? It was magic. Can I, Ma? Can I learn to play like that? Please?"

Nettie pulled the door closed behind them. She sighed. She should scold him for going to a stranger's room, but the enchantment of the music still swirled through her.

Neil's eyes were as big as full moons. His voice came in a whisper. "I want to do that. Please."

The music had spoken to her, too. If her son could learn to play like that . . . she gave him a hug. "We'll see. I'll talk to Herr Blumberg tomorrow." She swatted his behind gently. "Now, go. To. Sleep."

The next day, while Neil was in school, Nettie walked down the hall and rapped on Blumberg's door.

"*Hierein,*" he called out. "Come."

The old man sat at his table, eating a bare slice of bread. He gestured. "Sit. Eat?"

"No, thank you." Nettie sat across from him. "Uh, about my son—"

Blumberg's face lit with a smile. "Son. He learn. *Gut, ja?*"

Nettie nodded. "He wants to learn, yes. But I'll need to talk to my husband. Perhaps we can pay you a little something."

"*Nein. Nein.*" The old man clasped his hands across his chest. "I want . . . teach him. My joy. In old country, I teach *musik.* Here, *nein.*"

Nettie studied his round face. "Okay. I'll let him try it."

"*Gut, ja.*" The beatific smile came again, erasing the years and whatever hardships he may have experienced.

After school, Nettie accompanied a bouncing, babbling Neil to Herr Blumberg's room.

"Are you sure about this?" she persisted.

"*Ja, ja*. Is okay." The old man waved a hand toward the door, so she stepped out into the hall, where she leaned against the wall to listen, leaving her son to receive his first music lesson.

From that day on, Neil gobbled his after-school snack and slipped across the hall to play. Nettie often stood in her doorway and listened while the old Jewish man taught her son the fundamentals of playing the violin. She smiled to hear him. "Hunnert times," he would instruct Neil. "Hunnert times." To her surprise, Neil didn't object, but played a phrase over and over until he learned it to Herr Blumberg's satisfaction. Her pride swelled with the music her son was learning to play.

The next day she brought Blumberg a hot meal at noon. He tried to wave it away. "*Nein, nein*." But she saw his nostrils flare, and his eyes followed the plate as she set it on the table.

"Yes. You eat." She turned and left the room.

When she brought dinner again, he greeted her with a sparkling clean plate and a big smile. "*Gut, ja. Danke* you."

"Where are you from, Herr Blumberg, and how did you end up here in Montana?" Nettie tried to draw him out.

"*Deutschland*. Germany. *Das* war. Not *gut, nein*." He shook his head and wouldn't say any more.

But gradually over the weeks, in halting English, the old man revealed his story. How he had come to New York to escape the war, but he couldn't get a job teaching music, how he found a friend in Montana who invited him to come. But the friend died and Herr Blumberg still had no job.

Tears welled in Nettie's eyes as he pieced together his story. He had an extraordinary talent and it was obvious that he loved teaching. It was all she could do, but if giving her son violin lessons made the old man—and her son—happy, then she was glad to put together a meager hot meal for him every day, even if it was only warmed-up stew.

Jake came to town on Sunday and was astonished to hear his son already playing a simple classical tune. "Great, my boy. I didn't know we had another fiddler in the family. You'll be able to play for dances just like your grandpa." He winked at Nettie. "Maybe we'll have to go see if we can buy you a fiddle of your own one of these days."

"Can we, Pa? Can we go tomorrow?" Neil hopped around them, looking up into their faces. "After we go to the movies?"

Jake grinned at Nettie. "Sure, we can go look, anyway."

Nettie slipped her arm around her husband and smiled at their eager son. They were together, and she was content, for the moment.

⸻ ⸺

Nettie settled into a routine with Neil's school, music lessons, and reading. Occasionally one of the other women who lived in the hotel would invite her for coffee, but Nettie chafed at the bit not being able to work with her horses. She spent her days walking around the town, neatening their room, and reading Neil's library books, dreaming of summer and riding like the wind.

Just before Christmas a blizzard hit with the ferocity of a banshee. The wind whined in several different voices, screamed at the windows, dove away into the night and back again in a great moaning circle.

Nettie lay awake clutching her pillow and shivering. She pictured the cracks in the walls of Jake's shack, the snowdrifts piling in the corners. With this wind, he might not be able to keep a fire going in the cook stove. He could freeze to death. And the horses. She only hoped they had found shelter in the bottom of a coulee. *I have to help Jake find a place of our own.*

Finally, as the cold gray light of morning lightened the square of window, the wind settled into a drone, and she fell asleep.

Nettie paced through the days, her purpose defined by preparing dinner for the old man and supper for Neil. A cold empty feeling ached within. She just picked at her own food, and tried to forget everything by burying herself in books.

On Christmas Eve, Nettie awoke to a day cloaked in brilliant sunshine. Snowdrifts blocked the streets below, but soon townspeople were out shoveling, bustling about, apparently glad to end their forced hibernation. In the afternoon, she and Neil ventured out to shop for Christmas dinner. Snow crystals sparkled in the crisp, below-zero air and froze the little hairs inside Nettie's nose. She pulled her wool scarf farther up and tugged at Neil's. "Cover your face, honey, so you don't get frostbite."

At the Pay N Takit Merc, Donald Poole, the proprietor, greeted them with a smile. "Hello there. Nice to see everybody out and about again."

Nettie shook his outstretched hand. "It's great to get out. I was getting cabin fever." She looked around the store. "I think I'd like to get a bit of ham for our supper tonight. Do you have some?"

"I certainly do. How about some sweet potatoes to go along with it?"

Nettie's mouth watered. "Sounds good."

Poole put her items in a paper bag. Then he reached under the counter and brought out a bottle. "Some of the missus' chokecherry wine. Merry Christmas."

"Why, thank you." Nettie's face flushed with pleasure. "Merry Christmas to you both." She and Neil left the store, the bell tinkling behind them.

"Will Pa be able to make it to town in time for Santa to come?" Neil's face puckered into a worried frown.

Nettie swallowed her dread before answering. She fought to keep her voice cheerful. "I sure hope so, honey. But he might have to dig himself out of some pretty big drifts." Her words belied her own fear. "So don't worry if he doesn't come till tomorrow."

Back in their little room, she swept and mopped the floor, dusted the table and windowsill, and unpacked a tablecloth. That evening she fried the ham she'd bought as a treat. *Surely Jake will come. We won't have to spend Christmas alone.* Humming a lively tune, she set three places at the table, poured two jelly glasses of the wine, and lit candles. When she heard a loud thump in the hallway, she jumped and dropped the match.

A deep voice boomed. "Ho, ho, ho. M-e-r-r-y Christmas."

"Pa." Neil dropped his book and ran for the door.

Her cheeks flushing, Nettie smoothed her hair and untied the apron from around her waist.

Jake burst into the room, a big grin splitting his face. "Here I am, such as I am." He gathered them both into his embrace and held her so tight she couldn't move.

Neil disengaged himself and scrambled for the gunnysack his dad had brought in. "What did you bring, Pa?"

"Just wait, son. You'll see."

"Aw, Pa." Neil hung back, looking wistfully at the sack.

Nettie put her hand to Jake's cheek. "Oh, my gosh, honey. I'm so glad you made it." She smiled through happy tears.

"You know me better than that. Can't keep me away from my family on Christmas." Jake brushed a tendril of hair back from her forehead. Nettie widened her eyes to stare into his wind-roughened face.

"Ma was scared you'd freeze to death in that shack." Neil tugged the sack from the doorway to the middle of the room.

"Naw. I just left all my clothes on 'cept my boots and rolled up in the featherbed. Had a nice blanket of snow to cover me in the mornin'." He laughed, gave Nettie a quick kiss on the forehead, then turned to Neil and the sack. "I brought a little tree so we can have something to put our presents under." With a flourish, he pulled out a big silver sagebrush nearly as tall as Neil and held it up with pride. "What d'ya say, shall we pop some corn to trim it?"

"Yippee! Popcorn." Neil galloped around the room as if on a stick horse.

Nettie dissolved into laughter and clasped Jake's hand in hers. "A great idea. But supper's ready. Let's eat first."

After passing his plate for seconds, Jake raised his wine. "This ham dinner tastes as wonderful as any highfalutin dish served to a king."

Nettie clinked her glass with his, meeting his gaze with a smile. Warmth and love flooded the cold, empty void that had lived inside her since she saw him last.

Dinner finished, they took turns shaking the popcorn kettle over the hotplate burner. The hot, smoky smell of the oil and popping corn filled Nettie's senses with memories of noisy, laughing Christmases spent with her large family. While Jake propped the sagebrush in a bucket, she grabbed a needle and thread. Eating as much popcorn as they strung, she and Neil trimmed the "tree."

Jake pointed at the festooned sage. "You missed a spot. If you hadn't eaten so much—" He ducked, laughing, as Nettie threw a pillow at him.

"It's beautiful, and you know it," she teased.

Then Nettie lit tiny candles on the sagebrush, and they opened their few packages—tobacco and rolling papers for Jake, a music book for Neil, and a halter Jake had braided for Nettie.

After oohing and aahing over their presents, Neil coaxed the sweet notes of "Silent Night" from his violin, and Nettie snuggled contentedly beside Jake. The melody filled her heart with the wonder and miracle of that night so long ago, and the soft glow of the candlelight transformed the little hotel room into the cozy, warm togetherness of a home.

Christmas morning while Jake made pancakes, Nettie walked across the hall to invite Mr. Blumberg for dinner. His door stood open. She knocked on the doorframe and called out, but there was no answer. Stepping inside the room, she looked around in surprise. What few belongings the old man had were gone. And so was he.

A piece of paper lay on the table. *For Mosers: I go back to Germany to my familie. Happy Christmas und joy of Musik for Neil.*

Nettie bit her lip and smiled through her tears. Neil would miss the kindly old man. And so would she.

CHAPTER TWENTY-TWO

Saturday, January 7, 1933

Moved again. Rented a nice little house in Cut Bank. Seems a mansion after the hotel room. Sub-letting two rooms upstairs to oil workers. A little extra income to supplement Jake's job.

At first, with a profound sense of relief, Nettie swept the floors, cooked and baked for the boarders, and happily washed dishes. But not working outside with the horses wore on her. At the end of each day she was more tired from simply keeping house than she'd ever been out feeding hay and chopping ice. Only so many times could a person dust or rearrange their few pieces of furniture. She felt like a racehorse cooped up in a barn.

Afternoons, she looked forward to going outside. Along the railroad tracks, between the house and the school, stood a vacant lot, diked to hold water for a skating rink. She stayed to watch Neil and the other kids, some with skates and some without, slide and play tag on the ice until it grew dark and they finally had to go inside. Then, she and Neil would read or she listened while he practiced his violin.

During the day she explored the town. Today, as she often did, she ambled past O'Haire's Investment Company in the two-story National Bank building, stopped at the *Cut Bank Pioneer* office to peruse the daily newspaper, and bought aspirin and ladies' necessities at Delre's Drugstore.

Then she stopped to buy groceries at the Pay N Takit Merc. The bell on the door jingled as she entered.

"Afternoon, Miz Moser." Donald Poole wiped his hands on his canvas apron. "Can I help you find something?"

"Well, I came in to get some coffee. I think I'll just look around a bit."

A pot-bellied coal stove radiated warmth in one corner, and a scorched coffee aroma wafted from the tin coffee pot on top. Nettie wandered through the narrow aisles, an oily linseed smell rising from the worn wood floor that creaked beneath her steps. At the far end, she picked up a one-pound can of Maxwell House Coffee and read the hand-lettered sticker: thirty cents.

"You can save two cents by buying the two-pound can," Poole advised.

"That's true. Thank you." Nettie perused the shelves and studied the packages of cookies that Neil liked for his afternoon snack, twenty-five cents a pound for coconut macaroons. *Hmm, cheaper to bake them.*

She picked up a dozen eggs, eighteen cents, and then a two-pound can of baking powder for thirty-five cents. Walking back to the counter, Nettie set down her selections. "Town living sure does cost more."

Poole nodded. "Yeah, but things are lookin' up with this oil business. The newspapers say the Depression isn't hitting us as hard."

"I suppose." Nettie fished in her coat pocket for her coin purse. "It's sure helped us that Mr. Aronson hired Jake."

"More men do have jobs these days." The wiry storekeeper licked his pencil stub and began to list each item in a receipt book.

"But I still don't see anybody rolling in wealth." Nettie glanced at the posters and advertisements on the walls. One caught her eye, with a woman standing at an ironing board, a big smile on her face. The ad read: "Westinghouse Standard Ajusto-Matic Electric Iron, 70 cents a month for eight months. No Down."

Nettie smoothed her skirt. "That much money for just an iron. Who'd want to go into debt for eight months for that newfangled luxury?" Most of the places she'd lived didn't have electricity anyway. "I do just fine with the flat-iron on the coal stove."

"You're right. So does the missus." Poole chuckled and looked up from his ledger. "Comes to one dollar and eleven cents."

"Wait. Jake needs some tobacco, too."

"Hey, we got ready-made cigarettes, two packs for a quarter. Camels or Lucky Strike. Luckys are 'toasted.'"

Nettie frowned. "I don't know. Jake rolls his own."

"Lot easier, 'specially when he's out workin'. And it's cheaper to just buy the packs right now."

"Well, I suppose he could give 'em a try." Nettie dug into her coin purse.

"All right, that comes to one dollar, thirty-six cents. Anything else?"

Nettie spilled out the coins. "Oh, shucks, only have ninety-eight cents with me. I'll just take the one pack." She ducked her head to hide her flush. Cheap cigarettes or not, Jake's smoking habit was too expensive. "Do you have a smaller can of baking powder?" She would have to wait until Jake got paid mid-month to buy more.

"Naw, naw. That's okay. I'll spot ya the rest. I know you'll be good for it." Poole smiled broadly. "Let me know how Jake likes the Luckys."

Nettie walked home with her packages in the crisp cold, crunching through the remaining snowdrifts. As she approached the house, she saw a man sitting on the bottom step of the porch. He was dressed in torn, dirty coveralls, with a bandanna around his head and rags wrapped around his shoeless feet. She hesitated a moment as he rose. Something dignified in his posture belied his appearance.

He gave a little bow. "Howdy, ma'am. I don't intend to bother you, but I just wondered if you might be able to spare a slice of bread."

Nettie glanced across the ice rink lot toward the railroad tracks. One of the hobos. They were generally harmless. Just hungry. She turned to the man. "Sure. Come on in. Warm yourself."

While she heated a bowl of stew and sliced bread, he identified himself simply as "George" and told her his story. "I was a banker in St. Louis till the crash of twenty-nine. The bank closed. Lost every dime I ever had. My wife took the children and went back to her folks."

A chill ran through Nettie. A family split up because of finances. *We've lived apart a lot, but we're always together when we can be.*

George took a slice of bread and buttered it. "Several of my colleagues committed suicide." He took a bite. "I was about to do the same one night. I was ready to throw myself in front of a passing freight train."

A chill ran through Nettie. How desperate would someone have to be?

He paused and spooned the hot soup into his mouth, cradling the bowl with one hand for its warmth.

She sat at the table and watched his face, waiting for his next words.

"But then, at the very last second, something jerked me back and I fell to the ground. I lay there in the darkness, shivering with cold and fear. I had failed at death, too. Then I had a sudden thought. Why not hop the next train and see where it takes me?" He buttered another piece of bread. "I've been doing that ever since, and I've never been happier."

He finished the last of the stew and wiped the bowl clean with a chunk of bread. Leaning back in his chair, he closed his eyes and inhaled deeply.

"What happened to your family?"

"Still back east, as far as I know." He gave a half-hearted smile. "My wife just can't live without money. She doesn't understand what happened."

"Would you like to write her a letter, let her know you're all right?"

George smiled. "Oh, I did. But the letter came back, marked 'refused.' That's when I had the urge to relate with the train."

Nettie stood up to take his bowl. "Would you like more soup?"

"No, thank you, ma'am. My sufficiency has been suffonsified; any more would be obnoxious to my fastidious taste." He gave her a big gap-toothed grin, rose, and headed for the door.

Nettie looked down at the bloody rags on his feet. She flinched inside at the pain he must be feeling. Reaching into the coal bucket behind the stove, she picked up an old pair of Jake's boots. "Wait. Please take these. And these wool socks. My husband doesn't need them."

The man looked into her face for a long moment. He blinked glistening brown eyes. Then he smiled. "Thank you. Your hospitality is greatly appreciated." Bowing again, he left.

At the frosty window, Nettie watched him hobble through the snow toward the tracks. He was penniless but happy, riding the rails and begging for morsels. And here she was unhappy just because she was stuck in town, away from her husband and her horses. True, their dreams of owning a ranch or even a house had not materialized. But at least they had a roof over their heads. She hated being separated from Jake for long periods at a time and felt incomplete, but she still had her family intact. And although they didn't have a lot of money, they had enough to eat. Her life was luxurious compared to that pitiful man's. She swallowed her guilt.

Neil banged into the house, interrupting her thoughts. "Hi, Ma. Was that a hobo I saw walking away from the house?" His cheeks were flushed from the cold. "Did you feed him?"

"Yes, I gave him some soup. But he fed me, too." Nettie walked up to her son, who had a puzzled look on his face, and hugged him hard. "You'll get a kick out of what he said when I asked if he wanted more." She recited George's humorous reply and Neil laughed.

As he ran back outside to play, she could hear him repeating, "My sufficiency has been suffonsified . . ."

Jake moved into town while he tried to prepare the frozen ground of a vacant lot for a test well the oil company wanted to drill. He came home every night stiff with cold, his hands and arms bruised from the beating the fresno lever gave him. He huddled close to the stove. His teeth chattered as if the chill came from deep within.

"I don't know what they think they're going to accomplish in this weather." He grinned. "But as long as they keep payin' me, I guess I can stand it."

"And as long as you are here with me, I can stand it." Nettie massaged his shoulders and kissed the top of his head. He leaned back against her stomach, reached around and pulled her to his lap to give her a long, toe-tingling kiss.

Neil snapped his book closed. "Ah, mush." His feigned disgust broke them apart. He picked up his school bag and walked back to his bedroom. " . . . Any more would be obnoxious to my fastidious taste."

Jake raised his eyebrows. "Is that boy getting too much book learnin'?"

Nettie grinned. What a delight her men were. "No, I don't think so." She told him about the hobo. "You don't have to worry. He's so looking forward to summer when he can ride Paint again."

One gloomy February day, a letter arrived with "Marie Gibson" written in the return address. Nettie ripped open the envelope with eager anticipation. Marie had written:

> Tex Austin is taking a troupe to England again next year. Want to go? I thought I'd give you more warning this time, so you have a year and a half to get ready. Neil is old enough now to stay with his pa, isn't he? Alice and Marge Greenough from Montana are going. So are the 'big names'—Tad Lucas, Lucille Mulhall, Ruth Roach, Vera McGinnis, Rose Henderson—you'll get to meet them all. We had such fun ten years ago. You've got to come!

Another chance to go to London. To ride in big rodeos. The letter crackled in Nettie's shaking hands. She had no one to tell. Jake was working, and Neil was at school.

"Yippee. I'm going to London." She grabbed the broom for a partner and danced around the table, singing and whooping. "London Bridge is falling down . . . wahoo."

Then she dropped the broom and sat down, looking around the kitchen as if someone might be watching her frivolity. No sense in jumping the gun. She had to talk to Jake first.

Ideas and obstacles flitted through her mind. Would they be able to come up with the money for the boat trip any easier now than ten years ago? Last time, Jake could have sold a draft team. But now, nobody wanted to buy horses. With Jake still working for the oil company, moving here and there, Neil wouldn't be able to stay in school, if she were gone.

Nettie gazed into the distance, picturing the western festivities in that foreign city. She could see herself atop the biggest, baddest bull Tex Austin could find, holding on with one hand, waving the other to the cheering crowd. She would have a new shirt. Satin. Red. And a buttery leather vest and chaps. Yes indeed, she would give Prairie Rose Henderson a run for her money. And, as world-champion bull rider, she would be dressed in a bright-colored costume, riding in the Grand Parade. She laughed aloud.

With Jake working, they could surely afford it this time. And she would earn money during the show, especially when she won. Neil could stay with her folks or one of her sisters and still go to school. Her dream was about to come true.

Running her fingers through her hair, she jumped up and grabbed her coat and boots. She just couldn't keep this news to herself any longer. She had to go find Jake. The winter gloom vanished and she broke into a run toward the lot where Jake was working.

He pulled the team up, steam floating off their backs, and strode to meet her, his forehead crinkled. "Everything all right?"

She waved the letter in the air. "Marie. London." Panting, she ran to him and threw her arms around his neck.

"Whoa, whoa, little gal. What's all this? Can't understand a word you're sayin'. Something wrong with Marie?"

She burst into laughter. "No, no. Sorry, I got a little carried away. This letter is from Marie, and she says Tex Austin is taking a rodeo to London again next year." She stopped. "Jake, I'd really love to go if there's any way."

His face creased into a big grin. "Why, sure, little gal. You gotta go."

"Yeah, we can ride the circuit this summer, make some money, and with your job, we should be able to afford it, won't we?"

Jake's blue eyes twinkled. "I think so." He grabbed her in a bear hug and then swung her into a dance over the frozen ground.

CHAPTER TWENTY-THREE

Sunday, May 14, 1933

On the move again. Another abandoned shack for the summer. Got to go where the grass is. At least I'm out of town, back with Jake and the horses. Riding every day. Getting ready to put on a rodeo next month. Hope to make money for trip to London.

Nettie let the spring breeze blow her hair wild, and the warm sun on her back filled her with joyful song. It never ceased to amaze her how the countryside could go from tabletop drought to green lushness with just a few rain showers. And this spring the grass seemed greener than she'd ever remembered, even though it was still sparse. Just being back outside riding, she was once again a teenager, free from responsibilities. Town living, even with its amenities, could never take its place.

Jake still did dirt work for the oil company, and in between jobs, they went to as many rodeos as they could. Nettie tried her hand at riding bulls. They both won first place a couple of times, each time taking home a twenty- or thirty-dollar purse to sock away for her trip to London. Her excitement grew, along with the nest egg. She could hardly wait till next year.

She also tried competing in bronc riding with Marie and Alice and Marge Greenough, but she was hopelessly outclassed. Alice had just returned from a big win at the national Boston Garden competition. Alice, Marge, and Marie were riding the summer circuit to prepare for the big Madison Square Garden show in October.

At the Miles City Roundup Nettie joined the women behind the corrals after Alice's spectacular ride. "Did you hear what happened to Tad?" Alice sat cross-legged on a horse blanket. Marie and Nettie shook their heads.

"We were at the Chicago World's Fair a few weeks ago, and when she was going under her horse's belly in the trick-riding contest, she slipped. Lordy, I saw it happen. She was just hangin' there, her horse kicking her with every step as he kept galloping around the arena." Alice gestured with wide-eyed animation. "Finally she was able to roll free. Ended up with nothin' but a broken arm. But it's a bad break. At first the doctors wanted to amputate. She said, 'Absolutely not.' But they don't think she'll be able to ride again."

With a grimace, Nettie rubbed the wrist she'd broken many years ago. Tad Lucas was one of the highest paid women in rodeo. She'd been earning ten thousand dollars a year, even during these Depression years.

"Remember Fox Hasting at the Kansas City Roundup years ago?" Marge began another story. "After about four jumps, her bronc fell. On her. It kept tryin' to get up and every time it would fall back on top of Fox. She was tangled in the rigging. Her neck was so twisted it looked like it was broken. Cowboys came running from all corners, and they took her out on a stretcher. We thought sure she'd gone to the great arena in the sky." She paused dramatically.

Nettie peered into Marge's face. "What happened?"

"Then, just as the crowd was getting settled down again, here came this Model T with the top down and Fox waving to the crowd. She stepped out at the judges' stand and asked for a reride."

The Greenough sisters laughed, and Nettie joined in, but her heart contracted. What if something like that were to happen to her? Behind them, the crowd roared in the grandstands, signaling another successful ride.

"They gave it to her, and she rode that horse to the end," Alice added. "And later, as if bronc riding wasn't tough enough, she took up bulldogging."

"Didn't you have your horse fall on you that time in London, Marie?" Marge took out a small mirror and examined her teeth for lipstick smears.

"Yeah. It happened the first week out. Dislocated my knee. I had it wrapped and came back later for trick riding, but when I stepped off my horse, I felt it go again." Marie rubbed the old injury. "Went to a doctor to have it reset. He told me to lay off, but I had two days to rest, so I rode again. I had to have help saddling and mounting and they had to carry me from the stadium, but any prize money I might be able to get looked powerfully good to me." She chuckled. "And for just a shilling a day I got transported to and from the arena in a wheelchair. Felt like a celebrity. That beat walking any day."

Nettie shivered as though a dark cloud had passed over her. She gazed off into the arena, not really seeing what was going on, as the other women exchanged more injury stories. She and Jake had been lucky. He'd never had more than a few bruises or a sprained ankle, and she'd broken her wrist that one time when she first started. Of course, she hadn't ridden as much as these women. But what if she or Jake did get hurt seriously? What would become of Neil then?

"Gosh, my mama was right. Rodeoing is dangerous." Nettie looked into each woman's face. "Do you worry about that?"

"Aw, shucks, no. People get hurt all the time." Alice waved off the thought as though it were a pesky fly.

"That's the risk you take, because it's in your blood," Margie added. "When you love doing something, you don't think much about that."

Marie put her hand on Nettie's shoulder. "Don't worry about it, honey. It doesn't happen all that often. These stories are the exceptions. Just follow your dream, and do your best."

Nettie brushed dust off her denims. *She's right. I'm just not going to think about it.* "Tell me more about London."

"Oh, you'll have such a good time." Alice leaned back on her elbows. "The English people loved us. We would ride broncs and do our trick riding all day, then get all gussied up in our fancy dresses and stroll out to tea in the evening. And the locals kept asking the men where their six-guns were." She laughed.

"And they had such parties for us. We got to meet the queen at one of them." Marie took off her hat, fluffed her hair, and swished her shoulders as though getting ready to meet the royal monarch. "Here's how you curtsy to royalty." She dipped and flourished a hand as if holding out a skirt.

Alice and Margie jumped up and joined Marie. "C'mon, Nettie. Try it."

With hoots and giggles, the women curtsied to each other. A warm sense of belonging washed over Nettie. She had waited so long for this.

"I'm so glad I'm going with you this time."

❧

Nettie, Jake, and Neil moved twice more that summer, following available pasture as the horses grazed whatever meager grass they found before it dried in the blazing sun. Neil grew strong and brown and sneaked off to ride neighbors' calves every chance he got.

"Ma, can I ride a steer in the next rodeo?" Neil's amber-flecked hazel eyes gazed at her in sincere pleading.

"Oh, honey, I think you're a little too young yet." She cringed to think of her little boy atop a big brute of an animal.

"I'm almost nine. I rode that steer in the next pasture several times already." He stood with his feet wide apart, hands on his hips, and arms akimbo.

She gazed at her son, standing in her kitchen with so much bravado. "I know. But he's not as big as the ones they use in the competitions." She glanced at Jake, sipping his coffee. "And besides, you've been around him enough that he's used to you now. Those rodeo steers have only one thing in mind, to get you off their back and stomp on you."

"I could stay on 'em, Ma. I know I can."

Jake set down his coffee cup. "Aw, why not? He's gotta start sometime."

Nettie whirled around to face her husband. "Jake!"

He stood, arms out, palms up. "Okay, okay. I understand." He turned to Neil. "I guess you'd better wait a year or two."

Nettie swallowed an angry retort. "When you're fourteen, we'll have this discussion again." Seeing her son's smile collapse, she softened. "We'll be in Idaho Falls in September. Maybe they'll have some kids' calf-riding there and you can compete in that."

"Okay." He squared his shoulders and turned to walk off, whistling.

Such a confident little man. Like she'd been when she was that age. A chill washed over her. Now she understood what Mama must have felt when Nettie started riding steers.

She glared at Jake. "Don't ever do something like that again."

He caught her arm and brought her into his embrace. "All right, little gal, all right."

<hr />

Nettie leaned back against the headrest next to Jake. She closed her eyes, the rhythmic clacking of train and tracks taking her back to another train ride almost eleven years ago. This trip to Idaho took them back through Great Falls, where they'd been married. She reached out and took Jake's hand. He squeezed back. A lot had happened in those years.

Neil's voice broke into her memories. "Ma, this train is going really fast. The conductor said it can go fifty miles in an hour." He returned to his seat from his wanderings up and down the aisle.

"Yes, I know, honey. Isn't that great? It would take us three weeks to ride to Idaho." She grinned at him. "Sit with us for awhile?"

He inserted himself between them, cuddled against her, and soon was asleep. His little boy warmth soothed her. She dozed too.

The train rumbled south past Helena and Butte, through forested mountain passes, where Nettie gazed out the windows, remembering the cool, shady greenness from their long trail ride in 1930. Then, thinking of the steep, narrow Gibbons Pass where she'd first felt so sick, she shuddered, Thank goodness, she hadn't had one of those attacks since they came home to Montana. *I hope it isn't something in the Idaho air that caused them.* No, she was being irrational. It was altitude sickness, she knew that.

At the station in Idaho Falls, Marie and Tom Gibson met them with hugs and whoops. Then Neil joined a family with kids, and the Gibsons spirited Jake and Nettie off in a touring car to a restaurant, where a large group of cowboys and cowgirls had already gathered. With the end of Prohibition earlier in the year, beer and whiskey flowed openly, and the reunion lasted well into the night.

Finally, Marie stood and tugged at Tom's arm. "If we're going to be in any shape to ride tomorrow, we'd better get a little shut-eye."

With relief, Nettie rose to follow, Jake close behind. In their room, curled up next to him with his protective arm around her, she thought she would be able to drop off to sleep immediately. But she found herself staring at the dark ceiling, trying to contain her excitement. She calculated how much money they had saved for the London trip and how much they might be able to add if they both won tomorrow. Listening to Jake's soft snores, she dreamed of London and finally drifted off.

The September morning dawned clear and hot. Miniature dust devils swirled around booted feet as the competitors gathered at the arena, unkinked lassos, tightened cinches, and checked horses' feet. Steers bawled, broncs snorted, and racy language spewed as often as tobacco juice.

After sending Neil off to play with a couple of boys his age, Nettie met Marie behind the chutes and offered her friend a cup of steaming coffee. "All ready for the big ride?" Nettie frowned. The tiny lines around Marie's eyes seemed more pronounced this morning.

Her friend ran a hand through her shoulder-length hair, now tinged with gray. "Yeah, I guess. You know, I just want to get through the Garden show with a win and go on the London tour, and then I think I'm going to retire. I'm almost thirty-nine, so it's probably time I hang up my spurs."

"What?" Shock rippled through Nettie's chest. Marie giving up the rodeo life? She couldn't believe it. "But what would I do without you on the circuit?" Tears stung her eyes. "You've been living my dream. You've had a good career, won a lot of prizes and made some decent money. And you've always been so helpful to me."

Marie sighed. "It's a worthy dream and I hope you get to fulfill it. But those hundreds of miles on the road, the greasy spoons, the cheap hotels. And all the months I'm away from home, away from my family. It's about got me worn out."

"You're just tired this morning. We should've left the party a little earlier last night." Nettie reached out and hugged her friend. "Hey, you'll do great today. I have a feeling about that. And tonight, I'm going to see that you go to bed early and get a good night's sleep. Tomorrow everything will look a lot brighter, especially if you win the bronc riding today."

Marie smiled. "You're right. I am getting a little long in the tooth for late-night partying. I hope I draw a good bucker and you get a nice wild steer, and we'll both win today. Good luck. I'll be up there cheering for you." She clapped Nettie on the shoulder and walked to the chute.

Nettie climbed onto the top rail of the corral fence to watch, her mood deflated by Marie's pronouncement about retiring. *I'm going to hit thirty in another fifteen months. Instead of trying to make a comeback, maybe I should be thinking of hanging up my spurs too.* She sighed. But this was her dream. She couldn't just give it up.

After several mediocre rides by the men, the announcer's voice wound up. "And now, layd-e-e-s and gentle-men . . . on the back of Old Dutch . . . two-time Worrrld Champeen Cowgirl Bronc Riderrr . . . Ma-rieee . . . Gibson!"

The crowd rose to its feet, roaring its approval. The gate latch clicked and the white bronc lunged from the chute. On its back, Marie widened her smile beneath her sombrero, brown curls danced, her left hand waved.

"Ride 'im, Marie," Nettie yelled from atop her perch.

Rearing up, plunging forward, twisting sideways, the bronc fought the burden on its back with the fury of a thousand devils. Nettie shivered in the heat.

Buffeted and tossed like a tumbleweed in a storm, Marie gallantly spurred with each jump. Her raised hand never wavered, never strayed toward the saddle horn. Snorting and grunting, the white demon horse danced on its heels. It gathered its haunches like tightly coiled springs and kicked toward the dusty sky until it looked like it was on tiptoes. Over and over again.

Nettie's chest grew tight. She couldn't breathe. She didn't dare. Could Marie hold on much longer? Eight seconds seemed to take forever.

The sombrero went sailing, but her friend's grin never faded. Her free hand clawed the sky, while her spurs raked in front, then in back.

The whistle shrieked. A surge of relief swept through Nettie like a spring rain shower in the midst of a dust storm. Marie had done it. She had ridden the toughest bucker Nettie had seen in a long time. It was one heck of a ride. If that wasn't a prizewinner, then their shared name was not Antoinette. She grinned and slapped her thigh. "Good goin', Marie."

Old Dutch, oblivious to the meaning of the whistle, kept on bucking furiously. The pickup man galloped from the sidelines to retrieve the brave damsel. As he raced toward her, Marie's mount suddenly turned into his path. The two horses collided with a sickening thud that reverberated to the top of the corral where Nettie sat.

The pickup man's horse swerved and reared. Marie's bronc crashed to the ground. Her body flew in an arc over the horse's head. She came down, headfirst, onto the ground.

Nettie screamed. Her chest felt full of broken glass. The crowd hushed. Cowboys ran from the chutes with a stretcher.

Her heart pounding like the bronc's hooves, Nettie scrambled down from the fence and hurried toward her friend, lying crumpled on the ground. She sobbed. Marie's neck was twisted at such an odd angle. One of the men held out a hand to stop her from coming closer. Others lifted Marie onto the stretcher and ran with her from the arena.

"Is she all right?" Nettie swiveled her head, looking for someone to answer her. "Will she be all right?" Then Jake came running across the corral and gathered her into his arms. She pushed herself away. "I've got to find out how she is."

"It's okay, little gal." Jake attempted to placate her. "We'll go to the hospital in a bit and see."

"Come on. Let's go now." Nettie turned and raced toward the cars parked outside the arena. "Somebody! Give us a ride to the hospital."

"C'mon. I'll take you." A cowboy pointed to his Model T.

Nettie plunged through the crowd toward him then abruptly turned to Jake. "Where's Neil? Oh my gosh, I almost forgot him."

Jake put a hand on her arm. "He's okay. He ran into our ol' cook Shorty. They're catchin' up."

Her shoulders relaxed a bit. At least she didn't have to worry about her son. Nettie ran toward the car behind the cowboy. He stopped abruptly, looking around the parking area. "Dang. I'm all blocked in. Can't get out."

Nettie spun in a frantic circle. "I need a car." She ran up and down the rows of vehicles, shouting, "Who's got a car? Please help me."

Finally, at the edge of the field, another ranch hand stepped out from around his Model T. "I can help, ma'am. Where you need a ride to?"

"The hospital." Nettie jumped into the car and sagged against the seat. Jake slipped in beside her. The cowboy drove the Model T toward town like a runaway steer.

At the hospital, the waiting room filled with cowboys. Their spurs jangled as they paced with Marie's ashen-faced husband. Nettie rushed to his side. "Tom. She'll be all right. She has to be."

He nodded and slumped into a chair. But a moment later he jumped up to pace again. Nettie couldn't sit still either. She leafed through a magazine. She walked awhile with Tom, at times squeezing his arm or patting his shoulder. She sat. Then she jumped up to walk again and again to the nurses' station.

The white-clad nurse shook her head each time. "No word yet."

Finally the doctor came down the hall. The room hushed. Everyone stood, waiting.

Tom hurried forward, taking off his high-crowned hat.

"Mr. Gibson?" The doctor stopped and waited.

"That's me." Tom clutched his hat over his heart.

A chill went through Nettie, shaking her to the core. She bit her trembling lip. Jake slipped an arm around her.

The doctor led Tom just outside the waiting area, speaking softly and earnestly. As he shook his head, Nettie watched Tom's shoulders slump and his body sag against the wall. Oh, no. A tiny cry escaped from her mouth. Her knees threatened to buckle and she clutched Jake's hand. The doctor turned away. Tom stood frozen.

Nettie ran to him.

He stared down at his hands. "She . . . she's gone." His voice cracked. He sank heavily to the floor.

Nettie squatted beside him, putting her hand on his shaking arm. "Oh, Tom. I'm so sorry." She held him in her arms. "We loved her too."

———◆———

The cowboy gave Nettie and Jake a ride back to the arena. As she got out of the car, the noise of the audience and whinnies from horses assaulted her senses. "What?" She stopped in midstep and turned to Jake. "They're continuing the rodeo?"

She whirled around and ran for the chutes, her fists clenched, her breath coming in gasps. Reaching the holding pens for the rodeo stock, Nettie grasped the latch and flung open the first gate. "Git! Git!

Go on!" She shooed the broncs toward the opening, then ran for the next gate.

"What the—? Hey! Hold on there, lady!" A man jumped from atop the corral fence and chased after her. Just as she reached the next pen, he grabbed her arm. "What are you doing? Have you gone crazy?"

Nettie wrestled her arm away. "How can you keep going like this? Don't you know? She's dead." She felt her voice rising to a shriek.

The cowboy stepped back with a wide-eyed look, his palms upturned. Jake sprinted up to Nettie and wrapped her in his arms. "There, there, little gal. It's all right." Gently, he led her away.

Sobs wracked Nettie's body. She sat hunched in the dim light of their hotel room, nausea rolling over her like waves. "It was her best ride."

Jake held her, but she couldn't stop crying. "A perfect ride. Didn't matter." Nettie hiccupped another sob. "Not fair."

Neil sat on the bed next to her. "Don't cry, Ma."

Nettie looked at her son. "If that had been me out there—" She broke into a wail. Jake rubbed her shoulders. "Why don't you lie down awhile. I'll take Neil out for something to eat. Give you a little time. Want us to bring you back something?"

Nettie shook her head. Her stomach felt like a rock.

She closed her eyes to shut out the painful image of Marie's crumpled body. If that had been her, Neil would be left without a mother. Just like Lucien and Andy Gibson. Tears flowed again. Poor kids.

She shuddered as if she had the ague. Her life's dream had just turned into a nightmare.

She moved to the hard bed, burrowed under the blankets, and pulled them up over her head. Marie's voice floated on the periphery of her consciousness. "Don't worry about it, honey. You just gotta live for the day, pay attention to the dance, and do your best."

Finally, Nettie slept.

The next morning Nettie joined Jake and Neil for breakfast in the café near their motel, but she couldn't swallow her food. Jake speared another bite of pancake. "Well, guess I'm up to ride saddle bronc later this mornin'."

Nettie dropped her fork with a clatter. "No." She looked at Jake and Neil, sitting across the table, eating as if nothing was wrong. "This is it, guys. No more rodeo. I'm not doing this anymore. And neither are you."

"But, Ma." Neil looked stricken.

Jake leaned forward. "Now, little gal. Let's not jump the gun here."

A cold chunk of ice seemed lodged in Nettie's chest. "Just think of her boys. What if—?" She jerked her eyes toward Neil. He sat hunched over his plate.

Jake's sharp intake of breath told her she'd hit a nerve.

"That's why Marie insisted Andy and Lucien finish school and wouldn't let them ride broncs. It's too dangerous."

Neil sat up straight. "Ma. You said I could ride calves at this rodeo. I haven't got to yet."

"Absolutely not." Nettie's lip trembled.

Jake reached across the table for her hand. "Honey, you're still upset. This is not like you. You don't want to give up your dream."

"My dream died in that arena with Marie." Her voice choked.

❦

Back in town for the winter, this time staying in the Cut Bank Hotel, Nettie smoothed the newspaper clipping on the kitchen table and reread it for the twentieth time:

Antoinette Marie Gibson, internationally known rodeo star, was killed Saturday in a freak accident at the Idaho Falls Rodeo. As the 38-year-old World Champion from Havre, Mont., finished a successful ride, a pickup man's horse collided with her still-bucking bronc. The horse lost its footing and crashed to the ground. Mrs.

Gibson was thrown onto her head and died later of a badly frac-
tured skull.

Some of the words at her funeral described her life aptly: "She
died as she lived, hearing the applause of the people."

Mrs. Gibson is survived by her husband, Tom Gibson, and her
sons, Lucien and Andrew . . .

Nettie barely noticed the cramped hotel quarters this time. She
couldn't write in her journal. She could do only those mundane daily
chores required of her: getting Neil off to school, fixing meals, washing
their clothes.

Nettie's eyes filled with tears. Tears that could not wash away the
deep sorrow that lived permanently in her soul. Time and again she
thought of her baby sister, Esther, who had died of influenza the winter of 1920–'21. How Mama had grieved, nearly dead to the world for
months. The clipping shook in her hands. *It could happen to me.*

She didn't want to think about that day, or all the other women
and men who'd been killed riding. She had certainly heard about those
incidents when they'd happened, but most of those people she'd never
met, or had known only slightly.

This was different. Marie was her friend, the person who'd helped
her get on the road to her dream, the one who'd won Mama over and
gotten her to change her mind about Nettie's rodeoing. She was the
one with whom Nettie shared her triumphs and losses. She, more than
anyone besides Jake, understood Nettie's passion for riding. And now
she was gone. There would be no more letters from Marie. No more
surprise visits. No more shootin' the breeze behind the rodeo chutes.
No going to London.

Nettie got up from the table and went to sit on the bed in the
corner. Her dreams of becoming a rodeo star were as dead as Marie.
Slowly, thoughtfully, she folded the clipping again and buried it at the
bottom of her dresser drawer.

CHAPTER TWENTY-FOUR

Tuesday, June 5, 1934

Drought again. No rain for months. Grasshoppers mowing down the grass. What are we to do, another trail ride to Idaho?

Nettie rode the fence line to check for broken strands. She brushed stray hairs out of her sweaty face, feeling as wilted as the short spring grass under her horse's hooves. Another hot, dry summer in another abandoned homestead, trying to eke out a day-to-day subsistence. So many years of drought, so many moves. She might as well be living in the Sahara Desert, herding camels.

She stopped to pound a staple with hard, angry thwacks. This herd of horses was their life, their dream, their chance at building a ranch. But they weren't going to be able to hang on to that dream for much longer. Land prices were increasing, but wages were going down. Wearily, Nettie wrenched on a sagging strand of barbed wire. Her arms ached. Her head pounded. More and more farmers were giving up their teams and converting to gas-powered tractors, especially with the cheap source of fuel from the local oil wells.

Taking a drink from her canteen, she wiped the sweat from her brow. Even Jake's draft-cross horses weren't in as much demand for rodeos anymore. Fewer men had the money to produce the big events these days. Jake tried to put on some rodeos himself—she hadn't been able to talk him into quitting—but that took money they didn't have.

Lately, they'd been lucky to break even. Tired of arguing, she'd tried helping Jake with one, but just didn't have the heart for rodeo anymore.

Nettie gazed off into the distance. Clouds gathered like gray feather ticks on the horizon. As she swung back into the saddle, she wondered if they were going to be the kind that just blew a lot of dirt around and teased them with a few ineffectual drops of rain. *Hopeless.* She tightened her mouth and went on with her rounds of the fence. By the time she reached the house, the sky had darkened, the wind sighed through the sagebrush, and the air had cooled noticeably.

Jake and Neil rode up while she unsaddled. "Well, we got clouds. Let's hope they have rain in 'em." Jake threw the saddles into the shed, and stood with his face upturned as the first drops pelted them. Then the three of them ran for the house, whooping.

"It'll probably blow over in an hour or two." Jake's words belied the hopeful look on his face as he stood by the window with Nettie, watching the raindrops pockmark the dust.

"Probably." Yet she crossed her fingers, hoping at last there'd be enough to green up the countryside. She turned to light the lantern and then busied herself fixing supper, while Neil buried his face in a book.

The intermittent plop, plop slowly turned into a steady rhythm. Jake met Nettie's gaze with uplifted eyebrows and just the hint of a smile. She barely breathed, as if by holding herself still she could will the rain to stay.

The rain hadn't let up by the time Nettie shooed Neil off to bed and still hadn't when she crawled under the blankets. Jake stayed up smoking and watching the water cascade down the glass, his chair pulled over by the window.

Nettie awoke in the gray dawn. The beat intensified into a frenzied tattoo on the tar-paper roof. Jake's side of the bed was still empty. She now heard an additional plink, plink as water dripped onto metal. She slipped out of bed and walked into the other room, where Jake was just putting a bucket under a leak by the door. A candle burned, throwing long shadows.

Jake turned when he heard the floor creak under her footstep and laughed out loud. "Do you hear that? It's raining, real honest-to-God steady rain. Never thought I'd be happy to have a leaky roof." He grabbed her hands and swung her around. "It's raining!"

The soothing rhythm continued through the morning. Nettie fixed hotcakes for Neil and Jake and they lingered around the kitchen table, sipping tea, a luxury she hadn't enjoyed in ages.

Jake was suddenly jubilant and full of ideas. "With good grass this year, we won't have to move around so much. And we won't have to buy hay for the winter." He grabbed a pencil and scribbled on the back of an envelope. "If we save money on hay, and if the cowboys feel more like rodeoing this year, maybe we could find a place to lease, and some-day buy." He jumped up from the table and moved to the window, chortling as he looked out at the gray drizzle.

"Maybe." Nettie didn't want to say it out loud for fear of jinxing the idea, but it filled her with buoyant hope. Maybe, at last, they would be able to find their dream.

Two days later, the sun rose bright above steaming mud puddles. Nettie drank in the freshly washed air. With a buoyancy she hadn't felt in a long time, she helped Jake and Neil saddle up to ride out into the pasture. She could almost see the grass grow. The short, withered stalks from a few days ago were turning a lush, emerald green before her eyes. A red-tailed hawk swooped through the crystal blue sky.

Jake and Neil rode ahead, joshing each other and laughing. Suddenly needing a woman's companionship, she urged her horse into a trot to catch up. "Hey, what do you say we ride over and visit Mama and Papa?"

"Go see Gramma and Grampa? Can we, Pa, huh? Can we?" Neil squirmed around in his saddle until his pinto danced sideways.

Jake chuckled. "Why, sure. We haven't been to see them in awhile. Today looks like a dandy day to go visitin'."

Winding their way over the Sweet Grass hills, the three arrived at the Brady homestead after an hour and a half ride. Smoke spiraled from the chimney in a welcome greeting. Her mother stood hunched over in the garden, probably watching the peas grow.

Mama straightened at the horses' whinnies, and hurried up the path to meet them. "Why, this is a nice surprise. You're just in time for dinner." She held up a basket. "I was checking to see if I had any greens ready to fix."

Nettie dismounted and gave her mother a hug. Mama's hair was streaked with gray and the smile crinkles around her eyes deepened with delight as she turned to embrace Neil. "I'm so glad to see you, little partner. You're growing like a weed."

Then she extended a hand to Jake. "Come in. Come in. Papa should be back soon. He had to go check his fields. Isn't this rain a blessing?" She clucked and shooed them toward the house like a flock of hungry chickens.

A pang of—what was it, guilt? fear?—churned quickly through Nettie's gut. Mama was getting older. She must be about sixty-five. These drought years had been hard on her. Not to mention her whole life since moving to this homestead in 1911. Having eight children to feed and care for. Then Esther's death. Nettie shut her eyes for a moment. She hadn't visited her parents as often as she should have the past few years, what with their trip to Idaho and moving so many times since then. *I've got to visit more often, maybe come and help Mama with her garden and chores.*

Grabbing a broom from just outside the door, Nettie attempted to clean off the mud spatters the horses had kicked up on her and Neil's pant legs. They took off their muddy boots, and he ran inside, headed straight for the cookie jar. Nettie padded into the kitchen behind her mother. "How've you been, Mama? You look tired."

Mama waved off the question with a ladle in her hand. "Pshaw. I'm just fine. Even better, now that we've had some rain. Your papa was pretty near beside himself the last couple of days. Look at the newspaper."

Nettie opened the *Cut Bank Pioneer Press,* to read the giant headline:

THREE INCHES RAIN FALLS HERE!
The heaviest rainfall in years in Glacier County came just in time to save the crops. A long-needed nourishment for our soil, it's also been hard on the 'hoppers . . .

Nettie laughed. "Yeah, Jake stayed up all night the first night, just watching it come down."

Mama opened a jar of venison and added it to the stew cooking on the stove. "I was sure sorry to hear about Marie. She was such a nice woman."

Nettie put the greens into a large bowl to wash. She nodded, her voice suddenly too choked to speak.

Mama put a gentle hand on her shoulder. "It's been hard for you. I know."

Nettie was surprised to see a tear glisten in the corner of her mother's eye. She turned into Mama's warm embrace. Their shared bond, knowing the grief of loss, flowed into Nettie and she allowed herself to feel comforted. They stood that way in silence, hugging each other hard, until they heard Papa's greeting and Jake's answering voice outside. Then she let go with a forced smile, as if everything was all right.

Mama looked into Nettie's eyes and patted her shoulder before turning away. "Well, the men are probably starved by now. We'd better set the table. I'll get some coffee on." She bustled around the kitchen. Nettie opened the cupboard to get out the big soup plates.

As she put the fifth set of utensils on the wooden table, she heard the horses whinny, then shouts. "Hellooo. Anybody home?"

"Well, I'll be darned." Papa's voice came from outside the kitchen door. "It's the boys."

Nettie stepped to the window to see her three younger brothers ride up, along with her nephew Gary, waving their hats and whooping.

They dismounted with a flourish and greeted Papa, Jake, and Neil with handshakes and claps on the back.

She burst through the door. "Hey, you guys. Where have you been hiding yourselves?"

Ben, the oldest of the trio now at twenty-six, grabbed her in a bear hug. "Well, sis, we've been slavin' away on our ranch. Where you been?" The three boys together had leased a ranch about ten miles north, next to their brother Joe's place.

She grinned. "Just following the horses. Wherever they can eat, we go." She turned to give Ed and Chuck hugs too. "It's been too long. You're looking great. One of you must've learned how to cook."

"Yeah, we all took turns for awhile, but now Eddie's in charge of the chow." Chuck, at eighteen, stood tall and confident.

It seemed only a couple of months ago that he was the little four-year-old brother she'd played with on the floor in front of the stove on cold winter evenings. Ed, the shy one, looked awfully handsome. And Ben, always the doer, the talker, the leader.

"And Gary, I haven't seen you in ages. How's your mom?" Nettie stood on tiptoes to give Margie's son a peck on the cheek.

The boy hugged her. "She's well. Says it's high time you come for a visit."

"Well, since my favorite nephew came to see me, I probably don't need to go over there," Nettie teased.

"Come in, all of you, come in." Mama wiped her hands on her apron. "I just added another jar of venison to the stew. There's enough for everybody."

The men slathered chunks of bread with fresh-churned butter and dug into their bowls with gusto, punctuating their bits of conversation with jabs of their spoons. Nettie's heart warmed, watching the boys' friendly enthusiasm and Neil's animated face as he looked from one to the other, too enthralled to eat. She had missed this.

"This rain's gonna spark rodeo fever again this year, you just wait and see." Ben waved his bread in the air.

"Eddie just traded for a good-lookin' little bay that he's gonna use for bulldoggin' this summer." Chuck elbowed his brother in the ribs.

"Shelby's plannin' a big rodeo at the county fair in July. I'm gonna go. You all can ride on down with me." Jake looked from one to the other.

"Sounds good." Ed tipped his head toward Jake. "Are you goin' to put on a rodeo again?"

Jake gave Nettie a quick glance. "Yeah, I think I might."

"You goin' to ride steers this year, Nettie?" Ben leaned back from the table, tipping his chair up on its back legs. "You were doin' so good."

She stopped in mid-bite, her throat closing around the lump of stew. Gary looked at her with a grimace of sympathy. The ache swelled in her chest until she thought it would burst. She shook her head, got up from the table, and hurried outside before she disgraced herself by bursting into tears or vomiting. Why this empty hardness wouldn't fade away, she didn't know. She had tried to ignore it, but it surfaced at all the wrong times. Finally able to swallow, she leaned against the pump jack and gulped big draughts of cool, fresh air.

The screen door squeaked behind her and Gary put a gentle hand on her shoulder. "Sorry. Ben just plumb forgot about Marie. That was a terrible thing, what happened."

"Yeah. It was." Nettie searched her heart for the words. "And I just can't—"

Gary nodded. "I know."

Next to Joe and Jake, her closest bond of kinship was with Gary. Although only sixteen, he seemed to possess a quiet understanding of the depths of her soul.

They stood for awhile watching the shadows shift as the afternoon waned. "When you're ready, come back in. I think we might persuade your papa to get his fiddle out."

"I'm okay. I'll be right in. Gosh, we should've brought Neil's violin." Nettie smiled and reached out to squeeze his forearm. But would she ever feel normal again?

CHAPTER TWENTY-FIVE

Sunday, June 16, 1935

Living in our tent again this summer. Grass good. Horses fat. Jake working a green string to sell for saddle horses or rodeo stock. Neil and I help when we can.

Nettie leaned against a fence post and watched Jake working with an unbroken young horse. He had the dun gelding snubbed up against a post and slowly approached with a saddle blanket. Gently, he placed his hand on the horse's quivering withers and stroked its back, then offered it the blanket to smell. The horse blew through flared nostrils and rolled its eyes back toward his tormentor.

Jake rubbed the blanket back over its neck and shoulders, then settled it on the dun's back. The gelding pulled back against the rope, twisted, and kicked. The saddle blanket fell to the ground, and Jake repeated the process until the horse finally accepted the blanket. Getting him used to a saddle would be next.

When he was finished, he unfastened the rope. The horse bucked and snorted off to the far edge of the small pasture pen.

"I'll think he'll eventually make a good saddle horse." Jake coiled the rope as he walked toward Nettie.

"Nice work, as always." She smiled at him, admiring his strong, yet so gentle ways. Her love for him rose up like water from a newly dug well. She reached out to squeeze his forearm.

He bent forward and planted a quick kiss on her cheek. "You know what? I think we can afford to put on a rodeo this summer. It's time."

The fountain of her emotion trickled to an abrupt stop. Nettie gazed past him at the horse enjoying its newfound freedom. She knew the subject had to come up again, just wasn't expecting it right this minute. Almost two years since Marie had been killed, and yet every time Nettie thought of it, she could see the sequence of events as plainly as if they had just happened. She had to get past this. Rodeo had been such a big part of their life for so long. If she were going to overcome this mind-numbing fear, she'd just have to bite the bullet and ride again. It's like Papa had always told her, "When the horse throws you, you gotta get right back up on him."

She turned her head to look at Jake. He was peering into her face with a quizzical look. "What d'ya think, little gal? Are you game?"

"I don't know." She pursed her lips.

"You need to get over your fear." His eyebrows rose.

Nettie gulped. "I think I can help you get ready all right, but I don't know if I can ride."

"That's okay. You don't have to ride. Nobody's pushin' you."

Relief flooded her and she hugged him hard.

—◦—

The weeks that followed were like ever-moving dust devils. Jake contacted suppliers and picked out rodeo stock. Nettie rode into town almost daily to run errands and mail letters to cowboys, and Neil helped wherever he was asked.

The excitement slowly built, and she caught herself with thoughts of climbing onto the back of a bony steer or a saddle bronc. Her past triumphs and the cheers of the crowds played across her thoughts like a moving picture. How alive she had felt then. What promise the future held. Marie's advice kept playing across her thoughts. "You gotta live for the day. Just do your best."

Nettie drew in a deep breath. *I haven't been living.* This would be just a small community rodeo. It surely wouldn't hurt if she rode one steer. In time, her initial shudders of fear became little thrills of anticipation.

One evening as Nettie poured Jake his cup of after-supper coffee she blurted it out. "I'm going to ride."

He looked up from his jumble of letters, notes, and scribbles, his eyebrows arched. "You are?" Then he broke into his twinkling grin. "That's great, little gal. I'm glad."

She smiled back at him. There, she'd done it. She'd made the commitment.

When the day came, she awoke with the first pastel rays of the July morning sun slanting in through the tent flaps. She stretched dreamily, her eyes still half-closed. What a lovely morning this looked to be. Maybe she'd take a long, leisurely ride into the hills. Then a sharp pang of adrenaline surged through her middle.

The rodeo. For a moment she had forgotten all about it. She sat up and shook Jake's shoulder. "Jake. It's time to get up." She threw off the sheet, swung her legs over the side of the cot, and hit the floor running. "Neil! Rise and shine."

The day already held a promise of stifling heat as they arrived at the arena on the outskirts of Sunburst. Jake looked up into the clear sky. "Gonna be a scorcher."

Nettie turned a wooden box on its side to use as a registration table. "Yeah. It'll be good for business, though."

"See ya later." Neil ran off to help push calves into the chutes for roping.

The cowboys lined up, laughing and jostling, to pay their entry fees and list their events. Nettie was so busy dealing with the crowd she had no time to think. The events were going strong when she finally bundled up the receipts and walked to the chutes to get ready for the steer-riding contest.

Familiar smells of sweat, manure, and dust teased her nostrils. The shouts, cheers, and curses that punctuated bawls, snorts, and whinnies were like music to her. There was a rhythm to this life, a steady beat that made sense to her on some primitive level. She really had missed this.

"You're up next." Ben popped his head over the corral. "You ready?"

She ducked her head yes and climbed the fence into the chute where two men eared the steer's head down and a third checked the rigging. She swung one leg over the top pole and hesitated.

"We're ready for ya." The cowboy looked up at her.

Nettie drew a hard, quick breath and steeled her resolve. Just get it over with. She lowered herself onto the steer's back, grasped the rope, and dug in her knees. A picture flashed before her eyes. Marie's bronc and the pickup man's horse colliding, two thousand pounds of muscle and bone coming together at breakneck speed. A cold draft seemed to wash over her. She blinked rapidly to clear her head. No. She was not going to think about that today. But her arms and legs turned into a gelatinous mass. She couldn't get a grip. Her muscles wouldn't respond. Her chest felt like it was bound with leather straps. Her mouth was as dry as sand.

She felt the cowboys looking at her, waiting for her signal to let go. Frozen, she was unable to give the nod.

"You all right, ma'am? Ready to ride?"

Fear pushed forward in sobbing breaths. She panted. "No . . . can't . . . off . . ."

Arms reached down and pulled her off and over the chute. She collapsed on the ground. It was no good. She couldn't ride.

CHAPTER TWENTY-SIX

Sunday, May 10, 1936

Mother's Day. Neil picked me a bouquet of sweet peas. Jake roasted
a nice pheasant for dinner. Afternoon, visited Jake's sister Emma
and husband Roy.

Nettie leaned on the porch railing and gazed out over the green-tinged prairie. She breathed in the sweet air, tinged with the acrid aroma of the cigarettes Jake and Roy rolled and lit up beside her.

Roy took a deep drag and blew a smoke ring into the cool evening air. "The Jeffrey place here next to us is up for lease, if you're interested."

"It is?" Nettie hardly dared feel hopeful. Maybe they could finally quit moving every few months, quit living in town in winter. "Of course we're interested." She looked at Jake.

He grinned back at her. "Sounds good."

"Well, there is a catch," Roy said. "The current tenants won't be movin' outta the house till fall."

Nettie sighed. "We still have our tent."

Roy threw down his cigarette butt and ground it out with his boot. "Ya know what? Down yonder, I got an empty granary. You could camp out in there for the summer, let the horses graze on the Jeffrey place since there ain't no stock there. Then you'd be all ready to move into the house come fall."

Nettie wrinkled her nose. A granary. What next? For years they'd lived in tents, old shacks, hotel rooms. She'd made do, did the best she could to make a home. Now a granary.

Jake scuffed his boot on the wood floor. "That might work just dandy. But gosh, I been draggin' my poor wife around the country for so long." He turned to her. "Honey, I know you'd like to settle into a place. Could you put up with campin' out a little while longer?"

She pursed her lips. It was almost as if Jake knew what she was thinking. Here she'd been all ready to feel sorry for herself. He understood. And they would have a real house in the fall. She shouldn't be so selfish. Besides, there was no other alternative. They'd be camping somewhere anyway. Might as well be in a granary. At least it was a roof over their heads.

She grinned. "Sounds like a deal. I want to do this."

The next morning they loaded their meager belongings into a four-wheel trailer and the old Plymouth pickup Jake had bought with money he'd made working the oil fields.

Neil tossed one last bedroll into the pickup. "Who's gonna drive? Can I?"

"You don't know how. This is no time to learn." Nettie looked at Jake. She hadn't thought about this part. "Jake?"

"Naw, I'm gonna ride behind the herd. Neil, you come with me. Honey, you've driven before. Go ahead and lead us."

Nettie's shoulders slumped. "I'd much rather ride too. Couldn't we get Roy?"

Jake shook his head. "He had to go to town today." He winked at her. "You can do it. It ain't gonna buck you off."

Neil guffawed, his adolescent voice breaking.

Nettie shot him a killer look and crawled in behind the steering wheel. She started the engine, pressed one foot onto the gas pedal, and let up on the clutch. The pickup bucked and snorted like a bronc, then died.

"Dad-burned machinery." She never would get the hang of this driving business. Give her a good horse any day. "I don't see why Jake couldn't drive this thing," she grumbled out loud. "Neil and I could've trailed the horses behind."

She ground the starter again. This time the process went a little smoother. Towing the trailer slowly over sage-crowned hills and through still-muddy gullies, Nettie led the horse procession the fifteen miles to their new home. Accustomed to being fed hay from it during the winter, the herd readily followed the pickup. But she had to stop often to let them catch up, and sat fuming along with the vehicle's sickening exhaust.

Nettie drummed on the doorframe with her fingertips. Jake really should have found someone else to drive and let her ride. This was just plain silly. In his excitement over owning this pickup, Jake seemed to have forgotten the tried and true method of trailing horses. She shifted into gear and jounced forward once again.

The sun sat atop the crest of the spring-greened hills when she drove up to the weathered, wood-frame granary, only a little bigger than their two-roomed shacks. This might not be so bad. Nettie rolled her neck and shrugged her shoulders to ease the tension that driving for hours had caused. "Boy, I never thought I'd be so glad to see an old granary."

She opened her door and stepped out, stretching her legs and arms. She'd never been this stiff from riding horses all day.

Nettie walked toward the front of the building and stopped short as a horrible stench assailed her. Right in front of the door lay a dead horse. She swallowed rising bile. Oh, great. *Welcome to our new home.* She pressed her lips together, turned on the heel of one boot, and stalked back to the pickup. The perfect ending to a miserable day.

When Jake and Neil arrived, Nettie pointed toward the door. "Take a look at that."

Neil rushed ahead. Then he held his nose and made gagging sounds. "Phew. Pa, come 'ere, look't this."

Jake looked at the dead horse and grimaced. "Musta been winter-killed." He unhooked the trailer, then fastened a rope around the carcass's flanks, tied the other end to the truck bumper, and drove away with Neil to dump it in a coulee.

Nettie spread lye over the spot to kill the smell, the teeming maggots, and other insects left behind. Grabbing a broom from the trailer, she marched into the granary to conquer the dust. The tent was looking better all the time.

When the guys returned from disposing of the dead horse, Neil was still talking about the smell. "And you shoulda seen all the flies, Ma."

"I saw them here." She wrinkled her nose. "C'mon, help your pa and me get the trailer unloaded." They dragged in the kitchen range and their table and chairs, and then set up their beds.

She lit a lantern. "Sure dark in here, even in the daytime, isn't it?"

Jake grabbed a saw. "Where would you like a window?"

"How about over the table?" She pointed, then watched, bemused, as he cut a hole in the wall. "Will Roy mind?"

He shook his head. "Naw."

After unloading, he removed the three-foot-high cargo box from the trailer, turned it on its side, and installed roosts for the crate of Barred Rock chickens they'd gotten from Nettie's folks. Then he covered the open side with canvas. Jake stood back to survey his handiwork. "Now we'll have plenty of eggs."

Late that evening, Nettie fixed a small supper of bread, butter, and jam, then they all fell wearily into bed. Despite a diligent scrubbing, their "house" still smelled of musty old grain and mouse nests. She stared into the darkness. This was the pattern of her life. Pack up, move, clean, unpack, try to make the best out of the situation until they did it all over again a few months or a few weeks later. At first it had been a fun, outdoor adventurous life, but now she was getting tired of it.

Oh, the dreams she'd had as a young woman. The glamour, the money, the trip to London. It was all just a faded snapshot in her mind. Heck, she'd realized a long time ago it was just pipe smoke. Or had she? She always thought that someday she'd still be able to become a rodeo cowgirl. Now thirty years old, she knew better, but she'd hung on to the hope of that dream. Until Marie was killed.

She squirmed to find a comfortable position, and heard Jake's voice echo in her mind. "The drought can't last forever. We just gotta hang on," or "Just a couple more months working the oil fields, honey, and we'll have enough," or "There's a place up for lease we might be able to get into."

She plumped up her pillow and turned on her side. Despite the possibility of this Jeffrey place now, it seemed they were still grasping for wisps of smoke. No money in horses anymore. Slowly being replaced by the steam engine, the tractor, the automobile. Even Jake had given in. Trailing the horses behind a pickup, indeed. She snorted.

What use were dreams, anyway? She hadn't had to raise seven kids, but in some ways her life had no more meaning than her mother's. Mama had been plucked from a comfortable life in a city and stuck out in the middle of nowhere on a homestead. Drudgery. That's how she always saw her mother's existence. Nettie'd wanted better for herself. But this pattern of hers and Jake's, always moving, was just another form of drudgery.

The first gray light of dawn seeped through the lone window before she drifted off to sleep.

The next day, while Jake dug a pit for the outhouse, Nettie threw several colorful rag rugs on the rough wood floor and framed the window with bright checked gingham curtains made from flour sacks. The spring sunshine danced through the opening and highlighted these homey touches. She surveyed her handiwork with a satisfied smile. Things did look brighter in the light of day. This was not the dream she was looking for, but still it was another adventure with her husband and son. Might as well enjoy it. Who knew where this one might lead them? Dreams always came in different forms anyway.

She went outside to watch Jake and Neil set four posts at the corners of the hole and hang canvas around the outside. Jake gestured.

"It's got no roof or door, but it'll work. We'll just have to hurry if it rains."

Nettie laughed with him. "I don't suppose the chickens will peek in on us."

⸺ ❧ ⸺

One morning in late August, Neil dug out his books. "Where am I going to school this year?"

Nettie folded her napkin. "Gosh, I guess we've been so busy getting settled in, I hadn't even thought about it. Why don't we just have school here?"

"Aw, Ma. I want to go where there's kids." Neil scrunched his face into a frown.

"I guess it'll have to be Sunburst. Nothin' closer." Jake's words rippled through Nettie like a shock wave.

She looked at Jake across the breakfast table. "It's an eight-mile trip into town."

"Yeah. We're not likely to be able to make that every day in the winter." He stroked his chin and thought a moment. "What about those Johannsens, where we got your flat saddle? They take in boarders, don't they?"

"That'd be spiffy! Can I, Ma, please?" Neil bounced in his chair.

"Board him out?" Nettie's heart lurched. "No, honey. That's too far away." Sure, he'd be turning twelve in November, but she'd never been apart from him. He was her buddy.

Nettie closed her eyes. Already she felt the pain of loss. It was going to be too easy for her son to separate himself from her. She wasn't sure she was ready for this.

Then she remembered when she'd first met Myra. They'd both been pregnant and had taken an instant liking to each other. "That's right. They do have a boy about your age, honey, and another one a couple years older. They are nice people."

Neil stood. "Can we go to town and see them?"

Nettie looked at Jake, silently beseeching him for help. "I'm sorry. I just don't think I'm ready for this."

He reached over and took her hand. "I know, little gal. But you're always saying how important his education is. And it's only eight miles. He'll be coming home on weekends."

"Yeah, Ma. I won't be moving to Timbuktu."

Despite the feeling that her son was being wrenched from her soul, Nettie chuckled. "I suppose you're right, both of you." His education was important. He did need a good foundation for a better future.

And so in September, with great trepidation and a growing emptiness, Nettie rode in the pickup with Jake and Neil to move her son into the Johannsen household. She kept looking at him next to her, so tall and slender. Will he get enough to eat? What if he doesn't like what she cooks? She reached over to squeeze his arm and he grinned back at her. *I hope he gets along okay with the kids.*

While Jake and Cleve Johannsen wandered off to the shop to talk, Myra introduced Neil to four blond children lined up like stair steps. "This here's Virginia, the oldest, Russ your Ma's met, Jay is your age, and Margie's the youngest."

The kids greeted Neil and Nettie politely, and Jay stepped forward. "C'mon, I'll show you our room."

Myra turned to Nettie with a broad, warm smile as she served tea. "Don't worry. We'll take good care of him."

Nettie relaxed into her chair. "Looks like he's in good hands."

❧

Nettie barely had time to feel the full impact of her inner emptiness when Jake came home with the news that they could move to the Jeffrey farm.

"Hey, it's got a windmill. And a granary we don't have to live in. Even a chicken coop." He chortled with delight.

"Well, I'm just glad we don't have to live in the chicken coop." Nettie jumped up and started packing kitchen utensils. "An actual house with three rooms. And real windows. Won't Neil be surprised when he comes home next weekend?" Hope soared like an eagle through the sky. *This will be the one.*

One evening after they'd moved in, they sat at the table, listening to the radio and enjoying an after-supper cup of tea. Nettie hemmed curtains for the bedroom, and Jake scribbled figures on the back of an envelope. He stopped and cleared his throat. "What would you think of buying a few head of cows, now that we have a place to put 'em?"

Nettie looked up from her sewing, surprised. "Well, that might be a good idea, since draft horses aren't so much in demand any more. But, can we afford to?"

"Yeah, I think so. We still got some money saved from my dirt work. I was talkin' to a feller in town the other day who has some for sale." He chuckled. "I asked him how much he wanted and he says to me, 'Well, I'd sure hate to take less than fifteen dollars a pair.' So, I figure a dozen cow-calf pairs in the spring or pregnant cows now would give us a pretty good start on a herd."

Nettie raised her eyebrows. "That's a good price, isn't it?"

"I'd say so. Market report on the radio says cattle are goin' for about forty-nine cents a pound right now." Jake made a few more notations. "Say a cow weighs on the light side, maybe six hundred pounds, that's close to thirty dollars." He showed Nettie the envelope.

She bent her head close to his to look at his figures. "So we'd be getting a cow *and* a calf for half that." Excitement ricocheted around in her chest.

A huge grin lit up his face. "That's right. And if they weigh more than that, we're even better off. We've had enough rain the last year or two, it looks like the drought might be over. I'm thinkin' it's a good time to get into cattle."

"Then let's do it."

"And, not only that." He waved the envelope in the air. "We got three hundred sixty acres in farmland here. We can put part of it into wheat, and I want to try raising some rye too. I wonder if Neil will like farming." He jumped up from his chair and grabbed Nettie to twirl her around the kitchen. "Hey, little gal. We're on our way."

Caught up in Jake's dance, Nettie's face flushed with anticipation. Land. Cattle. Farming. If they could lease this place a few years, get a good start on a herd, make a little money on grain, maybe they could buy it. "This is our dream, honey. It's happening!"

Nettie looked forward to Fridays with great anticipation since Neil had gone to school. During the week, she kept busy enough feeding the horses and helping Jake fix up the fences and barn that she didn't have time to miss her son. When she did, the weekly trip to town gave her something to focus on.

But one Friday morning in late November, they awoke to howling wind. The view from the window was nothing but a swirling mass of white.

"Early this year." Jake stared out through a space he'd scratched on the frosted pane and smoked a cigarette. "I don't see that we'll able to go into town to pick up Neil this week."

"Please don't say that. Surely it'll let up in time." Nettie peered out the window, knowing even as she protested that it wasn't to be.

She sank back onto the bed in disappointment. Now they were housebound. She'd have to wait at least another week to see Neil, if not more. An empty spot loomed where her son should be.

The storm continued for the next two days, the cold finding its way through the thin walls. "We'll have to put more sawdust in the walls next summer," Jake remarked.

Nettie found a bag of rags and stuffed the cracks the best she could.

During the day she kept busy feeding the cook stove with coal. She was warm only if she stood within three feet of the range. Before they crawled between feather ticks at night, she emptied the teakettle so it wouldn't freeze solid.

In the morning Jake grumbled and cursed as he threw off his covers and groped for his cold, stiff boots. "Dadgummed fire's out. You stay here till I get it going."

Nettie burrowed deeper into the bed. Then the clattering sound when he shook the coals down in the stove woke her fully. She waited until she heard the fire crackling before she slipped out of the warm bed and shivered into extra layers of wool socks and sweaters.

This was going to be a long winter. But at least they were out of that granary.

On Friday morning, the third week of being housebound, the day dawned clear and bright. Jake came back into the house with a couple of rocks the size of bread loaves and put them on top of the stove. "Well, little gal, I've had about enough of your long face. I'm gonna check the sleigh and hitch up the team. We're goin' to town today."

Nettie looked up from the dishpan. "Really?" Her heart skipped a beat. "Oh, that'd be dandy." Suddenly it felt like a corral gate had opened. She would get to see Neil, maybe even bring him home for a few days. She shook soapsuds from her hands, dried them quickly on her pants, and threw her arms around Jake's neck.

"Yeah, I figure we need some groceries anyway, and I gotta go see about getting some more hay for the cows." He grinned at her. "Oh, yeah, and we can probably stop by and get Neil too." He ducked, laughing, as Nettie swatted at him. "Hurry up and get ready now."

Jake wrapped the hot rocks in gunnysacks and placed them on the floor of the sled to warm their feet. He tucked woolen blankets around Nettie, climbed in beside her, and gave the reins a snap. The sled runners squeaked over the snow as the Percherons trotted forward. Jake chuckled. "Good thing for these horses. They don't let a little snow stop them."

"Yeah. Not like those newfangled driving machines," Nettie teased.

Despite the brilliant sun that sparkled on the snow, the air frosted the insides of her nostrils. She pulled her knitted scarf up over her mouth and nose, leaving only her eyes exposed. Warm and cozy in her nest, she couldn't help but giggle with anticipation like a schoolgirl.

The sleigh skimmed through the white-blanketed emptiness. "You can't even see the sagebrush," Jake remarked.

"It's so quiet, almost like we're the last people on earth." The only things Nettie could hear were the horses' snorts and the crunch of snow as they traveled through rippled snowdrifts. By midafternoon the eight miles of white unrecognizable landscape gave way to the sight of oil tanks and derricks along the Sunburst skyline. The sleigh glided through the snow-covered streets, arriving at the Johannsen house the same time as the kids came home from school. The boys pelted each other with snowballs and wrestled in the drifts.

Neil looked up from the scuffle. "Hey. It's Ma and Pa." He ran toward them, and before the team came to a complete stop, Nettie burrowed out of the blankets and jumped off the sled.

She threw her arms around him. Oh, that felt so good. She gave him an extra-firm squeeze, then held him at arm's length, startled to look him straight in the eyes. "I think you've grown a foot since I saw you last. You look thinner. Are you getting enough to eat?"

Neil gave an embarrassed laugh and kicked one toe against the other boot.

Nettie swallowed. Maybe he was happier here than at home with her.

Jake cuffed him playfully on the shoulder. "Hey, pardner, wanna come home for a coupla days?"

This became the pattern for their winter. When the seemingly unending blizzards broke, they bundled up and went into town to see Neil and pick up supplies. The only hay Jake found contained mostly Russian thistle, a prickly weed with little nutrition.

"A poor excuse for hay, but it gives 'em something to chew on, I guess," he grumbled.

Before the first snow, he had built a cow shed with a flat roof made from chicken wire and covered with a layer of straw. As the winter went on, with ever more snow and wind, drifts built up against the shed like hillocks of granite. One morning when Nettie came out to help with chores she found that the cows had walked up the drifts to nibble at the straw. Jake was on the roof, fastening posts at the corners and stringing barbed wire to keep them off.

A sinking sensation came upon her as a picture of the drought years flashed into her mind. Then, it had been too little moisture and no feed. Now it was too much snow and yet again, no feed. She saw another dream becoming a nightmare. There was no middle ground for ranchers. She pressed her lips together and went to the chicken coop to deliver a pail of warm water and scraps to the hens.

CHAPTER TWENTY-SEVEN

Sunday, March 7, 1937

Long, dad-burned winter. When will it end?

Nettie was sure spring would never come and they would be doomed to endure this version of twenty-degrees-below-zero hell forever. How long could they continue feeding the cows? Jake was doling out bits of the last little pile of thorny hay.

As Nettie trudged along icy paths worn through the drifts, the wind shifted to the west. The needle-like sharpness of the air that usually froze the tears in her eyes felt softer. She picked up a bucket to get water for the chickens and suddenly she was too warm in her many layers of clothing. As she took off her heavy sheepskin coat, Jake came around the corner of the shed.

He whipped the fur-lined, ear-lapped cap from his head and tossed it into the air. "It's a Chinook."

By late afternoon the warm wind had raised the temperature to fifty degrees. The snowcap melted from the roof of the house, icicles dripped from the eaves, and streamlets of water followed the ruts of their path between house and barn. Nettie stopped to listen to the musical sound of running water everywhere, and tension flowed out of her limbs. A smile formed on her lips, slowly at first, as if her face had long been frozen and might crack with the effort.

She whooped and ran through the watery slush to the shed, where the cows stood blinking in the pen. "Winter's over, girls. We're not going to freeze solid after all."

Jake stood in his shirtsleeves, shoveled wet manure from the shed, and laughed along with her. Nettie knew this was only a short reprieve. Old Man Winter could still dump more snow and cold on them before spring really came. But now she was sure they could make it through the next storm, whatever it might bring.

April brought the inevitable spring blizzard during calving. Nettie had newborns nestled in gunnysack nests around the kitchen stove. She rubbed their stiff, cold limbs with a warm vinegar and water solution and fed them from a bottle of their mothers' milk until they were strong enough to get up and try to walk on the slippery wood floor. Then, one by one, Jake took them back out to the shed where their mamas mooed concerned little bleats and allowed them to suck milk-swollen teats.

May brought warmed earth and green shoots. Nettie looked every day for the next wildflower—the pale pink gumbo lily, the sunny sweet pea—to poke its head above the moist soil. Jake took on the role of farmer, tilling the fields and planting wheat and rye. He listened to crop reports on the radio, and sat up late at night figuring bushels per acre and cents per bushel.

"If that price holds, and we get some rain in June, how many bushels . . . ?" He chewed on his pencil and scratched his head.

Nettie watched, bemused, not quite understanding this new farmer side of her husband. He seemed to be settling in, and a warm contentment filled her formerly winter-frozen bones. Their new dream seemed closer to being real.

But one morning as summer approached, Jake started talking rodeos again and scribbling a different set of figures. "Honey, if we both ride the Montana circuit this summer, we'd probably win enough to put on a rodeo of our own toward fall."

The old ache rose up in Nettie, along with the specter of her failure. That picture of Marie's fatal spill would never go away. She could help him produce the rodeos, and she wouldn't stop him from going to them, but she just could not rekindle her desire to ride.

She gave an exasperated huff. "Oh, Jake. Why can't you just give up that pipe dream? We've got something else to work now, with our cows and our farming." She plunged her hands into the dishwater and scrubbed hard at an already-clean pot.

"But this has been your dream all these years too."

"Just a fantasy. A waste of effort."

"Now, little gal. That's just not true." Jake's forehead creased.

"Yes, it is. I used to imagine myself as the new Prairie Rose Henderson or Lucille Mulhall." Nettie rinsed the pot and put it in the dish drainer. "But reality is so different. Every time we get up on the back of a steer or a bronc, we risk life and limbs. And for what?"

Jake stared at her with a puzzled look on his weathered face.

"You know it's true. We've never made much money and I haven't achieved even a fraction of the recognition that Marie, the Greenough sisters, or Fannie Sperry Steele have."

"I thought we did it because we loved it." Jake chewed on the end of his pencil.

"Yeah, but we have to look at the practical side." Nettie forced her voice to stay calm, as if teaching a child how to approach a new colt. "We're getting a little old for this hard life. We have a son who is growing up to face a different world. And rodeo is changing."

Heck, so was she. After all those hopes of traveling the circuit, here she was, wanting to settle down, stop moving around so much. Fifteen years ago, she never would have thought this way.

Jake stood and gazed out the window. "I don't want our world to change. We have to fight to hang on to it."

Nettie threw her hands up. "And what is it worth? Rodeo isn't all glamour and money, even for the stars. They're always on the road, away from their families, with the possibility of getting badly hurt." She thought of Marie's crumpled body lying in the arena and swallowed a lump in her throat. "Or killed."

She walked to the window beside him. "And they don't always get paid."

"Yeah, I know. The 'bloomers' are ruining the reputation of guys like us when they run off with the entry fees and gate receipts." Jake turned to her. "I'm not like that."

She brushed at imaginary lint on his sleeve. "I know you are as honest as the day is long, honey, but sometimes you hardly take in enough money for a pay-off anymore."

Jake took out his tobacco and papers. "But we have to hang on, convince riders that rodeo isn't just a big con."

"Pffft." Nettie blew out an exasperated huff. "Even the Rodeo Association of America, with all its reorganization and rules, hasn't been able to do that." She rolled her eyes. "And now their 'sanctioned events' don't even include women riders."

Jake blew smoke from between his teeth and shrugged. "If you're givin' up on me, I dunno, little gal."

"I'm not giving up on you, honey." She reached out and brushed a sandy lock off his forehead, noticing a couple of grey hairs. "I guess I'm turning into my mother, looking at the practical side of life."

Jake nodded. "Yeah, I guess." He sat down with his pencil and papers again. "But I'd still like to figure out a way to put on at least one more rodeo before we hang up our spurs."

Nettie's breath caught in her chest like a bubble. "Yeah, if you do one more, then you'll want to do another and then another. I just want it to stop."

Jake didn't reply, just went back to his scribbling.

She finished the breakfast dishes and swept the kitchen with strong, broad strokes, as if she could discard her jumbled thoughts and memories along with the dust.

Overcome by a sudden urge to be a little girl again and feel her mother's comforting arms around her, Nettie threw the broom in the corner and headed for the door. "I'm going to ride over and visit the folks."

Jake looked up, eyebrows arched. "Why don't you take the pick—"

Before he could finish, she let the door slam behind her. No way was she going to drive that exhaust-belching, gear-bucking mechanical monster today. Besides, she could think so much better on the back of a horse. She saddled Tootsie and urged her forward.

So many thoughts raged through her mind that Nettie barely noticed the prairie flowers. "Bloomers," strikes, rules against women riders. What was the future of rodeo? Certainly not the way she and Jake had known it. One more rodeo, and he could get hurt. Then what?

Tootsie shied at a sage hen's sudden flurry in the brush. Nettie had her hands full for a few seconds, as the mare crowhopped and side-stepped. "Feeling skittish today?" She reached down and patted her horse's shoulder. "How about we run?"

She kicked Tootsie into a gallop. The wind loosened the hairpins that held her hair back and soon it was flying free. Nettie gave in to the wild abandon of the gallop, enjoying each powerful stride as her mare raced across the prairie.

"Yeehaw!" Nettie yelled, and reined Tootsie in to a walk. "Feeling better, girl?"

Yes, this was freedom. Riding with the wind over your own pasture whenever you wanted to. Just a woman and her horse.

Not being tied to a schedule. Not traveling for miles and miles to make it on time to some rodeo where you might not win or you might not get paid if you did. But rodeo did get in your blood, just like riding itself. She understood why Jake wanted to continue. Some people *had* to do it, like they had to breathe. She'd been that way. Once.

But rodeo was changing. Those cowgirls who had competed right up there with the men all these years must feel very frustrated by these changes.

Nettie shifted her weight in the saddle. About the only events available now were relay races and trick riding, and even that was more of an exhibition event rather than a contest. The Greenough sisters and many others were now in Hollywood, doing stunt work for the movies. It looked to Nettie like competition rodeo was on the road to extinction, at least for women.

The whole world seemed to have come around to Mama's way of thinking, that ladies just shouldn't be taking part in such a "dangerous" sport, that it was detrimental to their reproductive systems. How could that be? Women weren't fragile creatures. Nettie squared her shoulders. *We've already proved that.* Men got injured or killed, too.

❦

Papa stepped out of the barn as Nettie rode in. "Howdy, daughter."

She dismounted and gave him a hug. "Hi, Papa. Good to see you."

He took Tootsie's reins. "Your mama's inside."

Nettie stepped onto the porch of her childhood home. The door swung open. Mama took one look at Nettie's face and gave her a warm hug. "Come in, daughter dear. So good to see you. Let me make you a nice cup of tea."

"I know it's been too long since my last visit." Nettie sat at the familiar kitchen table, her hands tracing the scratches and stains from the spills and mischief of little boys growing up. And little girls too. She had taken a knife to the surface once herself to carve her name next to Joe's. She felt the ridges of the partial "N," all she'd been able to accomplish before Mama caught her and slapped her hands. Nothing accomplished. Was this to be her only legacy?

Her mother prepared tea and poured it into Grandmother's delicate china cups that she'd always saved for special occasions. As she worked, she sang snatches of a familiar tune from Nettie's childhood: " . . . You tell me your dream, I'll tell you mine. . . ."

Tears stung Nettie's eyes. "Mama, did you ever feel like you gave up your dreams to move here and homestead?"

Her mother sat down and gazed thoughtfully across the table. "Well, my dear, I'm sure that every young girl has lofty ideals. It's all a part of growing up. At one point I thought I would study music and become a famous singer or pianist." She sipped her tea. "But I soon realized that my parents didn't have the kind of money it would take. They were barely able to afford a few piano lessons for me."

Realization flooded Nettie like a ray of sunshine. So music was Mama's dream. All those years Nettie had been forced to practice piano when she was a child, it had never occurred to her that it was Mama's passion. She studied her mother's lined face and gray-streaked hair. This woman she'd always thought was so beaten down by life, too much work, and too many children had visions of fame and fortune too.

Mama swirled the tea in her cup. "Then I met your papa, and love, happiness, and children became my desire. He had some good jobs over the years and after you kids came along, we lived pretty comfortably."

She looked past Nettie with a faraway gaze. "Sure, I thought we would build a bigger, more modern house and become one of the well-to-do families in Coeur d'Alene. But his hunger was for the land. Because I love him, and he is the other half of my whole, that became my ambition, too."

"But didn't you ever feel defeated by not having your big dreams, your love for music, come true?"

Mama smiled in a serene way. "No, I really haven't. I think it's because I've simply been able to change it. Not give up on dreaming, but just allow another one to take the place of the one that was not to be."

She reached out to put her hand on Nettie's arm. "Do you feel defeated because you weren't able to rodeo professionally?"

Nettie sat up straight, blinking. She'd never thought Mama had any understanding of her dream. Her eyes filled, and she was only able to nod.

"And then your dear friend was killed, and that probably dashed what was left of the dream."

Nettie's throat thickened. "Yeah. I can't seem to get past Marie's death. Don't even feel the desire anymore. Jake keeps talking about producing another rodeo and riding the circuit this summer. And now

Neil wants to compete." She gave a wry smile. "I never thought I'd hear myself say this, but I actually understand why you were so against me riding steers when I was young. I can feel the danger now, the fear."

Mama chuckled. "Oh, I knew you'd understand, once you had a child of your own. Nothing is ever the same after that."

Wasn't that the truth? Especially for Mama, after losing one. Nettie sobered. "How did you ever get over—?" She stopped, unable to continue.

"Essie's death?" Mama's face sank a little. The lines around her mouth and eyes became more pronounced. "You never really get over something like that. But you eventually come to the conclusion that you have to go on, that you can't bury yourself with that loved one. I had you other children. There's still life to be lived, still dreams to dream."

Marie's words echoed in Nettie's head. *Just follow your dream, and do your best.* She rose from her chair and bent forward to wrap her arms around her mother. A new clarity seemed to shine, cutting through the fog in her brain.

Mama and Marie were so right. Instead of clinging to her hurts like a child, she would look forward to new dreams. She smiled. *I'm going to do something about those association rules, help other young women realize their dreams.*

CHAPTER TWENTY-EIGHT

Sunday, August 8, 1937

Jake's putting on another rodeo next Sunday. Couldn't talk him out of it. Helping him get ready. In debt up to our ears, but crops looking good. He has his own dreams.

Dust swirled, muddying the blue of the clear, hot sky. Cattle bawled and horses whinnied, creating a pleasant cacophony in Nettie's ears. She sat at the registration table by the entrance gate and surveyed the nearly empty stands. They'd had enough cowboys enter the rodeo events, but for some reason, the crowd hadn't shown up to watch. Nettie sighed. People just didn't seem to have the money or the interest in attending rodeos they'd had before the Depression.

Neil helped her count out the paltry gate receipts one more time, just to make sure some dollar bills hadn't stuck together. Nettie puckered her face in a frown. This looked like their own small version of the infamous Dempsey-Gibbons boxing match that had bankrupted Shelby in 1923.

Jake strode up and watched her count. "How bad is it?"

She shook her head ever so slowly. "We don't have near enough to cover the arena charge and the stock fees."

Jake pulled the Bull Durham sack from his pocket, rolled a cigarette, and lit it. He took a long drag and blew the smoke out between clenched teeth. "Well, we gotta pay that first. Riley'll be here any minute to collect. So I guess we'll have to take it out of the entrance money."

"But then the riders won't get paid. Not very much, anyway." Nettie chewed her lip. This was just what they'd always tried to avoid. But they had no extra money set aside to make up the difference.

Jake threw his cigarette down and ground it into the dust with his boot heel. "Them's the breaks, I guess." He turned and walked away.

"Pa's upset, isn't he?" Neil stared at his father's retreat with a twelve-year-old's childish, yet wise understanding.

White-hot needles pierced Nettie's chest. "I'm afraid he is. The riders are going to be unhappy with him."

Neil reached for his saddlebag. "He can have the quarters I been saving."

Nettie's heart filled with love for her son. "Oh, honey. That is so generous of you." She walked over and put an arm around his shoulders. "But you keep your money. It'll be all right."

"Well, if you change your mind, you know where I live." With a grin, Neil mounted his horse. "Guess I'll ride over to Johannsens."

Nettie waved after him, pride enveloping her. What a fine young man.

After the last event, the few people in the audience left, and the cowboys gathered around the judges' stand. Nettie heard Jake on the bullhorn and she walked closer to watch.

"Folks, bear with us. We had a pretty low gate today, and because of the expenses of putting on this rodeo, our purses are purty dad-gummed small. My apologies to each of you, and I thank you for participating. We'll make it up to you at the next one."

A murmur buzzed from the group. As Jake gave a few dollars to the top-ranked winners and apologies to the others, men filed past Nettie, muttering. She ducked back between the chutes so they couldn't see her.

"I didn't come here to bust my danged ass for nothin'." An older cowboy limped by, favoring one leg kicked by a bronc.

Another spat in the dust. "That Moser's nothin' but a bloomer."

A third added, "Good thing I won that bet. I'd be flat broke."

Nettie chewed on her lip. Oh, dear Lord, what had they come to? Being accused of cheating riders out of their winnings. That was the last thing Jake would ever do. But some of these cowboys had been burned before, and they didn't know her husband like she did. Dread settled on her shoulders like a dark, heavy cloud.

After tending to the stock, Jake walked toward her, that telltale slump in his shoulders. She looked down at her dusty, scuffed boots, waiting.

"Well, little gal, this was a bust." He sat down on the registration table and took his tobacco pouch out, but just stared at it.

"These things happen." Nettie tried to make her voice light. It came out weak and quavery. "It's a tough time for rodeo. I'm sure they understand." She hoped he hadn't heard any of their remarks.

He didn't answer for long minutes. He tucked the tobacco pouch back in his shirt pocket and slapped his thigh.

"All right. Enough feelin' sorry for ourselves. It'll work out. The least we can do is go buy them cowpokes a drink. At least I got credit at the bar."

A funereal mood enveloped Nettie along with the smell of stale cigarettes and yeasty beer when they walked though the swinging doors of the Rancher's Bar. She braced herself. This was the last place she wanted to be. She wished they could just go home.

Usually, after a rodeo, the saloon rollicked with laughter and shouts as the cowboys relived the highlights of their rides, embellishing the successes with each telling. Today the crowd was hushed. Men sat hunched over their drinks, and only a few forced laughs punctuated the low murmur.

Jake and Nettie settled on stools at the bar, and Jake summoned the bartender. "A round for the house, on me." He downed his whiskey in one gulp, then turned to the room. "Gents, ladies, I'm very sorry about today's poor purse. I'd like to buy you a drink to make it up to you."

The pitch of the conversation rose a notch. Somebody shouted. "Hear, hear."

"That's the least you can do." Another voice sang out.

A burly cowboy stepped up beside Jake. "It'll take more'n one drink to make up for this." With the speed of a rattlesnake, he drove his fist into Jake's jaw.

"No!" Nettie shouted.

Jake's head rocked back and he fell against the bar. His hand came up instinctively to feel for the damage to his face. Driving his weight forward, Jake ducked under a second punch. His return jab glanced off the cowboy's shoulder. The man spun to the side. He recovered his balance with a roundhouse to Jake's upraised arm.

The room erupted into a mare's nest of shouts and commotion. The crowd surged forward to surround the two men. Nettie scrambled over the top of the bar, her drink flying, to land beside the bartender. She grabbed his arm. "Help. Stop them!"

He merely shrugged.

The two men rolled on the floor. Grunts punctuated slaps. She couldn't tell who was landing punches where. The burly cowboy had Jake down.

No, now Jake rolled on top. He punched the cowboy in the nose. Blood squirted.

The cowboy heaved Jake off and swung a left to Jake's eye. The onlookers shouted encouragement. "Git 'im. Punch his lights out."

Nettie screamed. The din and confusion overwhelmed her with total helplessness. This couldn't be happening. She had to stop this insanity. Where were the other women? Gone. No help from them.

Nettie slipped from behind the bar and out the back door. Her boot heels thundering on the wooden sidewalk, she ran down the street to the sheriff's office and yanked open the door.

"Bar fight. Help!" she yelled and ran back to the saloon. Sheriff Ingram lumbered behind.

Inside, Jake and the cowboy were still rolling around on the floor, and a couple of small fistfights had broken out in the corners of the barroom.

"Stop." The sheriff's thunderous bass carried above the hubbub. The room quieted.

The crowd parted as Sheriff Ingram stepped through, leading with wide bull-like shoulders, a big meaty hand on his gun butt. "Get up."

Jake rose shakily, wiping blood from his mouth with the back of his hand.

The cowboy rose to his hands and knees. Then, with a hand from one of his buddies, he came to his feet, still reeling. Blood ran unchecked from his nose.

"What the hell's goin' on here?" The sheriff stood, glowering, arms akimbo.

Jake stood with his arms outstretched, palms up. "It's all my fault. Didn't have enough to pay my riders."

Her legs barely holding her up, Nettie took inventory. Jake's bloody face to his swollen hands to his legs and back up again, trying to assess how badly hurt he might be. She stumbled through the crowd to her man's side. With shaky hands, she held a handkerchief to his split and swollen lip.

A hot rush of anger sent strength through her body. She stepped forward and shook her finger in the cowboy's face. "You. You lily-livered spawn of a rattlesnake. This is the thanks he gets for buying you a drink?"

Jake put a hand on her shoulder. "Now, honey—"

Shrugging him off, Nettie spat out her words as though they were bullets. "Get out. I don't ever want to see your face again."

The man shrank back against his friends, his bravado deflated. He stared at the floor. As he turned away, Nettie heard him mutter, " . . . get my girlfriend t' beat you up."

Sheriff Ingram soon had the crowd calmed and accompanied Jake and Nettie back to the arena. "Heard what happened with the rodeo today. Sorry. Maybe you better lay low awhile till they get over it."

Jake nodded. "Thanks." His words slurred and one eye was nearly swollen shut now. He slumped onto a bleacher bench.

Sheriff Ingram left, and Nettie eased down beside Jake. Her legs and arms shook and her teeth chattered as if it were twenty below zero. "You need to go see the doc?"

"Naw." He turned and gave her a lopsided grin. "This ain't nothing. You saw the other guy." He winced as she slipped an arm around his waist.

Her heart breaking with his attempt at humor, Nettie leaned against him, trying desperately not to cry.

Jake's cuts and bruises healed, but Nettie sensed a deep inner hurt. In silence, he busied himself getting ready to harvest. Even what appeared to be a bumper crop didn't bring back his usual jovial self.

"Do you think Pa is mad at me?" Neil scuffed his boot on the kitchen floor one evening after supper when Jake had gone back outside. "He hardly talks to me anymore."

An ache constricted Nettie's heart and closed her throat. Oh, the poor kid. He thinks it was his fault. For a moment she couldn't speak. She moved closer to her son and put a hand on his arm. "No, honey. Your pa's not mad at you. He's just very sad right now."

"Because of what happened at the rodeo?" Neil's voice had begun to take on the husky quality of adolescence, with an occasional squeak.

"Yes. Being attacked like that and accused of being a bloomer. Everyone always likes your pa. He prides himself on being extremely honest, and he's never really had any trouble like this before."

Neil pursed his mouth. "I know. I just can't figure those guys out, why they blamed Pa for nobody showing up. That wasn't his fault."

"No. But sometimes people who are having a bad time just need somebody else to take it out on. That's the way of human nature."

"Well, it ain't fair." Neil shrugged and turned to go outside.

Nettie bit her lower lip. No, it certainly wasn't. She desperately wished she could wave a magic wand to put things back to where they were before this disastrous rodeo.

❦

A few days later the threshing crew came with their noisy, smelly steam engines, raised a cloud of dust, and separated grain from chaff. The men ate huge stacks of hotcakes and platters of bacon for breakfast, pots of stew and chili for dinner, and loaves of bread with butter and jam for supper.

Nettie thought sure she'd run out of grub before they were done. Like grasshoppers that munched their way through the countryside, the threshing crew finished the job and most of the food she had stored in the root cellar in just a few days.

Jake borrowed his brother-in-law Roy's two-ton truck. "We got ourselves a good crop first year out." He kissed Nettie's cheek and took off for town with Neil beside him, and for the first time in weeks, a grin on his face.

Seeing him smile, Nettie felt lighter too. Good, now they'd be able to pay off their bills for the seed and equipment they'd bought for planting. They'd be able to make their lease payment, buy feed and supplies for winter, and maybe even set a little aside. Maybe she'd look at a new saddle or a pair of boots. Nettie grabbed a bowl to collect eggs from the chicken coop. She'd make them a nice supper of scrambled eggs tonight, to celebrate.

As the sun lowered itself toward the hills, the big truck drove up. Nettie put slices of bacon in a pan to fry, bread in the oven to toast, and cracked the eggs. The truck doors slammed, and she heard men's boots clomping toward the house.

Neil came in first. "Hi, Ma. Brought you some peppermint sticks."

She grinned at her son. Always her thoughtful boy. "You remembered. Thanks, honey." He grinned, grabbed his book, and went to his room.

Jake came through the door. The grin was gone and his shoulders slumped again. Alarm sizzled through her. Oh, no. Now what? She gazed into his face, lifting her eyebrows in a question.

He sat heavily on the kitchen chair, reached into his pocket and threw a receipt on the table. "Eleven cents a bushel for the wheat. They won't even take the rye."

Her short-lived euphoria evaporated like a rain puddle on a hot day. Even with a yield of thirty bushels an acre, that price had brought them less than a thousand dollars.

"No. All that work." By the time they paid the threshing bill and the lease, there wouldn't be enough to pay off everything else. Let alone have any extra. She slumped into a chair across from him. Every time they thought they were going to be able to get ahead a little ...

Jake left early the next morning to return the truck. Nettie and Neil slogged through their chores, neither saying much. Her heart felt like the large, lichen-covered stone out in the pasture, weighing her whole body down. Things seemed so much simpler when they'd first gotten married, nearly fourteen years ago already. They had their horses, a leased place, and fresh new dreams. Now, they had horses they couldn't sell. A lease they might not be able to pay. A child to board out and educate. And debt. So much for dreams. She ground the heels of her boots into the dust as she strode to the well.

While Neil milked the cow, she watered and fed the chickens. At noon Jake still hadn't returned, so she fixed a sandwich for Neil and herself. Funny, it shouldn't be taking Jake this long to return the truck to Roy's. His place was only a mile away. Well, maybe they were talking. It'd be good for Jake to get his troubles off his chest.

A momentary longing came over her. Who was she supposed to talk to? She missed Marie. Her friend would've understood what they were going through. She couldn't be running off to visit Mama every few days. Jake's sister Emma just didn't seem to share the same ideas.

After they ate, she and Neil rode out together to check the cattle and horses. The animals grazed contentedly, flicking their tails to ward off flies, hardly a care in the world. They were lucky. They didn't have to worry about where their next mouthful came from.

Neil glanced over at her. "It'll be okay, Ma. I can get a job in town."

Tenderness softened her worry. "That's very good of you, honey, but there's no need for that. We've always managed before. We'll have calves to sell this fall." Even though the price per pound wasn't very good yet, she wouldn't tell Neil that.

Her nearly teenaged son touched the brim of his hat. "Okay, Ma." He rode off to check on the rest of the herd.

The languid heat of the September sun beat down on her shoulders. She gazed over the backs of the brown and white cows, across the tan prairie, up to the purplish rims of the Sweet Grass Hills. Breathing in the strong sage-scented air, she released a long sigh. This was their hope, their dream. With God's grace, they would make it work.

Neil rode up beside her. "They're all here. Nothing missing. Everything looks good."

Nettie smiled at her son. "Great. Let's go then. Race you home." She touched her heels to Tootsie's sides. The mare leaped forward into a run. Neil whooped and urged his bay into a gallop just behind. With laughter and shouts, they raced through the dense sage, down into coulees and over slight rises. Wind and energy flowed through her, leaving worries in the dust, and for a few minutes, she was the same age as her son, wild and carefree.

When they rode up to the barn, Roy's truck was parked at the corral and Jake worked some animals in the chute. Nettie heard grunts, thumps, and squeals, punctuated by Jake's shouted curses. She exchanged a puzzled glance with Neil and reined her horse up to the back of the truck.

"Pigs!" Neil dismounted and climbed over the fence to help, but Nettie remained in the saddle, too stunned to react. Her mouth hung open. She searched for words. Pigs. What on earth?

The animals finally trotted into a small pen next to the cattle shed. Jake strode back to where she sat, unmoving, atop Tootsie. He grinned, a little sheepishly, she thought. "Well, little gal, we got ourselves some pigs to eat that rye."

"Jake. Have you gone mad?" She stared at him, unbelieving. Using what little money they had to buy yet more animals to feed? A sharp bitterness passed through her.

"Hey, don't look at me like that." He reached up to help her off her horse. "Got 'em cheap at the auction. Figured we can feed them the rye, and we'll have pork to eat this winter and trade when we need something."

She slid to the ground and loosened Tootsie's cinch, shaking her head. Well, she guessed it did make some sense. At least they wouldn't starve. She forced a little laugh through her nostrils and gazed up at him. "You're something else, Jake Moser. Something else."

❧

Nettie's world settled into its preordained orbit. In September, Neil went back to school and to board with the Johannsens. Winter announced itself early and continued with frequent snowfalls. Jake fed his pigs, the cows, and the horses. He never spoke of the rodeo fiasco again. Nettie had to admit to herself that she felt some measure of relief, although a sense of loss hovered just above her consciousness. Rodeo had been such a huge part of their lives. Almost like that period of time after Esther had died and again after Marie's death, she felt an empty spot in her soul.

Jake decided to butcher a pig a few days before Christmas. Nettie boiled gallons of water to half-fill a barrel, while he bled and gutted the animal. They hoisted the carcass on a tripod of poles to dip into the scalding water just long enough to loosen the bristly hair. Then she helped Jake scrape hair from the hide.

While he cut chops, roasts, and slabs of side pork to cure in salt brine for bacon, Nettie made headcheese. Not much of the animal went to waste. The thick bacon rinds from the scraped hide would later be used to flavor pots of beans, after the rest of the meat was gone. Nettie rendered the fat into lard, and even washed the gut to use for sausage casings.

They hauled their bounty to town on the sled, half for the Johannsens to cover Neil's room and board, the other half to sell for five cents a pound. Even at that low price, they had to make several stops to find enough people who could afford to buy pork.

Neil came home with them for Christmas, and Nettie enjoyed the presence of her son once again for a week. He had turned thirteen in November, and stood a slim five or six inches taller than she. Last time he was home, he'd complained of frequent headaches after school. At first she was afraid he might have the same horrible headaches she had experienced in the mountains of Idaho. She still occasionally got one, forcing her to spend the day lying down in a darkened bedroom.

But, when they took Neil to the doctor, he chuckled. "As studious as he is, he just has bad eyesight. He needs glasses."

He was a handsome lad, with his round wire-rimmed spectacles and black hair slicked back from his forehead. Her throat tightened with pride. He could grow up to be a teacher, a musician, or maybe even a doctor. He was smart enough. No rodeoing for her son. She shook her head decisively.

CHAPTER TWENTY-NINE

Sunday, March 20, 1938

Spring again, finally. Glad to be rid of the snow, even though mud's up to our knees. Cows starting to calve. Jake's been out in the granary, sifting the wheat seed. Going to try farming again.

Nettie turned her face toward the sky, relishing the increased warmth of days that marched toward summer. Combined with warm breezes, the sun dried the fields enough so Jake could get out and plant. Neil came home on weekends to help. While the guys busied themselves with farming, Nettie happily rode and took care of the animal-related chores. This fall it would be two years since they'd moved to this place. It looked like they were settling in.

She urged Tootsie into a gallop, delighted with the freedom of wind flowing through her hair, the powerful muscles of her horse beneath her, and the fresh, clean smells of newborn spring. In these moments, she was fourteen again, sneaking away from housework, caught up in the exhilaration of getting away with something. Of course, being a mother now, she knew that not much had escaped Mama's eagle eye back then, even though Nettie thought she had at the time.

The cows foraged for tender shoots of new green grass, their young calves frolicking nearby. Calves were like works of art, with their shiny reddish-brown coats and white wavy curls etched onto clean, unblemished faces. Curious, they edged closer to her, heads out, nostrils flaring to catch the scent of human and horse. Then, as if propelled by a spring, first one and then the others leaped high, turned tail in mid-jump, and raced each other around the pasture. Nettie laughed out loud. Nothing in the world rivaled the boundless energy and enthusiasm for life that young animals displayed.

Refreshed and renewed, she cantered her horse back to the house to fix the noon meal. Her farmers would be starving by now. The easy, relaxed smile on her face turned to a puzzled frown as she rode up to the corral and saw a dark blue Buick parked in front of the house. She didn't recognize the car. Who was visiting in the middle of the day? Well, it looked like she'd have to cook extra for dinner.

Jake and Neil sat at the kitchen table with a white-haired, stoop-shouldered man. A cane leaned against the table and his hat rested on one knee. Mr. Jeffrey. The owner of their place.

"Hi, honey. Glad you're back." Jake rose and went to the stove for the coffee pot.

Nettie studied her husband's face. No sign of his usual, good-natured grin or joking manner. Must not be a friendly visit. What could be wrong now?

Jake grabbed a clean cup and filled it for her, then refilled the visitor's.

The man nodded to her. An icy finger skittered up her back. They'd paid the lease last fall. Hadn't they?

She put out her hand to shake his. "Nice to see you, Mr. Jeffrey. We sure love this place."

Jake sat. "Well, that's what he's here to talk to us about. Why don't you have a seat?" He looked over at Jeffrey.

"Yes, ma'am. I was just telling your husband and your son here." His arm swept the air. "I've had a very generous offer on my land from a gentleman back east."

Nettie's pounding heart plummeted. No. This couldn't be happening. Not this dream too. She looked at Jake. He had his tobacco pouch out. She thought she saw a slight tremor in his fingers as he shook the brown shreds into the paper. Her gaze shifted to Neil, his face solemn and pale, eyes wide behind his glasses.

"I would much rather be able to sell the place to you folks, since you're already here and you've done so much work on it in the last couple of years, but . . ." Jeffrey looked down at his gnarled hands and shuffled his feet.

But. They didn't have the money. Nettie clasped her hands to keep them from shaking. She wilted into a chair. A sharp pain shot through her head.

"Ah." Whose voice was that, anyway? She heard it as if from afar, cracked and weak. She cleared her throat. "If we could have just a couple more years."

Jeffrey pursed his lips. "I know, ma'am. We've been talking about the possibilities. But, you see, I'm a dying man. My daughter's married to a ne'er-do-well and they're not interested in farming. I feel the need to leave her well taken care of." He shuffled his feet. "So, as you can see, I really can't wait."

Nettie stared into the black depths of her coffee cup. It offered no magical solutions. She set the cup down deliberately to keep it from sloshing. Then with both hands braced on the table, she pushed herself slowly up from her chair.

"I'm sorry about your illness, Mr. Jeffrey. And I'm sorry we're losing our home." Then she walked out of the house to the corral, where she buried her face in Tootsie's mane.

She rested her forehead on the warm strong neck, letting the familiar scent of her horse comfort her. Concentrating on breathing in and out, Nettie forced away all thoughts. Her fingers stroked Tootsie's soft hair. It was the only way she could deal with this news.

It seemed she stood there for hours until Jake came up behind her. He rubbed her shoulders with a gentle hand, then put his arm around her and pulled her close to his side. They stood in the silence, just rocking and trying to draw comfort from each other.

Jake left for town early next morning. When he came home at sunset, he exuded a strange air of elation. It was as if the world-shattering news they'd received yesterday had melted away. When he gave Nettie a peck on the cheek, she caught the smell of whiskey. She turned away, her lips pressed in a tight line. "Easy for you to go drown your sorrows at the saloon, while I stay home and worry all day." She slapped the frying pan onto the stove and threw in some bacon. "We need to make some plans."

"We got a whole new adventure ahead of us." He poured himself a cup of coffee and sat at the table next to Neil.

Neil looked up from his book. "What adventure, Pa?"

With a self-satisfied grin and a twinkle in his eyes, Jake leaned the chair back to balance on two legs. "Guess. Just try to guess."

"We're going to travel the rodeo circuit?" Neil closed his book. Expectation glowed on his face.

"Nope." Jake winked at Nettie. "Hey, little gal. Come sit down and hear the news. Supper can wait a minute."

Nettie rolled her eyes. She took the pan off the stove and moved to the table as if her feet were caked with a sticky, heavy mass of gumbo mud. She sat heavily. What was the big adventure this time? "Okay. I give up. Where are we moving to now?"

"W-e-l-l. I happened to stop at the Rancher's Bar for just a minute. And who did I see, but Boots McClelland." He paused, as if to draw out the suspense.

Nettie frowned. "Boots McClelland? I don't remember him."

"Sure you do. From the Miles City Roundup a couple years ago. He's got a ranch over by Ingomar—that's about sixty miles northwest of Miles City—and now he and his wife want to retire. He jumped at the chance to lease it to us." He let the chair back down and leaned forward. "And, honey, that's still God's country. Not so many people out there. Not like here. This is gettin' way too crowded."

"Move to Miles City? Out of the blue. How can you expect us to do that?" Anger blurred her vision. She blinked and turned to her son. "You get your chores done, Neil?"

"Yeah, Ma."

She glanced around the kitchen, then grabbed a small bucket. "I think you forgot to get the eggs."

"But—"

"Go. Do what your mother tells you." Jake motioned toward the door with his head. Neil took the pail with a sigh and left.

When the door slammed, she turned to Jake, trying to come up with the words. "Jake, you've always said we're partners. But why don't you ever talk to me about these big decisions before you make them?" Nettie clenched her arms tight to her sides.

He looked at her with a puzzled expression. "Uh, I thought that's what I was just doin'."

"Well, it sounds to me like the decision's already been made and you're ready to pack up and head out tomorrow."

He rose from his chair, put his hands on her shoulders, and gazed into her eyes. "No, no, honey. I'm sorry. I never meant that. I didn't tell Boots yes or no yet, 'cause I did want to talk it over with you."

"Yeah?" She narrowed her eyes. "You sure?" Surely he hadn't already made a handshake deal with Boots. No. He wouldn't do that. Would he?

"Yes, little gal, I'm sure. We won't go if you don't want to."

She sighed, trying to remember how far it was. They'd always traveled by train to get to the rodeos there. It was clear at the eastern end of the state. Must be four hundred miles away. "It's even farther than Salmon. Would we have to trail the horses again?"

Jake took a swig of coffee. "Nope. The way I figure it, it's probably best we get out of the horse business. We've been losing money on 'em for years. Better to be in cattle these days, especially over there. That's real range country."

His statement hit her gut like the kick of a steer. Give up the horses?

— ~ —

The next few weeks stretched like a lariat on a roped steer. The decision was made. They would be moving. Jake went into town every morning, supposedly to talk to people who might want to buy the horses. He came home every evening smelling of cigarette smoke and whiskey, no buyers found.

Nettie left Neil to do the chores and rode out into the hills by herself. She dismounted atop a butte that overlooked the pastures. The April sky stretched in a crystal-blue dome above, unmarred by a single wisp of cloud. The prairie spread below her like a soft green blanket dotted with the browns and blacks and duns of the horses who grazed so peacefully.

Despite this idyllic scene, she sat for hours in a gray haze. That aura of hopelessness from those months of searing drought eight years ago haunted her. Then, she'd had visions of the horses' skeletons scattered around a dry waterhole. Now, she couldn't imagine what their fate would be. If no one would buy them, would they all end up in the glue factory? A sudden mass of fear rose and shifted inside.

She couldn't imagine life without the herd. They'd always been around. She had gentled and ridden scores of them, helped Jake break them to the harness, witnessed their foaling. Each one had a distinctive personality, and Nettie knew them all. They were her friends, their source of income in the early days, always the source of her pleasure.

She'd never known Jake without a herd of horses. They'd met over a horse deal. She'd gone to work for him, riding his green horses. Their love grew. Around horses. Nettie couldn't think of Jake without horses. She couldn't stand to think of herself without horses.

Tears streamed down her cheeks. But on the other hand, all the moving around they'd done had been because of the horses. Maybe this would be an opportunity to settle down.

When she finally rode home at dusk, Neil peered at her strangely. "Where you been all day, Ma? Are you all right?"

"No. Not exactly." Nettie brushed any further questions aside and went into the house to fix supper. She just couldn't deal with the boy's feelings on top of her own. Guilt pinged in her confused mind. Some kind of mother she had turned out to be.

She stepped back to the door. "Get washed up, honey. I'll fix you something to eat. Looks like your pa will be late again." She tried a smile. "Don't worry. It'll be okay." A lame attempt to fix the damage, but that's all she could manage right now.

Day after day, she sat on the lonely butte. A future as bleak as that of the dustbowl days intensified in her mind. Losing the horses. Moving far away from her family again.

At night, when Jake reached for her, she pulled away. He'd been happy about the prospect of moving, but not being able to sell the horses seemed to have turned him surly. He was burying his feelings in drink, gambling again. She couldn't even bear his touch right now.

Nettie lay awake listening to his snores, wondering if their marriage could survive this. What if she stayed here? She sat bolt upright, the thought scaring her as much as an unidentified sound in the dark. It was just silly. *I wouldn't be able to keep the horses.* What could she do? She certainly couldn't move back home with Mama and Papa. Rodeoing was out. Wouldn't be able to run a ranch by herself. Would she let Neil go with Jake, or keep him with her? A boy needed his father.

Nettie slipped out of bed, shivering in the cool night air. She clasped her arms around herself and went to stand in front of the window. The bright silvery light of a nearly full moon shimmered over the prairie. Oh, dear Lord, what was she thinking? Was she going crazy? What kind of a mother was she, thinking of giving up her son? Splitting up the family. All because of a bunch of horses.

She knotted her fists. Her fingernails cut into her palms, the physical pain welcome.

"Jake, we really need to talk about this." Nettie set a cup of coffee down in front of him after supper the next evening. "It's eating us both up. I can't stand it anymore."

"Okay. So let's talk." He took a sip.

"Do we really have to move clear across the state? Is there something else around here? What about my folks' place? They're getting up close to seventy. Maybe Papa would like to know the homestead will stay in the family."

Jake shook his head. "Naw. Your pa'll never be ready to retire. He'll work that place till he drops. Anyway, your brothers would be the ones to take it over." He clasped his hands above his head and stretched. "Besides, you know he and I could never work together."

"That's true." She was sure Papa liked Jake a lot, but on his place he would be the boss, and that would never sit well with Jake. He had to be his own boss. "What about another place around here?"

"You know I've looked around here, but all those abandoned homesteads are being bought up now by people like that feller that's buyin' this place." Jake shrugged his shoulders and held his hands out, palms up.

Nettie drew circles on the tabletop with her finger. "It's just so far from our families."

Jake chuckled. "Well, little gal, we got automobiles now. It'll be just a coupla days drive. It'll be a heckuva lot easier than all the miles we've traveled by horseback."

"Jake Moser, you always have all the answers. I can't win this argument." She stood, hands on her hips, knowing that what he said was true, whether she liked it or not.

"What argument?" He wrapped both arms around her in a breath-squeezing bear hug. She hugged him back, but an unsettled feeling niggled at her.

Nettie lay awake for a long time that night. So, it looked like they'd be moving somewhere near Miles City. Well, she'd been on worse trips. Their trail drive to Salmon, for one. But selling the horses. That had proved to be more difficult than Jake had thought. And despite his jubilance about this "new adventure," he surely had to be hurting inside as much as she.

Next morning, instead of heading off to town, Jake lingered over his breakfast coffee and picked up stray crumbs with his forefinger. Nettie washed the dishes in silence.

Finally, Jake cleared his throat. "Let's take a drive up to Ferguson's today. He's still in the horse business. Maybe he'd be willing to buy ours."

Nettie glanced over her shoulder at him. This was the most enthusiastic he'd been in weeks. She hesitated a moment. What good would it do, though? Surely Ferguson was in the same position they were. But at least they'd be doing something, not just sitting around brooding, she in the hills, he in the bar.

"Okay. Let's go then." She dried her hands on her denims, picked up her hat, and went out the door, calling for Neil.

Jake drove mechanically during the forty-five-minute trip to the Ferguson ranch. After a few cheerful attempts at conversation, Neil sat silent between them.

Nettie reached over to pat her son's arm. He was being a good sport about this. There wasn't much she could do to ease his confusion or soften Jake's obvious frustration. Her mood didn't help things either. But she couldn't seem to pull herself out of it.

The sage-dusted countryside passed by in a blur as she stared out the pickup window. Like the days of her life. All just a blur.

She ticked off the places they'd lived since she and Jake were married. Twenty-four times she'd picked up and moved since their honeymoon days on the Davis place nearly fifteen years ago. Twenty-four times packing up their few belongings. They'd never really stayed anywhere long enough to accumulate much. Twenty-four times of setting up camp in a tent, squeezing into a hotel room, or cleaning a mouse-infested abandoned shack, even a granary, for heaven's sake.

Moving around would've been different if they'd been part of the rodeo world. But that dream hadn't come true. Then she'd settled for the one about having their own place. Someday. Always someday. Did other women have to endure this kind of life?

How she wished she could talk to Marie. Her friend's words came back to her: *Live your life, follow your dream.*

Maybe she should go talk to Mama. No, she couldn't run home to mother every time she felt blue. Then she remembered what Mama had said: not to give up on dreaming, but just allow another one to take the place of the one that was not to be.

She twisted the ring on her left hand. Jake was a good man, good-hearted, hardworking. He'd had his ambitions, too, his visions blown away in the dust, swallowed by newfangled machines, strangled by the death throes of the only way of life they'd ever known. Easterners taking over farming, corporate ranches, machines making horses obsolete. What was to become of the life of the cowboy? Of Jake's life? Selling their horses could be the last straw.

She and Jake used to have the same dream: rodeo. Nettie's stomach knotted. That had been such a strong dream. Had she been clinging to that, even as she talked of focusing on a new dream, of having a place of her own? *What do I really want?*

But the ranch dream was still possible. Raising cattle would be a steadier income now in these changing times. People would always eat beef.

She did still love Jake, didn't she? How could she have thought of leaving him? It wasn't going to help things at all. He needed her support right now. She would just have to try her best to be strong. For her man. And for her son.

The pickup topped the rise overlooking the Ferguson spread. Below, at the corrals where she and older brother Joe had worked many a horse together as kids, a dozen vehicles were parked. Cowboys, horses, and cattle milled around, raising a haze of dust.

Neil leaned forward to peer through the dirty windshield. "Look. They're having a rodeo."

"By golly, you're right." Jake shifted into low gear and eased the pickup down the hill toward the activity.

Gosh, just what she didn't need, a bunch of people to smile at and talk to and act like nothing was wrong. Nettie concealed her sigh with a yawn and squared her shoulders. Okay. She could do this.

Jim Ferguson strode up to meet them as they got out of the pickup. "Howdy there, Mosers. You're just in time. We're havin' us an old-fashioned ranch rodeo. You ain't gonna find many of these no more."

Jake shook his hand. "Darn right. Dirty shame too." He jerked his thumb toward the parked cars. "Got somethin' to talk to you about." The two men strolled off. Neil followed close behind.

Nettie climbed up on the corral fence next to the chutes to watch the cowboys try to outdo each other. Their good-natured jests and laughter made her smile.

"I rode longer than you." And "Hey, your bronc just weren't as good a bucker." They were having a good time. That's the way rodeo used to be, the way it should be.

"Hey, sis, what're you doin here?" Joe's voice came from behind her.

She turned to grin at her older brother and cuffed him playfully on the shoulder as he climbed up beside her. "Came to see if you're staying out of trouble."

He snorted. "Nothin' but. With a wife and three kids, what kinda trouble could I find?" He put an arm around her shoulder and squeezed. "Seriously. How're you doing?"

Nettie didn't answer for a moment. Surely she didn't need to keep up a façade for her big brother. He'd always been there to listen to her and sympathize with her when she was a kid.

She looked down at her boots. Might as well tell him. "Well, we're going to have to move again. And Jake's looking to sell the horses. Came up to see if Ferguson wants to buy."

Joe gave a long, low whistle. "Horses are tough to sell these days, especially the draft-crosses. Hmmm. Where you going to next, you know that yet?"

She nodded. "Probably Miles City. Jake talked to somebody about a lease around Ingomar."

"Huh." Joe spat tobacco juice into the dust. "Hey, the boys are here. Gary too." He stuck two fingers in his mouth to whistle at their three younger brothers across the corral. Even though they now ranged in age from twenty-two to thirty, the family still called them "the boys." They waved back and ambled over. Nettie jumped off the fence and hugged them all.

"Good to see you guys. You still bachin' it on your place up here? Haven't heard any wedding bells ringing." Nettie grinned at her brothers, the perpetual bachelors, and hugged her nephew, who was like a little brother to her.

"Nettie and Jake are gonna be movin' out of the country pretty soon, down Miles City way." Joe dipped a finger into his snuffbox.

"What the . . . ?" Ben settled his hat back on his head with a frown. "Thought you were all settled in over there by Roy's?"

"We thought so too. But it's being sold. To some guy from back east." Nettie tried a smile but didn't quite succeed.

"That's what's happenin' all over." Ben scuffed his toe in the dirt. "Too bad."

A commotion off to the side caught their attention. Nettie turned to watch a couple of cowboys wrestle a big, rangy steer into the chute. A cowboy straddled the chute and twisted the animal's tail from above to encourage it into position. It pitched its horned head, bellowed, and kicked its hind legs up and outward, hammering the wooden rails.

The cowboy jumped to a higher rail in a hurry. "Whew. Good thing he didn't kick any higher." He faked a falsetto voice and spread his open hands in front of his crotch in mock horror, to the accompaniment of male laughter.

When he glanced over and saw Nettie with her brothers, he straightened up with a look of chagrin on his weathered face. "Sorry, ma'am."

She dismissed his embarrassment with a grin and a wave. "It's all right, Slim. Glad you're okay."

"Hey, one of you 'pokes wanna ride this beast? He's more Braymer bull than steer, way he's acting. Should make for a good ride."

Chuck and Ben shoved Eddie forward. "C'mon. You can do it."

He ducked his head and shook them off. "Naw. I'm waitin' for that black bronc over there." He turned and looked Nettie straight in the eye. "What about you, sis? I ain't seen you ride in a coon's age."

"Yeah." Ben chuckled. "Remember when we were kids and dared you, and you snuck off to ride that time? 'Twas some great day."

How could she forget? It was etched on her mind as though it had happened just last week. She was fourteen. It was a day about like today. Hot and dusty. A crowd of local ranch hands out on the prairie. How good it felt when she rode that steer to a standstill.

Joe put a gentle hand on her shoulder. "I always said you could ride just as good as any of those other lady bronc busters. What d'ya think? One last time, the five of us together?"

The flush of past successful rides warmed her. Then she froze with the picture of Marie falling headfirst. But she couldn't give in to that fear forever, could she? Papa always said you had to get right back on after you were thrown. She'd forgotten to do that.

Nettie suddenly itched to be on the back of that steer, pitching and spurring and waving. The anticipation. The dance. Subduing a mighty power. The cheering. It all rose up inside her like an oil well about to blow. She'd done this so many times before. What the heck. She could do it again.

She balled her hands into fists to stop their shaking. With squared shoulders, she stepped forward. "I'll ride him."

Slim reared his head back in surprise. "W-e-l-l, I dunno, little lady."

Nettie laughed at his expression. "Aw, come on, Slim, you've seen women ride before. Let me at this one." Spying the red bandanna around his neck, she reached over, untied it, and refastened it around her own neck, like Marie used to do. Nettie tugged leather gloves over her hands, jammed her hat tight on her head, and tried to swallow, but dust clogged her throat. Before she had time to think about it and maybe change her mind again, she scrambled over the fence and lowered herself onto the steer's back.

"And nowww . . . making her comeback . . . for the first time in years, riding the rankest steer on the ranch . . . we have Nettieeeee . . . Mo-ser," Jim Ferguson bellowed to the watching cowboys from the front of the chute as if it were a big-time rodeo.

The cowboy at the gate looked up at her, waiting for her signal. This was it. Now or never. Nettie took a deep breath. *The steer or me.* She nodded and the man released the catch.

The steer bolted from the chute and raced twenty yards down the length of the corral. What was this, all show and no go? Then, as she pressed her knees tight, the animal jerked to a sudden halt, gathered its great muscles beneath her, and exploded into a kicking, writhing frenzy.

Nettie strained to keep her balance and ground her teeth in a grimace.

The steer twisted high, then swooped low. Nettie stayed with him. Her spurs pumped. One hand waved. Their joined shadow danced across the dirt.

She sat high on the steer's back, matching his every move. Then a calm overtook her and the dance continued. Nettie felt herself blending with the animal. She could do this all day.

Gradually, she felt the steer slow. His efforts became half-hearted. At last he came to a dead stop with legs braced, panting in great snorts.

Nettie loosened her grip on the rigging. Someone rode alongside to swoop her off the steer's back. She wrapped her arms around the man's chest and pulled herself to safety.

"Good ride, little gal." The low voice rumbled against her ear. She looked up, straight into Jake's face, and broke into a grin.

This is the way it should be. The top of the world, as close to heaven as she could get. How could she have given it up?

Nettie whooped. She could have both dreams. They'd have their cows; they'd always have saddle horses. *And I'm gonna contact all those lady bronc riders. We can start our own rodeo association for women. No stoppin' us now!*

"Yes, it has been a good ride together, hasn't it?" Nettie hugged Jake hard and slid down to the ground. "And it ain't over yet. We're going to make it. Here's to a new life. In Ingomar." Giving him a lingering kiss, she doffed her hat and bowed to the group of cowboys, Neil waving from the top rail.

Their applause filled the air, singing to her soul, ringing in her ears.

About the Author

Heidi M. Thomas grew up on a working ranch in eastern Montana. She had parents who taught her a love of books and a grandmother who rode bucking stock in rodeos. Describing herself as "born with ink in her veins," Heidi followed her dream of writing with a journalism degree from the University of Montana and later turned to her first love, fiction, to write her grandmother's story.

Heidi's first novel, *Cowgirl Dreams,* has won an EPIC Award and the USA Book News Best Book Finalist award.

Follow the Dream, a WILLA Award winner, is the second book in the Dare to Dream series about strong, independent Montana women.

Heidi is a member of Women Writing the West and Professional Writers of Prescott, is also a manuscript editor, an avid reader of all kinds of books, and enjoys the sunshine and hiking in north-central Arizona, where she teaches memoir and fiction writing classes.

Married to Dave Thomas (not of Wendy's fame), Heidi is also the "human" for a finicky feline, and describes herself primarily as a "cat herder." Visit her at heidimthomas.com.

LOOK FOR THE NEXT BOOK IN THE SERIES, *DARE TO DREAM:*

Will Nettie be able to revive her dream during the 1940s, with family tragedy, dwindling rodeo opportunities, and World War II changing American lives? Ride with her as she struggles to overcome yet more obstacles in achieving her dream and as she discovers her rewards.